Hold You Against Me

Skye Warren

Be sure you sign up for Skye Warren's newsletter so you can find out when new books release! You can also join my Facebook group, Skye Warren's Dark Room, to discuss Hold You Against Me and her other works.

Tough Love is the short prequel novella that introduces Giovanni and Clara! It's available separately, but in case you haven't read it recently, it's also included here.

If you have already read Tough Love, jump to Hold You Against Me!

Or turn the page to start reading Tough Love…

Tough Love

CHAPTER ONE

THE MOON SITS high above the tree line. Somewhere beyond those woods is an electric fence. And beyond that is an entire city of people living and working and *loving* each other. I may as well be on the moon for how close I am to them.

A guard walks by my window at 10:05 p.m. Right on time.

I wait a few minutes until he's out of earshot; then I flip the latch. From there it's quick work to push up the pane with its bulletproof glass. I broke the lock a year ago. And almost every night since then I've sneaked down the ornate metal trellis—like a thief, stealing a moment to myself.

The grass is still damp from the rain, the ground beneath like a sponge, sucking me in. I cross the lawn, heart beating against my chest. I know exactly where the guards are on their rounds. I know exactly where the trip wires are that will set off the alarms. My father is too busy in his office to even glance outside.

The office I broke into this morning.

I breathe a sigh of relief when I reach the pool. I'm still out in the open, but the bright underwater lights make it hard to see anything on the patio. They make it hard to see me as I curve around the edge and reach the pool house.

The door opens before I touch the handle. “Clara,” comes the whisper.

I can’t help but smile as I slip into the dark. Giovanni always opens the door for me. It’s like some old-world chivalry thing, even though we’re just two kids sneaking around. At least, that’s how everyone treats me. Like a kid. But when I’m with him, I feel less like a girl, more like a woman.

He looks out the door for a beat before shutting and locking it. “Are you sure no one saw you?”

“You’re such a worrywart, Gio.” I let myself fall onto the couch, facing up.

“If your father ever found out…”

We’d be in so much trouble. My father is a member of the mob. Giovanni’s father is a foot soldier who works security on the grounds. Both our dads are seriously dangerous, not to mention a little unhinged. I can’t even think about how bad it would be if they caught us sneaking around after dark.

I push those thoughts away. “Did you bring it?”

Reluctantly, Giovanni nods. He gestures to the side table, where a half-full bottle of Jack Daniels gleams in the faint light. “Did you?”

I reach into the pockets of my jeans and pull out two cigars. I hold them up and grin. “Didn’t even break a sweat.”

He rolls his eyes, but I think he's relieved. "This was a bad idea."

"It was my idea," I remind him, and his cheeks turn dark.

Of course the little homework assignment was my idea. I'm the one ridiculously sheltered up in my room with the tutors and the gilded locks. Fifteen years old and I've never even been out to the movies. Giovanni gets to go to regular school. He's too young to get inducted, but I know he gets to be at some of the sit-ins.

"I just want to try them," I say. "I'm not going to get addicted or anything."

He snorts. "More likely you'll get a hangover. How are you going to explain puking to your padre?"

"Honor will cover for me." My sister always covers for me. She takes the brunt of my father's anger. Ninety-nine percent of the time, I love the way she protects me. But one percent of the time, it feels like a straitjacket. That's why I started coming to the pool house. And I'm glad I did. This is where I met Giovanni.

He examines the cigar, eyes narrowed.

"How do you even light it?" I ask. I've seen my father do it a hundred times, but I'm still not clear on how the whole thing doesn't just catch fire. Isn't it made from dried plants?

He puts the cigar to his lips experimentally. It looks strange seeing his full lips around something I've mostly seen my father use. Then he blows out a breath, miming how it would be. I imagine white smoke curling in front of his tanned skin.

"They don't let you use them when they do?" I ask.

He gives me a dark look. I'm not supposed to talk about the side jobs he does for his father. "I mostly sit in a corner and hope no one notices me. It's boring."

"If it's boring, then why won't you talk about it?" I know it's not a good thing to be noticed by men like our father, to be groomed by them, but sometimes that seems better than being ignored. I'm the younger one. And a girl. And there are rumors that I'm not even my father's legitimate child. In other words, I'm lucky my sister remembers to feed me.

He swears in Italian. "That's no life for you, Clara."

"And it's a life for you?"

"I would leave if I could," he says. "You know that."

"You turn eighteen in a year. Will you leave then?" My stomach clenches at the thought of him gone. I'm two years younger than him. And even when I turn eighteen, I won't be leaving. By then I'll be engaged to whoever my father picks for me.

Just like my sister. I shudder at the thought of her fiancé.

He shrugs. "We'll see."

I roll my eyes. I suspect he's making plans, but he isn't sharing them with me. That's how the men around here operate, keeping girls in the dark. Honor only found out she was engaged when Byron was invited over for dinner. He has the money and the power. She doesn't get a choice. Neither will I.

"If you go, you should take me with you," I say.

"I don't think Honor would appreciate me taking you away."

No, she wouldn't. And the thought of being without my sister makes my heart ache. Sometimes I give her a hard time, but I love her. I'd never leave her behind. "She can come with us. It will be like an adventure."

"Don't talk stupid, Clara." His eyes flash with anger and something else I can't define.

I jerk back, hurt. "It was just an idea."

"Well, it's a bad idea. Your father is never gonna let you leave."

Deep inside, I turn cold. I know that's true. Of course it is. Giovanni doesn't have the money or the resources to take us away from here. And even if he did, why would he want to?

I hate myself for even suggesting it. How desperate can I look?

Shaking inside, I stand up and grab the bottle of Jack Daniels. It's heavier than I would have expected, but I carry it over to a wet bar still stocked with decanters and wine glasses. No liquor though. There used to be huge parties here. When my mother died, they stopped.

We're supposed to have a party in a few days, though, to celebrate my sister's engagement. I'm not even allowed to go. I'll just be able to see the fireworks from the window.

Without a word Giovanni joins me, his heat both comforting and stark. He takes the glass from my shaking hand. He opens the bottle and pours the deep amber liquid inside. Then takes another cup for himself, twice as full.

"Why do you get more?" I protest, mostly because I like teasing him.

His expression is amused. "I'm bigger than you."

He is bigger. Taller and broader, though still skinny. His hands are bigger than mine too. They hold the glass with confidence, whereas I almost drop mine.

I take a sip before I can second-guess myself. "*Oh my God.*"

It burns my throat, battery acid scalding me all the way down.

His lips firm, like he's trying not to laugh. "Good stuff?"

"Oh, shut up." Then it doesn't matter because I'm laughing too. That stuff is *awful.*

He grins and takes a drink—more like a gulp. And he doesn't cough or wince after. "You get used to it."

"How much do I have to drink to get used to it?"

"More than you should."

I take another sip. It burns again, but I have to say, not as bad. It still doesn't taste good, but I'm determined to drink it anyway. This pool house is the only place where I can break the rules, where I can experience things. The pool house is the only place I even feel alive.

"Let's try mine," I say. My voice already sounds rougher from the alcohol.

He holds up the cigar. "Did you bring a lighter?"

"Oh, crap."

His eyes crinkle in that way I love. It makes my chest feel full, like there's no room for air. "It doesn't matter," he says.

"But I didn't hold up my end of the bargain."

He takes another drink. It looks so natural when he does it. "What bargain?"

"To do bad things," I say seriously. When your life is as controlled as mine, you need to plan these things. Tonight is supposed to be the night.

He looks down, a strange smile on his face. "Let's start with the whiskey. If that's not enough, we can knock over a bank or something."

I smack his arm. "You're making fun of me."

"Never." His eyes meet mine, and I see that he's not laughing at all. "I'd rob a bank if you wanted me to."

My stomach twists at his solemn tone. "I'd rather you stay safe," I whisper.

He reaches a hand toward me like he's going to cup my face, only half an inch away he freezes. I can almost feel the heat of him, and I remain very still, waiting to see what he'll do next.

He shoves his empty glass onto the bar and walks away.

I let out a breath. What is that about? Lately we keep having these moments where it seems like he's going to touch me. But he never does. I want to touch him too, but I don't. I wouldn't know where to start. I can't even imagine how he'd feel. Would he be like the whiskey, leaving a trail of fire? I'm scared to find out.

He's on the couch, so I join him there. Not touching, just sitting beside him.

"Gio, I'm worried about Honor."

He doesn't look at me. "She's strong. She can take care of herself."

"Yeah, but Byron is a jerk." And even she can't fight the tides. That's what men like Byron are. Tsunamis. Hurricanes. Natural disasters.

"Your dad wants someone who can take over. That's pretty much guaranteed to be an asshole."

He's not saying anything I don't know, but it's still frustrating. It's too dark to see his expression. I can only see the shape of him beside me, his neck and shoulders limned by moonlight. "This isn't the eighteenth century. This is Las Vegas."

"Marriage isn't about that. Not here."

It's about making alliances. It's about *money.* "He should make *you* the next one in line."

At least Gio has been around for years. His dad is trusted here, even if he's not high ranking. This Byron guy hasn't even been in Las Vegas very long. And he's a cop. I learned from an early age not to trust cops—even dirty ones.

Gio shakes his head. "No, thanks."

"Why not? You'd be good at it." I can tell he's biting his tongue. "What?"

"Good at killing people?" he asks softly.

I flinch. Most of the time we skirt around what exactly my father does. And technically Gio is a part of that. I've never asked him if he's killed someone. For all I know, he already has robbed a bank. He's still in high school, so they're keeping him light. But once he graduates high school, they'll want to induct him. I'd almost rather he did leave then. Even though it would kill me to see him go.

He shakes his head. "Anyway, if it were me being groomed, I'd have to marry Honor. And I couldn't do that."

The thought of him marrying my sister makes my stomach knot. He's only a couple years younger than her. It's actually not a bad idea. "Why not?"

"Because I like her sister."

I go very still. There's only one sister. *Me.*

"What did you say?" I whisper.

"You heard me." He leans close. He reaches for me—and this time, his hand does cup my cheek. The feel of him is shocking, startling, impossibly coarse and warm at the same time. He runs his thumb along my skin, rasping against me. My eyes flutter closed.

The old leather of the couch creaks as he leans forward. He must be inches away now. His breath coasts over my lips. Goose bumps rise on my skin. I'm waiting…hoping…

Suddenly his lips are against mine, warm and soft. God, I've seen those lips smile and twist and curse a blue streak, but I never imagined they could be this soft. Nothing like whiskey, with its fire. This is a gentle heat, a caress, and I sink into him, let myself go lax.

One second later, he's gone. Not touching me at all.

My eyes snap open. "Gio?"

He looks tormented. I may not have felt the whiskey burn, but he did. Pain flashes through his eyes. He stands and walks away. "No, Clara. That was wrong. I was wrong to do that."

"But why?" How could that be wrong? That was the best thing that ever happened to me. On a night when I wanted to be *bad*, I experienced my first kiss. It's the best bad thing I could have imagined. And it tasted so sweet.

He's still shaking his head, so vehemently I'm not sure who he's trying to convince—me or himself. "You've been drinking."

"One drink," I say, kind of insulted. I may be new to this, but I'm not drunk.

"One drink is enough."

"You had one drink too," I point out, accusing.

He laughs, the sound unsteady and harsh. "I'm bigger than you."

I don't know if he means the drink affects him less or if it's just another reason why the kiss was a bad idea—as if he might have overpowered me. But there is no reason why this is a bad idea. I've wanted him to kiss me forever. And judging by the way he kissed just now, he liked it too. Unless…

My voice is small. "Did I…do it wrong?"

He lets out a string of curse words. "No, *bella.* You did nothing wrong. This is me. I can't touch you when you've been drinking. I can't touch you at all."

Chapter Two

I GROAN AS light batters my eyelids. There's sound too. And something heavy pressing down on my head. I flutter my hand in the universal sign for *go away.* In case that wasn't clear enough, I add, "Turn off the light."

"That's the sun, silly," my sister says.

I peek one eye open and am totally blinded. If that's the sun, we must be going through some kind of apocalypse, because it's a hundred times brighter than I've ever seen it. And since when did she speak through a microphone? All I manage to do is whimper.

The bed dips as she sits down next to me. Her hand is cool and dry against my forehead. "Are you sick or something? You don't look that great."

"Thanks," I say wryly and then wince as the word echoes through my head.

Last night comes back to me with a crash. The Jack Daniels. Then the *kiss.* Then rejection.

Then more Jack Daniels.

We finished the whole bottle while very pointedly not discussing kissing. "I'm not sick," I tell her so at least she won't worry. Even though I feel worse than when I had the flu. I hope a hangover doesn't last for days.

"I'll take your temperature," she says, heading toward the bathroom connected to my room.

"No," I protest. The thought of something beeping in my ear makes me cringe. I force myself to sit up, to prove I'm okay. "See? I'm fine."

Honor is wearing a cream vintage blouse and black pencil skirt. She always looks so put together. I glance at the clock. Ten o'clock in the morning. Okay, I guess it's not that early. Still, she looks classy and stylish at any hour of the day. Her expression is tight. Because of me?

"I'm fine," I repeat.

The line of worry between her eyes fades, but her lips are still pressed together. There's something about her expression that's familiar. Then I realize… it's pain. Real pain. Not the kind of throbbing ache I'm experiencing now, an ache I completely deserve. This is something else.

I stand and approach her.

"We're meeting with the caterer in thirty minutes," she says. She's letting me sit in on the planning sessions so I can feel involved. The food, the cake. The fireworks.

Kind of crazy, having fireworks in the middle of a freaking drought. That's the benefit of having the fire inspector in your pocket. Or Byron's pocket.

Gently, I take her arm. I press the sheer fabric against her skin—and with the fabric taut, I can see. There they are, three bruises. "Did Byron do this to you?"

She pulls away. "I don't know what you're talking about."

I roll my eyes. "Maybe that works on other people, but not me. I'm going to go punch him in the face."

She looks alarmed, even though the punching thing is pretty unlikely. I'm not even tall enough. And he'd probably shoot me. I don't mind telling him off, though. He can't shoot me for that.

"Stay away from him," she warns.

"Or what? He'll grab me too? He probably hurts you other places, doesn't he? Places I can't even see."

She shakes her head even though I know it's true. She's not even really denying it. She's saying *leave it alone.* "Anything you do will just make it worse."

I hate that she's right about that. "Then we'll talk to Daddy. He can make him stop."

Pain flashes over Honor's face. "He already knows."

My eyes close. I'd been afraid of that. Afraid that Byron's connections and money were worth seeing my sister hurt. Byron may be relatively new to the scene, but he's ambitious. And like Brutus, an ambitious man is a dangerous one. He has money and connections. My father is old and growing weaker. The other factions could see it as an opportunity to take over. So he's solidified his rule by grooming Byron to take over—and marrying his oldest daughter to him as insurance.

I swallow hard. Our father never took much interest in me, except in the worst way.

Probably the rumors are true and I'm not really his daughter. I don't have the dark hair and olive skin that marks our family. I have strawberry-blonde hair and freckles. But he's always been fond of Honor. If he is willing to sacrifice her to assure our position, he must really have been worried about a takeover.

"What can Byron even do for him?" I ask, half angry, half wondering.

Honor lifts one shoulder. "He has everyone intimidated. Judges. Drug suppliers. He's working both sides."

I stare at the place where the bruises are. I can't see them when the fabric rests naturally away from her skin. I'm sure that's on purpose. She must keep an inventory of where her bruises are and make sure they're covered up. It makes me exhausted—and desperate.

"Then let's go," I say. We don't need Gio to take us away. We can leave ourselves.

She frowns, her delicate eyebrows drawing together. "What are you saying?"

"I'm saying let's run away. Just you and me." My throat goes tight as I imagine never seeing Gio again. And I tell her the same thing I told him, though my voice cracks this time. "It will be an adventure."

Her head is shaking *no no no.* "They'd find us. There's no way, Clara. Don't even say the words."

But I've already said them. And once they're out, I can't put them away. Not when I close my eyes and see the dark bluish imprint of Byron's fingers. "We'll find some way to hide. To go underground. It has to be better than this, than you getting hurt."

"And what will we do for money?"

"I don't know. Something. I don't need all this." I

wave my hand to indicate the ornate antique furniture and expensive artwork. These aren't things I chose for myself. They are part of the cage that keeps me here. Money and family and obligation. All of them bind me.

"It's impossible," she says, her voice wistful. "I thought of leaving once. I even had a plan. But…"

"But what?"

"But you're still a minor, Clara. You couldn't work. You couldn't even be seen."

My heart clenches. I would be a liability to her. "You could leave without me."

Her eyes flare with something—memory? Betrayal? Our mother left us both. The official story is that she died in a car crash. But everyone knows she wasn't allowed to drive. And the casket at her funeral was closed. If she did drive that day, she was leaving. And if she died that day, it means my father caught her.

"I will never leave you." She says it like a vow—fierce.

My eyes grow hot with tears. "Me either," I promise her. Even if Gio showed up, ready to take me away. Even if that girlish dream came true. I'd never leave without Honor. She's my sister. I love her. And that's why I can't stand by and let Byron hurt her. There's no fighting a man like that.

The only way to keep her safe is to take her away.

✧ ✧ ✧

THE NEXT NIGHT I creep across the grass. The bottoms

of my feet feel extra sensitive when I do this. Maybe my sense of touch is heightened because of fear. Or because I'm about to see Gio. I can feel every blade of grass tickle my feet, every bump and dip in the earth. Even the night air becomes a tactile thing, blowing gently against my skin, leaving goose bumps in its wake.

When I reach the pool house, the door opens. "Clara," he whispers.

I smile back, relieved. A part of me had worried that he wouldn't come tonight. He'd seemed freaked out by the kiss. All through eating samples of pork forestiere and shrimp kabobs from the caterer, I'd been thinking about him. What was he eating? What was he thinking?

The pool house is dark, like always.

I slip inside and toss myself on the couch, like always.

He looks outside to make sure no one spotted me. Like always.

Then he shuts the door and makes his way over to me. This is different, though. He's walking stiffly. Strangely. It stirs a memory in me. The way Honor sometimes walks when Byron has been rough with her.

I sit up. "Are you hurt?"

He doesn't answer. He just sits down—slowly. Carefully.

"You *are* hurt," I say, accusing. Then I'm up and by his side, hands hovering. I don't want to touch whatever bruise he has and make it worse. "What happened?"

"It's nothing."

I shut my eyes. The only two people in my life I care

about are being beaten, being abused, and I am helpless to stop it. "Your father?"

"Not this time."

I kneel beside the armchair he's in. "Who then?"

He sighs and leans his head all the way back. "Some assholes."

I run my hands over his leg that's closest to me—his thigh, his calf, his ankles. He doesn't flinch or pull away, so I hope that means this side is okay. "Where does it hurt? I can get some ice."

"No ice." His voice has gone deeper.

A part of me, some deep and ancient part of me, knows it's because my hands are on him. It makes me bolder. I move closer, between his legs now. "Or maybe some bandages? Did you have any cuts? You should put antibiotics in them so you don't get an infection."

His laugh is harsh. "No bandages, *bella.*"

God, his voice when he says that. I can almost forget he's injured. I can almost forget he's seventeen and I'm fifteen. I can forget that our fathers would kill us if they found us together.

"What then?" If I can make him feel better a different way, I will. I run my hands up his calves, his thighs—his hands grab my wrists, stopping me.

"No anything," he says, his voice thick with pain. Or with something else.

I don't fight his hold on my wrists. I let him keep me there. And I rest my head on his thigh. It's not really meant to be seductive, even though I can feel the slope of his jeans. Even though I can see the bulge just inches away from my face. I know he's not going to do anything dirty to me. I'd probably like it if he did, but he won't. Just like he won't kiss me again. But he doesn't make me move away.

Instead he lets out an unsteady breath and releases my wrists. I remain there, kneeling in front of him, resting my cheek on his thigh.

His broad hand brushes over my temple, my cheek. He plays with the braid of my hair for a moment before resuming his gentle, rhythmic stroking. He's not touching anywhere below my neck, but my whole body lights up with it, tense and languorous at the same time.

It's a strange feeling, like being a beloved pet. An owned thing. Cared for. Cherished.

It's somehow sweeter than being the unwanted bastard daughter.

"I shouldn't let you come here," he mutters.

"Don't," I say. I can't bear when he talks like that, as if he might not show up one of these days. It's a lifeline for me, a breath of air while I'm drowning. And if I run away with Honor, then each one of these visits could be my last. Tears spring to my eyes, dampening the denim of his jeans.

"Shh," he soothes. "I won't make you stop."

He traces the line of my jaw and the curve of my ear. His blunt finger trails all the way down my neck.

"So pretty," he says. "Do you know, *bella?* I hurt with it, how pretty you are."

And then I'm hurting too, his words like whiskey. They will take getting used to. I need so much more.

"Byron is hurting her," I whisper. Because it's the only way I know how to tell him. *We'll have to leave soon. I can't let him keep hurting her.*

His hand stills, and I think he must understand my secret message. "All the men hurt women here," he says. His tone is so dark, so unlike him.

I look up at him. "Gio?"

His hand encircles my neck, forcing my chin up. He just rests his hand there, his palm flush against my skin. Not squeezing. Just holding. "Are you afraid of me?"

I tremble because of the pain in his expression, in his voice. I am afraid—for my sister, for him. I'm afraid I'll break down and stay just so I can be near him, even if that means condemning my sister for life. But I'm not afraid that he'll hurt me. "No."

"You should be." He leans forward and whispers in my ear. "I've done things you couldn't imagine."

A tear slides down my cheek. Whatever these things are, they cause him pain. I see it in him. I feel it. And he has no choice—no more than Honor has a choice.

"You'd never hurt me," I say. My voice is wobbling because I'm hurting for him. But I mean every word. It's not the first time he's tried to scare me away. I'm not afraid of him.

The anger I feel in him slides away, replaced by something else. Desire.

His eyes are almost glowing in the moonlight streaming through the window. He removes his hand from my neck. His thumb brushes over my lips, back and forth. Back and forth.

My breath catches. Without even thinking, my lips part.

Then the tip of his thumb is pressing inside my mouth. He gently nudges my lips further apart. I don't understand all that's happening, don't know everything he wants, but I know how to take his lead. This is just like kissing, except instead of his lips and his tongue, it's his thumb.

He presses until his thumb is half in my mouth, and then it's only natural to close my lips and suck gently. He makes a soft sound, like a grunt. It sounds like need. Like relief.

The texture of his thumb is rough on my tongue. I slide it against him. He makes a hissing sound and shifts his hips. I never realized my tongue has this much power. Just a flick and the large frame of him tightens.

Before I am ready, he removes his thumb. It's still wet from my mouth when he rubs it along my lips, painting them, at first hot and then cold when he pulls away completely.

I feel like I'm in a trance when I stare up at him. He could ask me for anything, and I'd give it.

He knows that.

He leans forward and places a chaste kiss on my forehead. "Tomorrow," he says. "I'll see you tomorrow."

Chapter Three

I STARE AT the wood paneling, holding my breath. I'm not sure what I think this is going to accomplish. Still, I can't quite bring myself to knock. My father is waiting on the other side of that door.

Did he notice the cigars I took?

I'd be in trouble then. But even more trouble if he found out I've been sneaking out of the house.

My palms are damp, my breathing erratic. Once I knock on the door, I'll hear my father's voice. *Come in.* He answers that way every time. He's said those words to me more often than my own name. The sound of him saying them is both comforting and scary.

When I got the summons to come downstairs, I considered going to my sister. I needed her to give me a hug and tell me everything is going to be all right. But she has her own problems to deal with, including a puffy eye and split lip.

And I'm old enough now to know those promises are empty.

She can't make sure this turns out all right. Not for me and not for herself.

I take a deep breath and blow it out. Then I knock.

"Come in."

Shock races down my spine. I can't make myself move. I know exactly whose voice that is. Not my father's.

The door opens in front of me. It's not sweet, like when Giovanni does it. Not chivalrous. Byron looks impatient. "I said come in," he snaps.

I jump, imagining that voice snapping at Honor, those hands hurting her. He doesn't wait to see if I follow him—he already knows that I will. And I do, shutting the door behind me, a hollow feeling in my stomach. I regret not going to see my sister now, even though it wouldn't have helped. In fact she might have insisted on coming with me as a show of support, and that would just get her hurt even more.

If anyone's getting hurt now, it will be me.

"Sit down," Byron says more calmly, perching on the edge of the desk.

My father sits in his chair, watching me with a blank expression. Why didn't he tell me to come in? Because he's just a figurehead now. He knows it. I know it.

And Byron sure as heck knows it.

My father leans forward. "I've been talking to Byron about your work. I showed him some of your paintings."

My eyebrows shoot up. I thought he barely knew about my painting. And to think he showed them to someone else, like a proud father? My throat gets tight.

"It's important for young girls to have hobbies," Byron says. "I've been trying to get Honor to pick up riding, but she claims she's afraid of horses."

My eyes narrow, but I force them to look normal. Honor doesn't *claim* she's afraid of horses—she *is* afraid of them. And maybe if she wasn't busy dodging his fists and doctoring herself, she'd have more time for hobbies.

As if Byron senses my anger, he smiles. "But you are different from her, aren't you?"

Is that a jab at my parentage? I snap my gaze to my father. Something dark flickers in his eyes. And that's it. There was a time a man could be beaten for even implying dishonor. And here was this man, with his shiny shoes and his slick hair and his *butt* on my father's desk, getting away with everything.

It makes me angry. "Is there a reason you called me, Papa?"

"Byron and I would like you to attend the party."

Sweet. Finally I get to be part of something. And hey, it's my sister's engagement party. Even if she is getting engaged to a monster, I should be there.

Just as quickly, suspicion rolls through me. "Just last week you were saying I'm too young. Why did you change your mind?"

My father's hard expression slips, and just for a moment I see the desperation underneath. He's a man holding on to the ledge. And one of these days, he's going to get a push—from the man sitting on his desk.

Byron's genial expression doesn't fool me for a second. "I convinced him you were a big girl," he says with a wink. "You are, aren't you?"

What a creep. "Of course I am."

The look he gives my body then is bold and disgusting. His gaze settles on my breasts, and *big girl* takes on a totally different meaning. The corner of his mouth lifts in a slight sneer. I feel like I could shower for days and never get clean.

"Can I go now?" I ask, keeping my voice as even as possible. "I have to figure out a dress if I'm going to the party tomorrow night."

"Of course," my father says, waving me off.

"Oh, and Clara." Byron fingers a pen in a way that somehow looks menacing. "Be sure to look your best. There are some friends of mine I'm having you meet."

I WASN'T EXAGGERATING about the dress. Having spent most of my life cooped up in my bedroom or the library, I don't have the kind of fancy dresses everyone will be wearing tonight.

"You can wear one of mine," Honor says when I tell her the good news. Well, *somewhat* good news. The prospect of going to the party seemed less exciting after that creepy look from Byron. And his mention of friends. I have no desire to meet anyone he'd call a friend.

Still, I can't deny that I'm excited. My first party.

"There's no way that's going to work," I tell her honestly.

Honor is slender. And I'm…not. I'm five years younger than Honor, but somehow my bust is actually bigger. So are my hips.

She rolls her eyes and still manages to look classy and mature while she does it. "We'll make a few alterations if we have to."

"*If* we have to? Oh, we'll have to. And by alterations, I'm guessing you mean adding an entire extra dress. Like if we tie two together, there might be enough fabric."

Her lips twist disapprovingly. "We aren't that different, Clara."

Yeah, right. We're different in every way. Her black hair to my pale. Her smooth olive skin to my pink freckled skin. Her slim body to my full one. "Have you looked in a mirror lately? You're beautiful."

"What are you talking about? Clara, you're gorgeous. There are women who'd love to have your curves. And your pretty hair."

I just stare at her. I don't believe her at all.

She sighs. She must know I'm a lost cause. "You have no idea how adorable your freckles are, do you?"

"Just what every girl wants to be. Adorable. You look like Audrey Hepburn come to life."

That makes her laugh. "Wouldn't that be nice. I could go off on a holiday in Rome."

"You'd have to escape first," I remind her. That's how the movie goes. We've both watched it a hundred times. There's only so many things you can do while stuck in a mansion. Read a book. Practice yoga with a DVD instructor.

"Well," she says lightly. "That can be for later. For

now, we need to get you dressed. And I have an idea."

She digs through her closet and comes up with a black wrap dress. The fabric has enough give that I can fit into it. It expands to accommodate my hips, falling above my knees instead of below, looking flirty instead of vintage. It's cute.

I stare at myself in the mirror. Really cute.

Except…

"That's not going to cut it," Honor says, staring at my cleavage. It's hard not to stare. My cleavage is practically busting out of this dress, straining at the top.

So much for looking my best. "I'm hopeless."

She shakes her head. "Nothing a little double-sided tape can't solve. We'll add a shawl that covers up the rest."

She disappears to find this magical tape and shawl that's going to fix me. With her gone, I suck in my stomach and lift my body, in what I guess is a seductive pose. The truth is I have no idea what seduction would be like. My mind flashes to Giovanni's hand stroking my hair, my neck. His thumb brushing my lips. And then slipping between them, resting on my tongue.

My whole body flushes warm.

I imagine Giovanni in the room with me. What would he think of this dress?

What would he think of this cleavage? I wonder if I'll get a chance to show him. He might be at the party. My mind is awash in fantasies. Dancing on the ballroom floor. Stealing a kiss in the garden.

I know they're stupid dreams. His father is a foot soldier—they don't often get invited to these kinds of affairs, much less their underage sons. And even if Gio came, would he dance with me? Or would that tip off our fathers that we knew each other?

There are a hundred reasons why it's a bad idea. But sometimes it feels like if I want it enough, if I wish hard enough, it might happen anyway.

WE ARE LOUNGING side-by-side on the old, musty sofa. One earbud is in my left ear, the other is in Gio's right. Above us, dust floats in the moonlight. I'm back in my standard jeans and tank top. No longer glamorous or over-the-top sexy. But this moment feels so perfect it almost hurts. I want a million of these moments, strung like beads on a necklace, one after the other.

When the third *Glee* song comes on, Giovanni slants me a dark look that makes me giggle.

"What?" I ask, going for innocent. But I don't quite succeed. I like making him suffer with fun songs. He doesn't tell me that much about his life outside of these nights, but I know there's not enough fun in it.

"Really?" he says.

I sing along. "*Don't stop believing…*"

He groans, but I see the smile that plays on his lips. He likes it. "You know high school is nothing like that show, right?"

"Duh," I say. "That's not even realistic. It's obviously

more like *Buffy the Vampire Slayer*."

He flicks his thick fingers lightly against my arm. "Smart-ass."

I stick my tongue out, which probably proves him right. I don't care. "Hey, it's not my fault I never got to go. If it were up to me, I wouldn't have to guess what high school is like. I would already know."

"I don't agree with much your father does, but I think he got that part right."

Stung, I face the ceiling again. "Whatever."

"I'm just saying people would know who your father is. It makes you a target."

"So I should just never live, is that what you're saying? I should just stay locked up and marry whoever he tells me to and dress however Byron says—"

"What the fuck are you talking about? What did Byron tell you?" He's facing me, eyes a little wild.

Unease rolls through me. Gio and I, we've had our little spats. It's part of the teasing ups and downs we do. But I've never seen him quite so intense. Except maybe about his father. But then he mostly shuts down if that topic comes up.

He's not shutting down now. His expression is furious and expectant.

"He didn't tell me anything," I say, trying to calm him down. "He just said I was going to the party. And that I should look my best, whatever that means."

Gio swears in Italian. I mostly don't understand the words except to know they're bad.

"That fucker," he says.

Okay, I know that one. "It's not a big deal."

"It's a big fucking deal. He needs to keep his filthy fucking hands off you—"

"He didn't touch me." I prop myself up on one elbow, concerned. Cautiously, like approaching a wild animal, I rest my hand on Gio's arm. "He didn't touch me, okay?"

I watch Gio take deep breaths in and out. He calms down slowly, though I sense the rage is still simmering beneath the surface. After a beat, I lie back down. The song changes to *Angels We Have Heard on High*. It's early May, but I love Christmas music any time of year. It's so hopeful. I especially love the *Glee* version.

Maybe I did think high school was a little like that…

"I thought you weren't allowed to go to the party," he says, his voice low.

I shrug. "I guess they changed their mind."

"It's not safe for you."

Umm… "Everyone will be there."

"That's exactly why it's not safe."

"Will you be there?" I ask hopefully. I'm not worried about the safety of this party. I mean…it's a *party*. But I want him to be there anyway. "You could protect me."

He lets out a disgusted sound. "No. I have a job that night."

A job. That sounds ominous. It's not like he's got shifts at a movie theater or something. A job means something for his father. Something for *la familia*. What if something goes wrong? What if he gets hurt? He still has bruises from whatever awful thing happened the other night. How dare his father send him into violent, dangerous situations.

Then again, that's exactly what my father is doing with Honor.

"We'll see each other after," I say. I was thinking of telling him we'd skip that night, but lying here with him now, that feels too painful. And now that I know he has a job, I'd just be worried about him until I saw him again.

"The party will be late."

"I'll leave early. I'll tell them I feel sick or something." I don't mention that I already feel sick. I've wanted to go to a party, to *anything,* since forever. But now that it's here, it feels all wrong. This isn't about dancing in ballrooms and getting kissed in the garden. This is being paraded in front of Byron's friends while Gio is off somewhere risking his life. "Please. I need to see you after the party. Meet me here."

He grunts, still looking at the ceiling. "Maybe."

CHAPTER FOUR

THE PARTY IS a success. I know this because at least five people have told me so. How good the food is. How pretty the flowers are. How grown up I look in this dress. It makes me wonder if they want something from me.

Maybe I'm just being cynical. The people do seem very nice…if a little superficial. Every conversation I've had has been about the weather and the best wine vintage. And the weather again.

I miss lounging on the couch, choking down whiskey or listening to music. I miss resting my head on Gio's strong thigh, feeling the warm weight of his hand on the back of my neck.

I miss him.

"Dear?"

My attention snaps back to the woman in front of me. It's almost hard to see her face with all the diamonds crowding her neck and earlobes. "I'm sorry, Mrs. Donato. I didn't hear you."

It helps that the ballroom is crazy loud. It makes it less weird that she has to keep repeating herself to me. "Call me Ines," she says with a knowing smile. "You're practically a woman now. One of us."

One of us. But who is that exactly?

It's like there's a secret handshake that no one ever taught me. I understand what Gio meant about staying in the background and hoping not to be noticed. There's something almost creepy about all the smiles and the wealth. And the congratulations for my sister, when everyone here knows what a monster Byron is.

Heck, everyone here *is* a monster.

All the jewels dripping from wrists and necks were bought with blood. But I'm supposed to smile and say, "I'm so thrilled to be here."

She clucks. "It's so hot though. More than usual, don't you think?"

"Yes, it has been warm this year."

Which is a lie. We live in Las Vegas. It's basically a giant oven, a kiln that's been baking the cracked clay earth for centuries. The grounds of my father's estate are lush green, a testament to what huge sums of money and half the city's water supply can accomplish.

We've made our own little oasis. But that doesn't make it any less of an illusion.

I scan the crowd, but I'm too short to see above the black tuxes and fancy hairdos. "Have you happened to see Honor around?"

Mrs. Di Donato winks. "I saw her leaving the ballroom with Byron a few minutes ago. Young love is a beautiful thing."

I manage some kind of nod that convinces her before

making my excuses. Then I'm crossing the ballroom. I readjust the shawl as I go, making sure it's covering my cleavage. My feet are aching after hours of standing in heels—seriously, whoever invented these was a masochist. Or a sadist. But they don't slow me down. Whatever is going on between Honor and Byron, it's not love. I have to check on her.

A man stops in front of me. I start to go around him, but he touches my arm.

I flinch back. Only then do I realize he was stopping me on purpose.

He smiles. "Are you Clara?"

I've never seen this man before. And I have no desire to meet him now. "Excuse me. I'm looking for my sister."

He grins, mouth stretching wide. He looks kind of like a movie star, and I don't like it. "I'm afraid she's indisposed at the moment. I hope that will give you a few minutes to talk to me."

I'm standing in the middle of hundreds of people, but I've never felt more alone. I don't know where Honor is. She could be anywhere in the house. Heck, she could have left the house. And with Byron, who is no doubt hurting her in some way. He will always hurt her. There's no way we can stop him. As I stand in the crowded room, a deep and sorrowful certainty takes root.

We have to go. Leave. There's no reason to wait.

There's no reason to hope things will get better.

The only thing to do is leave—and never see Gio

again.

"Excuse me," I say again, this time more quietly. I'm breaking apart inside. "I think I need to be alone."

His expression turns apologetic. "Actually, Honor sent me to check on you. She knew she'd be busy and wanted to make sure you had someone by your side."

I narrow my eyes. Is he flat out lying to me? It feels that way. Honor would know I don't want some weirdo stranger hovering around me. But then again, she does get protective sometimes. Maybe she did worry about me in the ballroom by myself.

But why not send someone I actually knew? Or at least introduce me to him first?

Then again, it's not like Byron would have given her time to do anything. If he says to jump off a cliff, he's already pushing you off. That's how he operates.

I look back at the party. I *do* feel sick now. Sick of smiling. Sick of pretending. I want to be in the pool house, teasing Giovanni. But it's still my sister's party. And I don't need to listen to my intuition to know she might be hurting right now. I have to find her before I go. I'll make sure she's okay. Then I'll make excuses so I can sneak to the pool house.

"Can you bring me to my sister?" I ask the strange man.

"Of course." His smile disarms me. He actually looks pretty nice when he's not blocking my path and being pushy. "She just stepped outside for some air."

✧ ✧ ✧

THE LIGHTS STRUNG up over the patio cast the rest of the lawn into darkness. I can't even see the outline of the pool house from here. A couple is making out, half-hidden by a bush, but they stop when they see us. Actually, not us. Him. Whoever this guy is, he makes their eyes widen and they run inside, straightening their clothes as they go.

"Where's my sister?" I say.

He absently scans the dark landscape. "She'll be along."

It's not only secluded here. It's quiet. Much quieter than the voices and five-string orchestra inside. It makes me feel a little stranded, being out here alone with him, with no one to hear me. "Umm, what did you say your name was again?"

"Markam," he says with an easy smile. "Javier Markam."

My eyebrows shoot up. Wasn't he in the news about some big controversy? "The governor's son?"

"Does my reputation precede me?"

I can't remember what he'd supposedly done. But no one in that ballroom has clean hands. Not even me. We all benefit from the criminal enterprise in some way, even if it's only the bed we sleep in or the guards that lock us in. "Not really."

"Good." A glint enters his eyes. "I don't want us to get off on the wrong foot."

Suspicion is a dark knot in my chest. "Are you friends with Byron?"

"Good friends, yes. We go way back."

My heart pounds. Honor would never send one of Byron's friends to me. She wouldn't trust him any more than I do. "He said something about wanting me to meet his friends. Was he talking about you?"

Dark eyes study me. "Direct. I like that in a girl. I hope we can speak frankly with each other."

"Why would that matter?"

"Because we're going to be seeing a lot more of each other. At least, if I have my way." He winks to lighten the words, but I can read between the lines. He always gets his way.

"I don't understand."

He shrugs. "You know how these things work. Powerful people make powerful enemies. We need to stick together. Like Byron and Honor, for example."

We are nothing like Byron and Honor. They're engaged. And if that was a marriage proposal, it was seriously lame. "I'm fifteen."

That earns me a chuckle. He has handsome features and an expensive tux, but he's twisting and distorting while I look at him. Everything looks exaggerated, fake. His smile. His hair. Even the good humor in his eyes. It's a creepy kind of humor. "I know you're too young for anything serious. We're just getting to know each other. Getting to know if…there'd even be a point in pursuing this, understand?"

No. "And if there is?"

"Then you'd still stay here, finish your studies. You'd

be under Byron's protection. I'd visit from time to time."

In other words, he'd be free to play the field while I'd stay locked up in here. Gross. "I'd like to find my sister now."

"Look, Clara." He drops his head. It's an endearing move. A practiced move. "The truth is, Byron didn't only introduce me to you because of the family connections we could make. He thought I'd like you…and I do."

Somehow I don't think he's talking about my personality. "Why would he think that?"

"You have a certain innocence. A youthfulness I find appealing."

It's called being underage, jackass. "Well, thanks. I guess. I'd like to find my sister, though. I'm worried about her."

"You never have to worry about her. Byron would never let anything happen to her."

That's what I'm afraid of. I take a step back. Then there's a hand clamped around my wrist. Javier's hand. "Let me go."

He pulls me closer. I wobble on my high heels, almost falling into him. The shawl comes lose. His gaze drops and darkens.

"Clara, I think you and I really get along."

"Let go of me *now.*"

He walks forward, and I have no choice but to walk backward, stumbling as I go. One of my shoes twists off, and then the other. I'm off balance, almost falling, except that he's holding me up, fingers clenched into my skin, wrenching me. The trellis is at my back, the same metal trellis I use to climb down, the one I use to escape, and now it's part of my prison. I'm caught between those unforgiving bars and his body, breath coming fast. Now I understand how Honor feels. I understand why she puts up with it—because she has no choice. I knew it before, but I never experienced it until now, never felt fear like a living thing inside me, clawing its way up my throat.

I kick at him, even as part of me knows that will only make it worse. I don't have the poise and class and core of steel that Honor has. I can't endure this, even when I know I have to. I can only fight.

"You little bitch," he snaps as my knee connects with his shin.

He twists my wrist, and I'm facing the wall. The scarf is long gone, and my breasts are pressing into the metal criss-cross. Javier is holding me in place, his breath hot against my temple. "I want us to get off on the right foot, Clara. I told you that."

And this is the right foot. Violence. Coercion. Tears stream down my face. There's no way out.

This is how Honor must feel. *Trapped.*

There is a sudden cry and groan from the man holding me captive, and then he's up against the metal grate himself, flat with arms spread wide, while Giovanni punches him again and again. The only reply Javier makes is a groaning sound that makes the hair rise up on my neck.

"Giovanni, stop!" He'll kill him, and that will be so much worse. He's the governor's son—and worse than that, he's Byron's friend. "Stop!"

Giovanni turns to see me, and the rage parts like dark clouds, long enough for me to see *him* looking back. Him, the boy who spent those nights in the pool house, cracking jokes and letting his hand brush against mine. The haze clears. "Clara?"

I'm crying, my hands clenched together as if in prayer. Begging. "Giovanni, please."

He turns and faces Javier. For a minute I think he's not going to listen. He's just going to keep beating him until Javier is dead, and then what will we do? I don't even know what we'll do if he's alive. We're in so much trouble. This goes beyond trouble.

Giovanni speaks low, so low I can barely hear him. "How does it feel without your buddies backing you up, huh? How does it feel one-on-one?"

Then he slams Javier into the wall one last time. Javier's eyes are closed as he slumps to the ground.

I stare at the unconscious man, his nose bloodied, his crisp tux rumpled and torn. "Is he…dead?"

Giovanni wipes his brow with his forearm. "No."

"Is he the one who did that to you? The bruises?" *With his buddies.*

"It doesn't matter."

"Yes, it does. Why would he—"

"We need to get out of here."

Right. What would happen if we were found out here? Every man in there is packing heat. Some of the women too. "We have to find Honor."

"There's not time." He puts his hand out to me. He doesn't grab me. Not like Javier did. His eyes are as dark as the night behind him—unfathomable. They scare me just as the night too, but I trust him. No matter how much he's tried to scare me away. No matter that he once stroked my neck, that he once held it in his hand.

I put my hand in his. "Let's go."

He doesn't wait. We run toward the pool house together. We don't even have to discuss it first. We both head toward there like it's our north star, our home.

I'm out of breath when we stumble inside. Adrenaline is like lava in my veins, making it too hot to stand still. Too hot to sit down. I can only pace in the small space, running my hair through my hands. "What are we going to do? Oh my God. *What are we going to do?*"

Gio takes my hands in his, and I finally stand still. I'm breathing hard, trembling.

"You have to go," he says. "It's not safe for you here anymore."

I know it's true. I knew it from the moment he first punched Javier, from the moment when Javier attacked me. I knew it even before then, when it was only Honor being hurt. But it's still hard to hear the words. This is my home, the only place I know. And for all that my father has been distant—and maybe not even truly related—he's the only parent I know.

"You're the one who told me my father was right to keep me here."

Gio swears in Italian. "He isn't fucking in charge anymore. You aren't safe here. You won't ever be safe here again."

I swallow hard. "Honor?"

"She'll go too. She won't fight it once she knows about Javier."

"And you, you'll come with us, right?"

He rests his forehead against mine. "Clara."

Panic rises in my chest. "Gio, you have to. He'll wake up. He'll tell them it was you."

Chapter Five

THE DOOR BURSTS open. I jump back from Giovanni, guilty and afraid of being caught touching—even though we have worse problems than that. It's not my father. Not even Byron. It's Honor.

Her gaze snaps to Giovanni, but she speaks to me. "Clara, I need a word with you. *Now.*"

She must have heard about Javier. I can tell by the strength of her voice—and the tremor hiding underneath. "You can say it in front of Gio," I tell her. "He already knows."

Honor's eyes narrow. She's wondering if we can trust him. She doesn't know him like I do.

"You have to get her out of here," Giovanni says. "There's not much time."

Slowly she shuts the door behind her and leans back against it. "I know."

"Take my car," he says. "It's gassed up. It should get you a few hundred miles. Then you'd better switch vehicles."

Honor nods. "That's better than the bus. I know they'll be checking."

Giovanni crosses the room and stands on the back of

the sofa. I can only stare as he reaches up to the vent that had been above us all those nights. He unhooks the grate and pulls out a black bag. "This has money," he says. "It's all I've got."

My sister takes it without question. "Thank you."

"Don't tell me where you're going," he says.

I can only stare at him. *Don't tell me where you're going.* As if he's not coming with us. As if he might get tortured for information. I grab Gio's arm. "What are you talking about? You need to come with us."

"Security," he says. "They're staying farther back from the house, but there's even more than usual around the gate."

"That means none of us can get out."

He shakes his head. "I'll cause a diversion. Distract them long enough so you can get out."

What? "No way."

"It's the only way."

I look at Honor. "This is crazy. Tell him he needs to come with us."

Her eyes are sad. Sadder than I've ever seen them. But also accepting. Of all people, she understands about sacrifice. "We don't have much time. The party is the best time to run, when they're distracted, when it will be hard for them to search the house. Especially if he can pull the guards away from the gate. We need to go now."

"No." I take a step back. "This can't be happening."

Gio looks at my sister. "Can you give us a minute?"

Her dark eyes study me. After a beat, she nods. "I'll

go scout the best path out of here."

"But the guards?" I tell her.

A ghost of a smile crosses her face. "I still have some friends here."

Then she's gone, leaving only Gio and me. Alone together. Just like we have been every night. Except totally different. Because this time tomorrow I'll be gone. And Gio will be…where? Here. Except if they find out he helped us, they'll hurt him.

And once Javier wakes up, they'll kill him.

"Gio, no."

He runs a hand down my arm—so lightly. His fingertips barely brush my skin. "Are you hurt?"

"I'm serious. We aren't doing this. I'm not kidding."

"I'm not joking." He sighs. "You don't know they'll take me. I'm not going to go easy."

"Yeah, but up against Byron? *Against all of them?*"

His gaze dips to my chest. "This dress, Clara."

The scarf is long gone, and all the running and freaking out have left my breasts almost popping out. I look like some kind of bombshell. I don't feel like a bombshell, though. I feel like a bomb that's about to go off if someone doesn't *listen* to me. The two people I love most are making plans about my life without me. Very serious plans that involve Gio getting hurt.

And I'm afraid nothing I say can stop them.

"You can't," I say, my voice soft and desperate.

"I just need a minute," he says, still staring at me in this dress.

"To what?"

"To remember this."

Fear grips my heart tighter than anything before. This can't be happening. I'd have let Javier touch me if I knew it would lead to this. I would let Javier do anything if it meant keeping Gio safe.

I can't stand him looking at me. Not because I don't want him to see. Because he's looking at me like a dying man would—as if he knows it's his last sight. As if drinking his fill.

My breath stutters. I need to be closer than this. This place we're in—this is water. And he is air. I push up to him, pull him down to me. I meet his lips in a gasp.

Then he's kissing me back, his lips demanding, tongue fierce. And his hands. Those large, beautiful hands that have done violence tonight—for me. They cradle my head so sweetly. How can something so good feel like pain? How can this be the end?

I shove him back. "We'll find another way. Something. Anything."

"There is no other way. This isn't the first time I've thought of how to get you out of here. And if you stayed here, you'd condemn your sister too. Byron would make everyone suffer."

And now it will only be Gio suffering. The canapés from the party turn in my stomach. My hands curl into fists, useless. "You wouldn't let me do this. You wouldn't let me sacrifice myself for you. So how can I let you?"

"You're not letting me do anything, Clara. You don't have a choice."

Angrily I shove the tears aside. This isn't a time to be sad, because this is *not* happening. We're not leaving him behind. So why can't I stop crying?

Why does it feel like I've already lost?

"Gio," I say, my voice breaking.

His forehead touches mine again, his hands cradling my face. I feel so delicate when he holds me like this. I feel loved. "Let me do this for you," he says roughly. "I couldn't protect you before. I don't have anything to offer. I never did. But this?"

"No, no," I sob.

He pushes me tighter against him, cheek to cheek, and I swear these tears aren't only mine. "You care too much, Clara."

"How is that too much? It's the right amount. I care too much to leave you here. How is that wrong?"

He is silent a moment. "It's not wrong. But I care too much to let you stay."

His arms come around me, holding me in. They feel unbreakable. They are castle walls, his arms. They are a drawbridge rolled up and a moat. They keep everyone out. Only with him do I feel completely safe. Maybe I'd always known how much he'd do for me. He'd fight for me. He'd die for me.

And that's what he's going to do. And at the end only rubble will be left.

"I'll be fine," he says, but we both know it's a lie.

My hands clench in his shirt. "How can you be?"

"Just go," he whispers fiercely. "You think this is about me sacrificing for you? No. I need you to do this for me, Clara. I need you to stay safe."

I cry until his shirt is dark and wet. These are silent tears. They fall without my consent, while my face is solemn. I can be stoic for him. I won't beg now. I won't plead.

Not even when Honor comes in and tells me it's time to go.

It feels like dying to walk away. Feels like dying to look back and see him watching me go. Feels like dying as I cross the dark lawn.

Honor holds my hand, but doesn't say anything.

I think she knows. It's the worst thing I've ever felt, to leave him behind. And it's nothing compared to what he'll go through.

We're near the gate when we hear the explosion behind us. *Fireworks.*

Those are the fireworks that would have celebrated her engagement.

Only fitting that they'll end it.

It's not hard to find Gio's beat-up Pontiac Grand Am parked down the side lane. The radio is broken. The gas tank is full. We drive in silence until the blasts fade to nothing.

There is only empty road in front of us and empty

road behind.

I need you to do this for me, Clara. I need you to stay safe.

And so I do.

That's the end of the prequel Tough Love! I hope you loved meeting Giovanni and Clara. Turn the page to begin reading Hold You Against Me, the novel-length conclusion to their story…

Hold You Against Me

"I want to be inside your darkest everything."
—Frida Kahlo

Prologue

Giovanni

The sound of running water pulls me out of the darkness. Soft and pleasant, like a babbling brook. That's how it seemed the first time I heard it. Only the clench of my gut told me it would be different. And the sight of the black-soot concrete ceiling.

It's become my sky, that ceiling. Instead of finding shapes in clouds, I see skulls in the dark growth and water stains lining the top of the room. The walls and floor are similar, but I don't get to see them much.

They only take me down from the table when I pass out.

They only put me back on the table when it's time for another round.

A faint whoosh is my only warning before ice-cold water lands on my face. I sputter, coughing, feeling a thick liquid in my mouth that isn't only water. Blood. Old blood. The metallic taste is almost the same as the rancid water they use.

"Time to wake up, you stupid fuck."

My vision clears to reveal my tormenter, one of them, holding a bucket that used to be blue. Now it has black growth all around it. *Unsanitary.* I think I said that to him once. It's dumb to antagonize the men, but sometimes it's impossible not to. After hours of questioning. Days? I can't be sure. It feels like an eternity.

"Did you miss me?" I say, my voice thready and rough.

His large nostrils flare. "So it's going to be a hard day, is it? You stupid fuck."

That's always what he calls me. *You stupid fuck.* Not a very imaginative insult, especially when he says it fifty times a session. I'm pretty sure I told him that once, too. And I lost a tooth for my trouble.

I'd never seen him before I woke up strapped to this table the first time. I nicknamed him Troll in my mind, because I imagine him living down in this torture basement, never seeing the light of day.

I don't mind this one much. As torture goes, his is predictable.

A handful of bruises, another broken bone. Could a single bone break in more than one place? I'm running out of things to hurt, but I'm sure he'll find something.

The sound of footsteps on metal stairs makes me tense. My body remembers something worse than pain. That's all Troll can dish out, but the other man messes with my mind.

Javier Markam strolls into view, his suit impeccable, his smile deceptively charming.

I want to rip his throat out. My fists tighten, wrists straining against the bonds holding me here.

He laughs in a way that is sickeningly pleasant. "Good evening, Mr. Costas. I see you're eager to get started." His smile fades, his eyes as flat as a snake. "I am too."

"Can't wait to put your hands on me again," I manage, though the memory of yesterday's torture is still fresh enough to make me vomit. Luckily I haven't had anything to eat in days.

His expression darkens. "I have a new game for us to play."

Are you flirting with me? I can't force out a comeback, though. Not with my entire body twisting, fighting. It's determined to survive even though I know I have no hope.

No, my best chance is with Troll over there. If he gets careless, hits a little too hard, I won't wake up.

That's the best case scenario for me.

"Fill up the bucket," Markam says.

Both of them disappear from view, and there's that water again. So peaceful. So horrific.

Then Markam is back, holding up a wet washcloth. "Do you know what this is?"

I want to tell him exactly where he can shove that, but my throat is too tight to speak. I'm guessing I know what's coming, and the thought has me sucking in a deep breath. *Shit.*

He smiles a little. "Where's Clara?"

I hate that I'm trembling, but this is going to be bad. Fear. He gets into my mind. "Have you checked up your ass?"

That terrible smile is the last thing I see before the wet cloth slaps my face. One second. Two. That's how long it takes for the air in my lungs to get used up, for my body to exhale and reach for me. Except there's no more air, nothing but wetness—and it feels like I'm drowning. Every muscle fights, but I barely move at all. I only manage to use up more of my oxygen, to drown faster.

Then the cloth is gone, and I suck in air so sharp it slices me up inside.

I'm panting, staring at Javier with a promise to kill him. I know better than to think I'll actually get to, but I swear on everything I believe that if I get the chance, I'll do it. And I'll make it slow.

"Where's Honor?"

"Fuck you."

The cloth is back on me, and I count. That was ten, and this is nine. It helps sometimes, counting.

Then my body fights again, and I forget everything. Forget numbers, forget anger. All I know is a bone-deep fear, the instinct that kept humans alive for thousands of years. Survival, except this doesn't feel like survival. It feels like death.

The cloth disappears, and I choke on air.

"Tell me where they went."

It's a relief that they never told me. There are times I'm so delirious from the pain, I can't be sure what I've said out loud. There are times I've actually seen Clara in this room like a damned mirage. But I can never give away her location. I don't know where she is.

The cloth is more wet this time, and water fills my mouth, my nose, before I can take another breath. I'm fighting from the first moment. *This is eight,* I think. *Fucking eight.*

He's looming over me again. "You're only making this harder on yourself. We're going to find them, and then what use will you be? Tell me now, and I'll show mercy."

There is one sweet thing about this torture—while this happens, I know they haven't found Clara yet. She's safe as long as I'm in pain. I want it to go on forever.

"Clara," I say, voice like rusted metal.

"Yes," he says, soothing. "This is her fault. She doesn't deserve your loyalty."

She deserves more than I could ever give her. "You'll never touch her again."

His fist hits my stomach just as the cloth lands on my face again. *Seven.*

And so it goes on, more questions. More fighting. Sometimes I think he knows I don't know where they are, that he just likes fucking with me because I got in his way. Other times I think he must be really desperate. I know he wanted Clara. I saw the way he looked at her, the way he *touched* her in the garden while she told him no. Thank God I was there to intervene, even if it did lead to this.

Six. Five. Four.

But it's more than that. He's friends with Honor's fiancé, who would have gotten power out of the alliance. I have no idea what Javier wanted to get out of the deal. He's already the governor's son, already rich and powerful. For men like him, it's never enough. *Run, Clara. Never stop running.*

Black spots dance in front of my eyes. I'm blacking out, muscles too locked up to do anything but clench. Javier is talking to me again, but my oxygen-deprived brain can't make out the words.

Three.

Instead I see Clara's face—wavery, as if I'm watching her from underwater. She's smiling at me.

This is all she ever wanted, to be free.

Two.

"You're going to fucking die in this room," he hisses into my ear. "You're going to rot in this basement until only your bones are left. And when I find your pretty little girlfriend, I'm going to fuck her until she bleeds."

Somehow my body finds the strength to fight again, and I lunge against the restraints, slamming my head into Javier's. A sickening crack fills the air. Then a fist lands on my temple and everything becomes muted. In slow motion I see the washcloth coming down toward my face. I'm still too dazed from the punch to suck in a breath, my body spasming and out of control. *Clara. Clara. Clara.* Her name a wild beat in my ears, a thousand feet pounding the pavement.

One.

CHAPTER ONE

Present Day

I SEE HIM everywhere. He is the memory of a dream when I wake up. He's the man at the street corner, gone the moment I blink. He's my last regret as I go to bed. The boy I left behind. The boy who died for me. Some days it feels like I'm living a normal life—the one he wanted me to have, free from my mafia family, going to art school like I always dreamed. Other days I feel like a ghost, like I died back in that gunfight with him, never really free.

"Earth to Clara."

I blink, coming back to myself. My friend Amy waves her hand in front of me, an exasperated look on her face. The windows are already dark, the light in the studio reduced to shadows. When did that happen?

A twinge of pain courses through my hand, and I look down. My fingers are stained with black. Charcoal. I don't remember drawing, but the result of it is splayed across the page.

I move to cover it, but I'm not quick enough.

"Again?" Amy sighs. "Let me see."

Reluctant, I push the paper across the smooth table

as if it means nothing. And really, it doesn't. I have a hundred of those stacked up at home.

Amy studies the harsh lines and shading. "Your composition is perfect," she says a little wistfully. "Even when you aren't trying. I might hate you."

That makes me smile. "It's a sketch. It doesn't mean anything."

"Mhmm, and what about the hundred other times you've drawn him?"

"Those didn't mean anything either."

She laughs softly, because she's seen his face drawn in charcoal, scribbled on napkins, and traced in watercolor. He's never what I set out to draw, but he's always where I end up.

I crumple the paper into a tight ball and toss it into the trash can. "Let's talk about something else."

"Like your big debut?"

"Like that." My gaze sweeps over the big empty place in the corner where I spent the last three months sculpting. It was my first commission and my largest piece. It turned out more beautifully than I'd envisioned, and it's now installed on the fountain where it will stand, awaiting its official unveiling tomorrow night. I should feel proud. I should feel accomplished.

Instead a sense of dread has taken root in my chest, soaking up all the happiness, spreading through my limbs. I should be focused on my dreams or, at the very least, enjoying life as a college student. We aren't on the run anymore, but in my darkest hours I can't shake the feeling that we should be.

A hand covers mine, and I look up to see Amy's eyes full of concern. "It's beautiful, sweetie. Everyone will be blown away tomorrow night."

I force a smile. "I hope so, but I'll settle for not totally hating it."

"It's going to blow their minds, and I'm still bummed you won't let me be there to see it."

Her family is extremely uptight, and the fact that the Grand used to be a strip club means that it's off-limits. Technically almost anyplace off campus is off-limits, but she sneaks out often enough. She's determined to rebel, but I have to admit, it isn't a safe part of town. The only way my own sister lets me go is with her and Kip as my escort.

"You've already seen it." The statue is an angel reaching up, both sensual and pure, a representation of how I see the girls who stripped at the club. It may be a burlesque club now, may be respectable, but there was something beautiful and raw about what it had been. Survival and sex.

"Not installed."

"Use your imagination," I say, teasing. Her medium is paint, and her work is incredibly imaginative. She has a soft dreamy style, kind of like Alice in Wonderland with an Instagram filter.

She sticks out her tongue. "Well, you better call me after and tell me all about it. I bet you get a million new commissions."

I look down at the blank sheet of paper. She's not totally wrong about the commissions. The guest list to the opening gala is highbrow because the club owner, Ivan, has more money than God. And I learned a long time ago that money erases every sin. The hint of impropriety will just make the art that much more desirable.

But I'm not sure that I can fulfill those commissions. I'm not sure I want to. It's every artist's dream, but the lingering imprint on the blank paper, leftover pressure from charcoal, a mindless drawing, proves that I'm really dreaming about something else entirely.

"HERE COMES YOUR trophy boyfriend," Amy mutters.

I glance back to see a bunch of frat guys approaching, Shane at the head of the pack. The way they're weaving down the street, it's clear they're wasted. I feel myself tensing, because Shane can get a little intense when he hangs out with the boys after football practice. Which is most of the time, these days.

"Don't call him that," I say absently, hoping she can't see my worry.

"Why not? That's the only reason you're with him. Don't tell me it's his charming personality."

Shane knows how to be charming. He pursued me with the full weight of that charm. There are boys at the art school, but they're usually more interested in having me pose for them than actually dating. Shane made me feel desirable, coveted—at least until he started to change.

I don't answer her and instead paste on a smile for the guys. We're on the edge of campus, and the streets are still busy with students walking home after late-night study sessions or heading to a club. Light rain mists the air, leaving a sheen on everyone's skin.

Shane grins at me as he gets close, all swagger and sweaty male. A certain appreciation sweeps through me, but it feels detached, the way I'd view a beautiful piece of art.

"Hey, babe," he says with a sloppy kiss.

I hide my wince. Definitely drunk. "How was practice?"

"Killer. Coach made us lap the stadium ten fucking times." He grabs me around the waist, and I stumble against the pull of him. "But I'm feeling no pain now."

A grin tugs at my lips. "I bet you're not."

"We're heading over to Club X. Come with us."

Two blocks down is the clubbing district. Party Row, it's called. The clubs open up in warehouses with cheap couches and heavy beats, only to get shut down a few months later, usually related to drugs or sex work. Club X is the latest hot spot, which means Shane wants to go all the time.

I look down at my clothes, a tank top and jeans. Sandals. No makeup. "I'm not really dressed for it."

He pulls me close, his hands wrapping around my ass. I squirm because his friends are totally watching.

"Shane," I whisper.

His lips are close to mine. "Go back to your place and get dressed. I'll watch."

Unease twists my stomach, along with guilt I don't want to examine too closely. "Amy will come with me. You go ahead with the guys."

Shane might be a jock, but he's not stupid. He knows a rejection when he hears one. His lips firm. He tightens his hands on my hips, and for a tense moment, I think he's going to do something crazy, something violent, right here in front of everyone. His impatience has been getting stronger, his temper more extreme. Always in the privacy of a dark corner or his apartment on the rare occasion I visit him.

Always followed by an apology and a promise never to do it again.

"Hurry," he says finally, his voice sharp. "You don't want to miss all the fun."

Then he's gone in a swirl of testosterone, the raucous laughter of his teammates bouncing off the stately brick facades of university buildings.

We stand in silence, watching them go, until they round the corner at the end of the block, their shouts melting into the persistent clamor of Party Row. Even two blocks away you can almost feel the bass in the concrete beneath us, the sex and the glitter and the casual expectations.

"You okay?" Amy asks quietly.

I haven't been okay in years. Not since the night my sister and I went on the run. Not since the boy I loved gave up his life so we would be safe. "Of course. Why wouldn't I be?"

She frowns. "I don't like the way he looked at you."

"He's drunk."

"And you're making excuses." There's a pause, dark with speculation. "Are you still holding out on him?"

There's that shame again, but for all the wrong reasons. Shane and I have been dating for months. I've let him get to second base, but we haven't had sex. This isn't freaking middle school. Who does that?

I do, apparently. He would be humiliated if his teammates found out.

I'm just not ready to give up my virginity. *Not when you saved it for him.*

Which is crazy, because the boy of my teenage fantasies is dead. Shane is alive and so very willing.

"We'll do it soon," I say, but that sounds like a lie.

A small part of me feels guilty for stringing Shane along.

Most of me feels guilty for even considering having sex with anyone who isn't Giovanni.

"Oh, Clara." There's a wealth of meaning in those two words. *I don't think you should be with him. Doesn't it mean something that you won't have sex with him? Something is holding you back.*

I've heard it before, and I can't even deny it. I can't explain it either. Giovanni is my secret, a shard of glass buried so deep in my soul it would kill me to remove it.

"Let's hurry," I say, my voice hollow. "We don't want to miss all the fun."

CHAPTER TWO

I DECIDE ON a dark skirt and a black slinky sleeveless top that drapes low in the back. I finish the outfit with a glitter-gold headband that looks half-vintage, half-party girl. I'd love to wear my low black heels so I can dance the night away—it's more fun than sitting on Shane's lap while he trades mildly sexist jokes with his buddies. Instead I pull on my four-inch black heels studded with gold Swarovski crystals.

"Gorgeous," Amy says, but I hear the judgment in her voice.

"They *are* gorgeous." I don't have any right to be indignant, because I'm only wearing them for Shane. He likes me to look a certain way when we go out. That kind of control seems weird to Amy—and, well, maybe to most girls my age. But I was raised to be a mafia princess, someone who shuts her mouth and looks pretty. It's not a destiny I've fulfilled, but some of the lessons never go away.

Amy sighs and adjusts her silver dewdrop choker in the bathroom mirror. She borrowed a silver dress with ruffles and a short hem from my closet so we wouldn't have to stop at her apartment. "Aren't you going to

Honor's house tomorrow?"

"Regular Sunday night. Why? You want some real food?" We usually subsist on the food stands scattered around campus. There's a pretzel-dog guy outside the art history museum who knows my order before I say a word. Ever since my sister got married, she's turned into a regular Martha Stewart. Her house is like some country-chic magazine spread with fresh-baked muffins on the counter.

Amy clips a strand of pink hair and shakes her head so it blends. "Nah, I'm good." There's a suspicious pause while she adjusts hair that already looks fine. "You should bring Shane. Introduce him."

My heart stops. That would be a disaster. I can only imagine Shane swaggering into my sister's picturesque bungalow like a bull in a china shop. "How about no."

"Why not? At some point you have to tell Honor about him."

My sister, Honor, is already overprotective. Kip used to keep a cool head, but he's turned into a regular caveman now that they're married. They'd probably bar the door as soon as they saw him—and his flashy Viper. "You just want me to tell because you know she'll freak out."

"Anyone who cares about you would freak out," she says. "He's not good enough for you."

I focus on the bracelet clasp I'm fighting with, blinking against the sting in my eyes. "Why can't you just be happy for me? You're my best friend."

Her gentle hands take the bracelet from me. In a few seconds she has it attached around my wrist. Then her arms enfold me in a tight hug that steals all the air from my lungs.

"I'm sorry," she whispers fiercely.

My eyes squeeze shut, and I breathe in her familiar scent. Her arms are more comforting than Shane's have ever been. "Why can't you be a guy?"

She pulls back, grinning. "If I were a guy, I'd bang you in a heartbeat."

My laugh is a little watery. "Thanks."

"Hey," she says. "We don't have to go out tonight. Forget boys. They only bring drama, right?"

"Nah, we should go. We both look fabulous."

"That's right. Let him see what he can't have."

I wince because that's not what I'm trying to do.

And I know that Shane won't accept this forever.

"Do me a favor?" I ask softly.

"Anything."

"Leave the Shane thing alone for tonight?" There was a look in his eye, a hardness that made me shiver. He doesn't like being denied. He comes from a wealthy New England family. He's not used to being told no. "One night. That's all I'm asking."

She meets my gaze, and the solemn concern makes my insides clench. "One night," she says.

I know I'm only postponing the inevitable. Amy will bring this up again, and she's right. Eventually I will have to introduce my sister to Shane. Eventually I'll have to give in and let him have sex with me.

History is repeating itself…

That dark little voice in my head reminds me this is all I'd ever been meant for. Shut up and look pretty. The mafia princess who wasn't even a legitimate daughter. At least that's what the whispers said. So I tried even harder to be perfect—to be quieter and prettier.

Only my sister was strong enough to defy what was expected of her.

To escape the cruel fiancé chosen for her, we went on the run. We came to Tanglewood to hide. Honor met Kip, who protected her when we were found.

And now we're safe to be with whomever we want.

Except the only boy I want is the one who died to save us.

✧ ✧ ✧

THE LIGHT DRIZZLE from earlier has turned into a hot summer shower, so we order an Uber and wait under the overhang until it pulls up. The art department uses the older buildings in the university, without the glass and smooth granite bricks of the engineering building. Of course it's a campus joke because the art department doesn't have much money or resources. But I actually like the crumbling old buildings, the feeling of history, of being a part of something bigger than myself. Maybe that's because most of the time I feel so small.

My loft is a one-bedroom apartment just off campus, as ancient as those old buildings. Honor wasn't thrilled about me moving out, but it was just too stifling knowing she worried about me every time I came home late. So I moved here last semester with the promise that I visit at least once a week for Sunday night dinner.

We get to Party Row when Saturday night is in full swing, flashing neon signs advertising clubs and tattoo parlors and thinly veiled illegal pursuits. The car stops at the end of the street, where barricades are set up and a couple of rent-a-cops flirt with a group of college coeds.

Drunk guys and girls move from bar to bar, in the street. There are some old folks who come out, a shirtless guy in a rainbow Speedo, a man in a cowboy hat shouting at people who walk by. A couple of people have pamphlets that promise to save our souls.

Pretty much a regular Saturday night.

Amy and I hit the sidewalk and head toward the opposite end of the street where the newer, shadier clubs open up. Of course that's where Club X would be.

"Hey, girls, let me show you a good time," a guy yells to us from across the street.

His friend laughs at him. "You fucking wish."

Amy rolls her eyes but puts a little sway in her step for him. As much as she gives me a hard time about Shane, she enjoys the occasional drunk frat boy. *They have their purposes,* she says mysteriously. She means sex, and usually I nod along as if I know what that's about—even though she knows I don't.

We get catcalled all the way to Club X, where the line is halfway around the block.

"Not waiting," Amy says. "Tell your boyfriend to come get us."

Shane has a way of getting what he wants. Most of the time people just have to look at him. Something about him screams privilege, and they instinctively defer to that. But if that doesn't work, he doesn't mind slipping a couple twenties to get his point across.

Except if he has to leave his friends, he's going to be grumpy.

"Come on," I say, taking Amy's hand.

I lead her up to the bouncer and give him my best smile. I don't bother trying to be seductive, since I have exactly no clue how to do that. That's Amy's job. And besides, I have a decent track record with my innocent look. Maybe they think I got lost on my way to the library?

The bouncer gives me a once-over. He's built and really pretty hot in a tight-black T-shirt. Occasionally they get upperclassmen for this job, but this guy looks a couple years older—and definitely unimpressed with the college-girl tricks. "Back of the line."

"Please. My boyfriend is inside."

He doesn't even blink. "Tell him to come get you."

"His phone's dead." The lie comes easily. "But he's expecting me to meet him. He'll be mad if I show up late."

One eyebrow rises. "And that's supposed to convince me to let you in? Girls shouldn't be afraid of their boyfriends."

The words resonate inside me, a blow that echoes through every tense moment with Shane, through every moment of my childhood—where I learned that men are best obeyed if I don't want to be hurt. "I'm not afraid," I say, but my voice sounds hollow.

The bouncer doesn't appear convinced.

I'm saved from his dubious expression when Amy steps closer. The dewdrop choker she's wearing emphasizes the expanse of bare skin the silver dress exposes. Her shoulders are slender, her breasts small. The bouncer's lids lower in appreciation. They seem an unlikely match, the heavily muscled, tattooed bouncer and the pixie-sized good girl, but that's what Amy wants. She comes from doctors and investors and engineers, each with their own set of impressive credentials and awards and hefty bank accounts. Her art major and the rough-looking bouncer amount to the same for her. Freedom.

Oh, and I can understand that. That's what I've wanted my whole life, except now that I have it, I still feel tied down. Constrained by the expectations of my sister, my boyfriend. Unable to let go of the past.

Amy whispers something in the bouncer's ear, and even though he hasn't officially let me in, I scoot past him. She'll keep him occupied for a while at least, and if she's lucky, he'll occupy her right back.

Chapter Three

THE CROWD HAS already heated up, moving as one large ocean, liquid heat filling the dance floor. I slide between bodies and duck waving arms toward the back of the club, where sofas and chairs are haphazardly arranged. There isn't much seating in clubs like these, so usually people claim them fast. It doesn't matter when Shane shows up, though. He can clear the best seats with a few crisp bills or even a smile.

That's where I find him, holding court with one of his friends and several girls.

Two of the girls are chatting with Rick, a guy I've always found a little creepy. The other girl leans against Shane while he looks down her dress.

As I watch, he brushes his hand up her arm.

When I reach the table, Shane looks up. Guilt flashes in his eyes, and he gives the girl a shove that I find more disturbing than his flirting. She wobbles on her high heels before shooting me a venomous glance.

"Babe," Shane yells over the heavy thump of music. "I thought you'd never make it. Get your pretty ass over here."

Part of me wonders what would have happened if I

hadn't joined him tonight. Would he have kissed that girl? Would he have had sex with her? What bothers me most is how little that worries me. I know there's something toxic in our relationship, but toxic is all I know.

He grabs my wrist. Then the world is tilting sideways as he drags me onto his lap. I let out a small squeak before settling on his thighs. This close, I can smell the sweat on him, the faint musk of grass from the field. It's not unpleasant, exactly. It's just a little too intimate for comfort.

As is the erection pressing into my ass. I squirm to get back on solid ground.

He wraps his arm around my waist like an iron bar on a roller coaster. "Where you going, babe?"

"Yeah, *babe,*" Rick says, smirking. Everything dumb and dangerous that Shane has done while we've been together has been with Rick at his side. Bad influence doesn't begin to cover it, but it's not my place to tell Shane who his friends should be.

"Please don't call me that."

I know better than to challenge him, and sure enough, his lips widen. It's not a nice smile, especially when you factor in the calculation in his eyes. "Your girl needs to lighten up," he says, his gaze trained on mine.

"Yeah," Shane says, voice low. He's too busy feeling me up to realize we are wading into danger. He has one hand groping my ass, the other playing with the neckline of my dress.

"Stop," I whisper, but of course he doesn't hear me.

It's way too loud for that. I scan the crowd, hoping Amy will magically appear. Maybe that's cowardly of me, but I just want this night to end without a fight.

As if Rick reads my mind, he asks, "Where's the smurfette?"

He calls her that because her hair was blue when they first met. Since then it's been pink, purple, teal, and every color under the rainbow.

"I don't know," I say because I don't really. She might be at the front of the club, flirting with the bouncer. Or he might have taken a break and found some empty office for them to make out. Either way, I'm not sending Rick in their direction.

His eyes narrow. "I know she came with you."

Crap. "She went to the bathroom."

Rage flashes over his face—he doesn't like being lied to, but most of all, he hates that Amy isn't interested in him. She likes to rebel, but she's not stupid.

Shane grows bold enough to push his hand inside my dress and stroke my breast.

My whole body goes stiff. I grab his wrist. "Stop."

"Fuck," he mumbles, his face buried in my hair. He's hard as a rock underneath me, almost rolling his hips into me. This is bad. He's too far gone to say no right now, and if we were doing this at my apartment, I might have to go along with it. But we're not in my apartment. We're in the back of the club. As much as I'm trained to avoid conflict, I can't let him undress me in public.

"Shane, I mean it. Stop that."

"Why should he stop?" Rick says, his voice taunting. "It's nothing he hasn't done before, right?"

Oh no, this is bad. I figured Shane wouldn't tell anyone that we haven't had sex yet. It might make people question his virility. Maybe it sounds weird, but I'm fine with everyone assuming I've put out even if I haven't. Except the way Rick's eyes have lit up, he must know we haven't.

Shane's body tenses, his fingers tightening on my ass and on my breast. "Shut the fuck up."

Maybe I should be glad my boyfriend is finally sticking up for me, even though I know it's more about himself. But my conditioning kicks in. I stroke his arm, trying to soothe. "Don't worry about him. Let's get out of here. Let's just go."

He's still taut with anger, with frustration. "Why do you fucking do this to me?" he says, bitter and sharp. For a moment I think he knows how toxic we are together.

I think he hates it too.

"Too fucking uptight to spread your legs," he adds, and my hope withers.

"We'll go back to my place," I say, placating. This feels like a pot boiling over, and I'm desperate to remove the heat. So what if I have to sleep with my boyfriend to do it. Girls do that all the time. At least that's what I tell myself.

He rocks his erection into me, and I know it's working.

I close my eyes for a moment. This is how it will be,

the throbbing rhythm, the darkness. With my eyes closed I can pretend he's someone else. Best of all, I can pretend I'm someone else.

"You've waited this long, man," Rick says, breaking into my fantasy. "Why stop now?"

I feel the heat go up a couple of degrees. "Let's go," I say, pleading.

"You got some magic pussy, is that it? Some fucking unicorn tits under that dress? Because I've seen my share of tits. Not sure why you're hiding yours like they're something special."

Shane shoves off his chair, and I tumble off his lap. The ground hits my knees hard, my palms harder. I shudder out a breath. God, this is messed up. And I don't even care. I don't want a great relationship with a nice boy. I don't want Shane either. But I can't have what I want, so this is where I end up, on my hands and knees in a dirty club.

I turn in time to see Shane haul Rick out of his chair.

Rick is either too drunk or too stupid to care. He laughs, loud and cocky. "Her sister is a fucking stripper. And your girl won't even let you touch her."

Oh, that's too damn far. I'll do almost anything to avoid confrontation, but I draw the line where my sister is concerned. She's not a stripper—not anymore—and when she was, she did it to protect me.

I don't get a chance to defend her honor, though, because Shane tackles him. They fly into the table behind us, knocking it over. People scatter, forming a circle to lock us in. Making this into a circus act.

My stomach turns over, and I push myself unsteadily to my feet. People don't move out of the way for me like they did for Shane and Rick, but I shove myself between them, blind, sick, heading sideways until I see red lights that spell EXIT.

Humid air wraps its fingers around my throat. The rain seems to have stopped, leaving every surface glittering. I lean against the damp brick wall, sucking in moist air that's surprisingly fresh for an alley. My head falls back, and I stare up at a heavy blanket of dark clouds.

There are no stars. There are never any stars.

A harsh metal sound warns me that Shane's not done with me tonight.

"Clara!" He barrels into the alley like he's still spoiling for a fight. A bruise darkens the side of his face. And judging from the glint in his eyes, he blames me.

My heart leaps into my throat. "You're scaring me."

He pushes right into my face, hands flat against the brick on either side of me. His hot breath blows across my cheek. "You've been leading me around by my dick since we met."

"That's not true." We met at a coffee cart outside the art building. He was in his third year, taking a basic art class to satisfy his business degree requirement. He was ahead of me in line after class, and when I stepped forward to order, I discovered he'd paid for my drink. After I got my coffee, he introduced himself, using the charming smile that made everyone fall in line—even me.

He took me to old movies at a local theater that served themed menus to match. And on Valentine's Day he sent so many roses that my room had overflowed. He told me that he liked my innocence so much he didn't mind waiting for me.

His eyes narrow. "I think you like this shit, giving me blue balls. Making us fight over you."

"You weren't fighting over me! Not like that. He was just being an ass." I'm not sure when the anger started, the accusations. It feels like it came slowly, creeping up on me. By the time I realized how bad it had gotten, I was almost afraid to end things. How would he react?

Shane scoffs. "All my friends want to fuck you, and I'm tired of fucking lying."

"So don't. It looked like Rick knew anyway."

"He figured it out, because I was—" He cuts off with a dark glare. "And now he won't fucking shut up. I get it, you're hard to get. Message received."

My breath catches. "You think this is a game?"

"It is a game. You're playing me, and I fucking played along. I waited for you longer than any other guy would have."

That isn't exactly true. Giovanni waited for me longer than a couple months…and we never got to be together. *But he's gone now.* I can't keep living in the past.

And maybe Shane is right. Maybe this is a game, but not like he thinks. I wasn't trying to make him jealous. I was living in an imaginary world where Giovanni was somehow alive, where he'd find me and we could be together. I was playing pretend.

"Okay," I say softly, giving up more than my virginity. I'm giving up the dream of another boy in another time. "Let's go back to my place."

"No," he says.

"Yours then."

"And give you time to change your mind? No fucking way. Here. We're doing it right here."

Shock leaves me cold. This isn't the charming boy who paid for my latte. This isn't the hot guy sneaking a feel underneath the table on a date. This isn't even about sex. I saw what my sister did, both at the strip club and in our previous life—the way sex became about power. That's how this feels, like Shane is trying to prove a point.

That's not how I want my first time to be. *Cruel hands on my back, hot breath on my neck.* I swore to myself that my first time would be with someone I loved. I may be able to break that promise for Shane, but at least I want the illusion.

I make my voice soft. "Please, Shane. I'm sorry I made you wait so long. Let's just find a bed, and I promise—"

"I said no. Did you hear me? We're going to lift that short skirt of yours right here, right now, and I'm going to get what I've been waiting for."

My shock hardens into anger. I would do a lot to

avoid conflict, but I won't lose my virginity in a back alley. I know I seem soft—it's why my sister is so protective of me. But underneath I'm forged in steel. Even she doesn't know how that happened. She doesn't know what our father did and she never will.

I push against his broad chest, and maybe in surprise, he takes a half step back. "I said no, Shane."

And then he does something horrible—he laughs. The most disturbing thing about that laugh is that I've heard it before. It doesn't sound particularly sinister. It's an ordinary, fun-loving laugh from an ordinary, fun-loving guy, except he's laughing about something dark and twisted.

"No one will care," he says. "You've been dating me for months."

My chest feels tight. I've been in this situation before, with a man who wouldn't take no for an answer. Last time I had a protector. I had Giovanni, but I'm alone now. "Stop," I say. "This isn't you."

His lips brush over my cheek. "You don't really know me."

Then I feel his hands on my legs, pushing up. I shove my skirt down, but I'm no match for him. The cold air rushes between my legs—and then this hand is there, groping, feeling, taking.

No, I won't let this happen. I make fists and hit him anywhere I can reach: his shoulders, his neck. Only when I manage to get the bruise on his face does he swear roughly. It seems to enrage him. Hard hands shove me back into the wall. The brick catches me in its cold net. My breath rushes out of me. Spots dance in front of my eyes.

Shane leans back to reach for his zipper.

A blur flashes in the corner of my eye, something dark and fast.

It crashes into Shane, and they slide along the gravel into the shadows. The sound of fists smacking flesh makes me wince. My hands shake as I cover my mouth. Oh God, this is just like before. Except I don't know who had come after Shane. A stranger? I can't see into the deep part of the alley, and I'm not getting any closer than I have to.

Without even meaning to, I take a step back toward the street. Then I turn, and I'm running to the entrance. The bouncer's still there. Amy, too.

"Someone's fighting," I manage, breathless. "In the alley. Please help them."

The bouncer doesn't seem surprised. He mutters something into a mic attached to his shirt before taking off around the corner. I have to trust that he'll break up the fight, but I don't want to be here when he does. I don't want to give Shane another chance to attack me.

"Oh my God," Amy says. "He's fighting again? Are you okay?"

No, I'm not okay. Not like she means. I'm not injured, but I'm cracking open inside, because for the briefest second, it had seemed like Giovanni was saving me. That's impossible, I knew. He died years ago. It's just some kind of flashback, a memory from when he saved me before.

More wishful thinking.

"Let's get out of here, please," I beg.

Amy doesn't ask another question. She grabs my hand and steers us toward the side street where cabs line up. We get into the backseat without another word and take the ride home in silence, my shaking hand in hers.

Chapter Four

When I reach my building, I bypass the front door with its key-card entry. Instead I head into the alley beside my loft apartment and climb the fire escape. These are the kind that slant at a steep angle, more like skinny stairs than a ladder.

Sure enough, a matted bundle of blonde-brown fur wriggles on the second-floor landing.

"Hey, Lupo," I murmur, keeping my voice soft and my movements slow.

He backs up until he's at the corner of the bars, his small body trembling with anxiety. We've done this dance for weeks now, but he still doesn't trust me to get close.

I think he belonged to whoever used to live here. Either that or he just likes to climb. The first time I caught a glimpse of shaggy fur, I opened the window and he raced down the stairs. After that I started leaving scraps in a bowl outside the window. Only when I come up through the stairs do we even get this close.

Sometimes I imagine snatching him up into my arm and bundling him inside. I could brush the knots out of his fur and feed him from my hand.

Then I worry that startling him will set us back. Will he still trust me if I keep him trapped inside? So for the time being I'm content to coax him gently, to show him I won't hurt him, night after night.

Whispering sweet nothings, I push the window up from the outside and pull out the food I left there this morning. Slowly, slowly I scoot the bowl to his side of the landing.

"Aren't you a pretty one," I croon as he sniffs at the food, then begins to eat. "Aren't you sweet."

I remain like that, crouched on the metal grate, watching as he downs the whole meal. Only then do I step in through the window. As soon as I'm inside, no longer blocking the stairway, Lupo rattles the steps on his way down.

"Good night," I whisper into the damp night air.

The only response is the tinny sound of a trash can knocked aside. With a sigh, I pull the bowl in and shut the window. On impulse I turn back and push the window open again. My sister would freak if she knew I was doing this, but Lupo might come back while I'm sleeping. He might be curious enough to peek his nose inside if he knows it's safe.

I drop the empty bowl in the sink and grab an orange from the counter for a late-night snack. Settling into the drawing table that I use for both my art and my schoolwork, I toss the peel into the trash can and set the split pieces on the pencil ledge.

The loft is really a single room with thin hardwood

slats set diagonally on the floor and a high, peaked ceiling. A small kitchen frames one corner, the door to a small bathroom in the other. The open window splits the space between a twin bed and nightstand and a lounge my sister found at an estate sale. The drawing table and small wardrobe for my clothes round out the rest of the space.

It's an ordinary apartment in this part of Tanglewood, except for the paint. I've covered almost every surface I can find. My landlord agreed that I could paint the walls as long as I paint them back before I move out. He probably thought I meant a soft beige or maybe a trendy sky blue. Instead there's a patchwork quilt on one side and a mountain vista on the other. The starry night surrounding the window and a gothic Rapunzel on the other side. Not even the furniture escapes my brush. The squat wooden legs of the chaise are fashioned into chess pieces. Thorny vines wrap around the tall spindly legs of the drawing table.

Heavy sketch paper sits on top of the table, waiting for me to draw. Except I don't want to see Giovanni's face again, not like earlier. I'm haunted by his ghost, but he isn't around me. He's inside me.

I could do some studying instead. Or maybe browse Buzzfeed until I'm tired enough to sleep.

They would both be safe enough.

But there's some kind of demon inside me that flips open my laptop. Some horrible impulse that clicks the bookmarked link. Why do I keep doing this? I can't seem to stop myself.

The obituary is short and unbearably impersonal. There's no picture.

> *GIOVANNI COSTAS, 18, of Henderson, Nevada, passed away of unknown causes.*

Unknown causes. My mind had filled in a thousand horrifying possibilities in the years since I found this record online. What happened to him after I left? I remember his slight smile in the dim moonlight, the warmth of his body as he lay beside me. Those memories are bad, but even worse is my imagination—his body beaten, bruised. A bullet in his heart. Someone had hurt him, *killed* him, most likely because he had helped me. Whatever he did to distract them so that my sister and I could escape, cost him his life.

The temperature in the large room seems to drop a few degrees, and I shiver. On my darker nights I imagine that he haunts me. Selfishly I sometimes wish that he would, if only so I can see him again. The loft remains empty, light wavy on the knotted hardwood floors as clouds cross the moon.

The trill of my cell phone makes me jump.

I slam the laptop lid shut, feeling guilty and somehow afraid. I never told anyone about seeing Gio's obituary, even my sister. Especially not my sister. She worries about me enough without knowing that I'm grieving.

Sure enough, the phone screen flashes her smile. I

snapped that picture while Kip was behind her, pressing his face into her hair. The bliss on their faces burrows under my skin, uncomfortable and hot. Like anyone who's been burned by love, it hurts to see two people so happy together. I can't stop looking, though. Can't stop pressing on that bruise.

"Hey, Sis," I say into the phone, my voice a little husky with lingering emotion.

"Are you okay?"

"Of course I am." Only barely, I refrain from saying that I'm always okay, that she has me wrapped up so tight that it sometimes feels stifling. I know it only comes from a place of love, but sometimes I long to break away from her caring arms as much as from my father's harsh grip.

"I haven't seen you lately," she says, her tone contrite. She knows she can be overprotective, and she tries to curb it. Well, Kip helps her with that.

I may have missed a couple of Sunday dinners.

"I'm sorry. I've been busy with school." And with not telling her about my boyfriend. At least I won't have to keep that secret anymore. After tonight I'm officially done with Shane. "How have you been?"

"Good." The smile comes through the line loud and clear. "It's our third anniversary."

I flop onto my bed, her happiness stealing away my earlier gloom. At least one of us can be lucky in love. "So what did he get you?"

"Too much. This gorgeous ruby necklace, an all-day

spa gift certificate—for two, by the way, so I expect you to come with me. We'll make it a girls' day."

"I don't want to think too much about this, but are you sure he didn't mean for you two to go together? Isn't that a thing people do? Couple's massage or something."

She gives a snort-laugh that still manages to sound delicate. "There's enough money on this thing for two full days of body wraps, facials, massages, and who knows what else. Either you're doing this with me or they offer an entirely different kind of couple's massage at this place."

A flush crosses my cheeks like it always does when someone mentions sex. You'd think being friends with Amy would have inoculated me to this kind of embarrassment. "Okay then, count me in."

"I can schedule us for the day after tomorrow? After the big reveal, we'll have something to celebrate."

I blow out a breath. "Sounds great."

"Hmm," she says. "Nervous?"

This is one of the upsides of having an overprotective big sister. She knows when I need to talk. "Only a lot. People are going to take one look at it and think I'm a hack."

"You mean the amazing, creative, breathtaking piece of art my talented sister made? Yeah, I don't think so. They're actually going to think it's too good for the Grand, considering it used to be a strip club."

"Umm, they'll be attending a re-opening gala at said strip club."

"Hypocrites come in all income brackets."

"I feel like that should be on a fortune cookie."

"And don't worry. Actually, forget I said that. I know you're worried. That's part of the artistic process. But while you're worrying, know that people who love you are going to be standing by your side tomorrow night. And we all see what a shining bright star you are."

"That should *definitely* be on a fortune cookie."

"Trust me, grasshopper. Everything will work out."

Her words are the warmth and reassurance I need. "Thank you."

"Anytime. Kip and I will pick you up tomorrow night at six."

"I can drive."

"Ha! In that neighborhood? Kip would have a heart attack."

I'm not sure it's Kip who would have the heart attack, but I can go along with this. "Okay, pick me up at six. Then the next morning, all-day spas. I want something completely wild and luxurious, like a gold-leaf body wrap."

"Done." I hear the smile in her voice. "Now get some sleep."

"Good night."

I click off the phone. The orange pieces linger on the pencil ledge, uneaten. I'm not hungry anymore, but I gather them into my hand and carry them across the room. They roll and rest around the glass of water that sits there, half-empty. I take a sip, and the coolness soothes my throat. *Stop thinking about ghosts.*

The whole apartment is humid from the open window, the evening's rain steeped in moonlight. I stretch beneath the sheets and curl my body around a pillow. The streetlamp winks at my window, and my eyes fall shut, again and again, snapshots in the dark.

A space between sleep and waking suspends me, turns me inside out. I can't quite breathe, but I can't drown. I try to pull myself awake, but exhaustion weighs me down.

Minutes pass, hours.

The sheets wrap around my limbs, trapping me. Sweat slicks my skin, but I can't fight the heat or the damp. Can't do anything but fight.

Giovanni's face hovers above me, incorporeal and wavy. "You grew up," it says, harsh and accusing.

"Wait." I know he isn't real, he *can't* be real, but that doesn't make me any less desperate. My arms reach out, grasping at nothing. "Don't leave me."

I wake up panting, alone in my apartment. A dream.

That's all that's left of him, of us—a memory.

Streaks of purple break the sky in half. Morning is here. I don't feel rested at all, even though an entire night has passed. Maybe I'm getting too old to visit clubs so late. Without Shane, I won't have any reason to. That's probably for the best. I don't need another night like this.

Today I have studio time reserved at the university. Since I'm up so early I can walk the halls of the university's art museum. It doesn't open to the public until nine, but department students can get in anytime.

With a small groan, I push out of bed and check my phone.

There are a bunch of texts from Shane. I don't want to read them.

Something dark compels me to.

WTF? Where are you? I get fucked up and you run out on me?

At the emergency room. Hope you're happy.

I cringe a little at that one. Part of me feels like I should have stayed with him, taken him to the hospital, and taken him home at the end. Except he's the one who wouldn't take no for an answer. How messed up is it to want to comfort your own attacker?

At least I have a text from Amy to boost my spirits.

That bouncer was big in all the right places

That pulls a smile from me—and a blush. I'm glad she went back and had some fun, even though my night ended early. I send back a wink emoji. *His heart?*

You are such a dork. I love you.

The clock reads 5:30 a.m. If she went back to see him after midnight… *Why are you still awake?*

Walk of shame

A smile tugs at my lips. *Didn't want the big bad bouncer to wake up and see you?*

Boys are so needy

After Shane's behavior last night, I can't really disagree. Needy, pushy. *I'm done with them,* I type. While I wait for her to answer, I delete his messages and block his number.

For real?

I know she doesn't mean all boys. She wants to know if I'm serious about breaking up with Shane. *You were right about him.*

I'm sorry

Don't be. I'm over it.

She sends me a sad-face emoji. *Do you need help finding a rebound? I know a bouncer.*

That makes me laugh. *No rebounds, but I do need hair and makeup for this thing tonight. And maybe some wine.*

Then I'm your girl. I'll come over at four.

I set the phone on the nightstand beside the glass of water. An invigorating breeze wafts in from the open window. I might have to leave it up more often. For now, I close the window and flip the lock.

A quick shower strips the lingering anxiety from my dream. By the time I'm dressed in slouchy pants and a purple cami, my hair tied in a wet knot, I'm ready to face the day.

I take a campus bus to the art building and my student ID lets me into the museum wing. There's a Rembrandt and Van Gogh in here, though not the recognizable pieces. The collection is eclectic, built through decades of different curators and styles. I love turning a corner and finding something new to examine in a painting I've already seen.

But this morning I head for a picture I've looked at too long to be surprised. My favorite piece in the exhibit. This one was done by a university student, who went on to some acclaim before settling down to teach art at a high school in Toronto. Such a mundane end for an artist who created this, a photography piece. Not my usual medium, but only film could have captured the eerie flash of night, the splash of trees, the faint silhouette of a face framed by leaves and sky.

I see Giovanni everywhere, even here. Sometimes it's a comfort that I can still remember him. *Don't leave me.* Other times grief twists my stomach inside out.

Why can't I forget?

Only here, alone in a maze of white walls, staring at a dusty old print, do I realize. The orange pieces I opened last night, the ones I left on my nightstand—when I woke up this morning, they were gone.

CHAPTER FIVE

THE STATUE I made for the Grand is an angel, my tribute to the women who worked on that stage. To my sister, to Lola, to Candy. They danced with strength and with grace, rising above the base lust of their customers. They danced to survive. The angel's dress drapes her body, revealing more than nakedness, the stone fabric wet. Her lips curve in a tempting smile while her eyes are solemn. The vixen and the innocent, wrapped into one holy package.

That piece came easily to me because I knew what it should be. Gratitude for my sister, reverence for the other girls. They drove my design just as much as the proportions and measurements.

My plan is to sculpt the counterpoint next, the archangel Gabriel. Except whenever I draw even the simplest of sketches…I see him instead.

The blank page yawns in front of me, but I can already see the shade beneath his cheekbone, the curve of his eyebrow, the pillow of his lower lip. Frustration burns in my stomach. I want to move past this. I want to move past him.

"You need a model."

I jump, almost tumbling off the hollow metal stool I'm on. Amy slouches against the large table behind me, messenger bag slung over her shoulder, the scent of fresh pine radiating from her. She raises one eyebrow at me, and I know she's right. Most sculptors work from models. I've done it before, and I'll do it again. But the angel came from a different place, a deeper place. I want Gabriel to be the same way.

"No models."

"But they're so pretty. And so naked."

I scrunch my nose at her. "You just want dibs on him when I'm done sculpting."

She drops her bag on the table and begins pulling out her work. The quilt in the corner covers a wire-frame mermaid that looks a little like me. I modeled for it, but the shape of wire is loose enough that it's not entirely obvious. Which is a good thing because the piece will be shown in our class gallery at the end of the year, where my sister and her husband will be.

"Maybe," she says, her eyes flashing with…worry? "Then again, maybe not. You could ask Shane to do it. And in that case, I think I'd have to pass."

My eyes narrow. "Why would I ask Shane?"

"Well…he's already here, for one thing. And looking pretty desperate for a way to make things up to you." She shrugs. "He does have the muscles for it."

"Oh my God." I glance around wildly as if Shane is going to suddenly jump out from under a table. The studio space is large, designed for multiple students to use, but we have to reserve time so it's not too crowded at any moment. "What do you mean, he's here?"

She pulls out a worn leather satchel that contains her wire-cutting tools. "Downstairs. I didn't let him follow me in."

Like the museum after hours, art buildings require our student IDs on the weekends. I rush to the window and peer down at the stone steps, where a very rough-looking Shane waits. His clothes look rumpled, his jaw covered in a sheen of dark-blond scruff. From one story up I can see the dark shadow of a bruise on his cheek and a cut on his lip. "Oh no," I murmur.

"Ignore him," Amy says in a tired voice, as if she knows I'm not going to listen.

She's right. I can't leave him down there, especially once I spot the bouquet of roses hanging from one fist. I'm not going to get back with him, but I can't ignore him either.

He has the grace to look abashed when I open the door.

"Shane," I say, but I don't know where to go from there. *Why did you come here? It's over.*

"I know you're mad." He holds out the flowers, waxy petals glistening in the sunlight. "I fucked up. I had too much to drink, and Rick was being an ass—"

"Rick is always an ass."

"You're right," he says, contrite. "You're completely right. I'm done with him."

"You can't be done with him. You're both on the

football team."

"I mean it. No more late nights. No more partying. I know you don't like it, babe. Last night was a wake-up call for me." He runs a hand over his bruised jaw and winces. "I'm ready to make a change."

Tenderness swells up inside me. Maybe that's crazy, considering the way he pushed me against the club wall last night. But I've always had a weakness for dangerous men, part survival instinct and part reckless desire. "I can't do this anymore, Shane."

"That's what I'm saying, babe. Let me fix this."

"I can't see you anymore." Can't continue a cycle that isn't healthy for either of us. And most of all, I can't pretend I'm not in love with a dead man anymore. "I'm sorry."

His expression flickers with hurt, with anger. "You're pissed. I get it."

"I'm not angry." My voice comes out mournful enough that I know he believes me. "I'm done."

He sucks in a breath. "Don't do this to me, Clara. I need you."

It's one of the few times he's used my real name, and it transports me back to that first meeting at the coffee cart, his uncertainty, his charm. The need clenching his fists in my hair the first time we kissed. There's some part of him that does want me, need me. But nothing can really happen between us. It's not only about his asshole friends or his tendency to drink. It's about me being hung up on another man.

"Shane…what happened after I left? Who was the guy who stopped you?"

A scowl darkens his face. "I never saw the bastard clearly. By the time that fucking bouncer came around, he was gone."

Something trembles inside me—uncertainty? Hope? God, I'm so messed up. A shadowy image flashes through my mind, a familiar face. I've sketched it so many times. "They didn't catch his face…like on a security camera or something?"

He snorts. "Security camera? It was fucking nighttime. Besides, no one was looking at tapes. The bouncer told me to get lost. Said I wasn't welcome at that club anymore, that he'd blacklist me from the entire Party Row."

I can't help but wonder how much of his sudden desire to stop partying comes from that. "Shane," I say as gently and as firmly as I can. "I'm sorry, but it's over."

His expression hardens, and I see the sharp edges of the man who hurt me last night. Cold eyes rake over my cami and loose pants, my toes peeking out the bottom in my flip-flops. "I can't believe I waited for you. Rick was right about you. You're just a frigid bitch after all."

The sun flicks through leaves, blinding me for seconds at a time. I watch Shane cross the plush green university lawn.

I know I did the right thing in breaking up. Shane's parting words proved that, if nothing else. But it still lends a somber air to the afternoon. Tonight is my big break, but I can't shake the feeling of danger. Of dread. I had the same feeling the day my sister and I had to run. The same day Giovanni died.

CHAPTER SIX

"WITHOUT FURTHER DELAY, please let me present to you all an incredible artist and lovely young woman."

Candy hands me the microphone with an encouraging smile.

I climb the small steps to the temporary stage, my heart thumping inside my chest. A hundred of Tanglewood's wealthiest people fill the courtyard, swathed in linen and silk and jewels. Some of these same people frequented the Grand when it was a strip club, anonymous and furtive. Now they're here with a mixture of pride and disdain—and the same prurient curiosity as before.

My hand shakes as I hold the microphone tight. A sharp, high-pitched sound arcs over the crowd before falling silent. I hold curved metal close to my mouth and speak.

"Thank you for having me tonight." My voice comes out shaky, so I take a deep breath. This is important. Not just for my career, but for my sister. For my friends.

Candy overcame the odds to be standing here tonight, looking glamorous and confident. No one would know she once shivered in a dirty white shift under the control of a cult leader. She's the one who turned this place into a burlesque show.

I grip the microphone tighter. "It's an honor to be here tonight, sharing my work with you. But this night isn't about me. And it's not really about all of you either."

There are a few soft gasps in the audience.

"This is about the women onstage, the ones who dance under those bright lights, night after night. Their costumes are beautiful, their makeup flawless." My voice grows stronger as I look at my sister, tears shining in her dark eyes, Kip's arms around her. "Their dancing is powerful and elegant, but that's not why we're here either."

I look at Lola, who overcame so much just to grow up. Things most people take for granted. A home, parents. Enough food to eat. She started stripping at the Grand to support the only foster parent who ever cared about her.

"We're here to celebrate the women inside, beneath skin and muscle, bone-deep. The resilience of the human spirit. We're here because we want to bask in their strength, if only for a few hours. As if even the sight of them raised up will lift us too."

My voice cracks on the last word, and I can't shake the dread from earlier, the danger. Can't shake the feeling that this is goodbye. I nod to the men dressed in suits on either side of the fountain. They reach for the black silk covering the angel and pull it away.

The crowd audibly sucks in a breath at the sight of the angel, standing proudly in the center of the fountain—her wings stretched as if to take flight, her eyes with all the dark knowledge of this earth and all the painful hope for more.

I step down, my insides still quivering from being onstage, and the crowd sweeps me up. *It's gorgeous, transcendent. Who was your model? Do you take commissions? What's your availability?*

Honor manages to squeeze in beside me and encircles me in a hug. "You were wonderful up there," she whispers.

"Thank you," I say, eyes wet with tears.

She hands me back my silver clutch before people press their way between us again. I knew that I might get a commission or two out of this event, but I'm unprepared for the deluge of interest. I answer the questions as best I can, feeling overwhelmed.

I didn't use a model for this piece. I'm not sure what my availability will be. No, I don't have a website. No agent either.

It feels like I've been fielding questions for hours even though it's probably just been twenty minutes. I'm out of breath and flushed.

"Excuse me," I murmur to an older woman dripping in diamonds.

Without waiting for her response, I stumble away, ignoring the calls and the hands that reach for me. Is this how my sister felt when she danced onstage? Except worse because she was naked—and the men thought they had a right to her body.

I stumble across the courtyard, over the threshold of wide double doors, across velvety carpet. The first private places I see are the small vestibules that used to be VIP rooms. They've been converted into ticket booths, but they're not operational right now because this is a closed, invite-only grand opening event.

Leaning back against the door of one, I close my eyes and breathe deep—trying not to think about all the things that have happened in these four-by-four feet of space: favors paid for, things taken without permission.

Once my breathing evens out, I reach into my clutch and pull out my phone. It's blinking with notifications, which isn't surprising. A bunch of my classmates are on Instagram with me…and now that I think about it, I guess I could have given this URL to the people asking about my website. Then I remember the goofy picture Amy and I took with the shot glasses shaped like high-heeled shoes. It's probably best I didn't tell them about my account.

There's also a text message from Amy.

Hey—this is going to sound weird. You know the guy you always sketch? I think I saw him.

My heart immediately races faster than it did onstage. The shadowy shape of him that night in the alley. The missing orange pieces. I tell myself I'm imagining things, but it doesn't help.

With trembling fingers I type, *That's not possible.*

After a minute my phone rings. "Hello," I breathe. "What happened? Where did you see him?"

"It's probably nothing," she says, but her voice sounds strange, like she's just seen a ghost. "I left my makeup bag at your place, and I have a date with Mr. Bouncer tonight, so I went back to get it. I used my key and went straight to the bathroom. I was just packing up the eyeshadow when I heard this sound in the apartment."

"Oh my God."

"I went out and I didn't see anything, so—I don't know why, but I walked over to the window and looked down. There was someone at the bottom. I just saw a flash of his face with the streetlamp. Then he was gone. It freaked me out, that's all."

"Of course it did. That's scary." The neighborhood isn't exactly the safest. Not as dangerous as where I am now, though. "What did you do?"

"Nothing. I peeked out at the street before I left, and waited until the Uber pulled up before I stepped outside. But I didn't see anyone. Just some students walking around."

"I'm sorry it scared you, but I bet Lupo got spooked and that got your attention. Then you saw some random guy—"

"But he looked like *him*, Clara. I must have seen a hundred sketches of him by now."

Something that feels uncomfortably like hope shifts

in my chest. I push it down. "I wish you were right, but it's just not possible. He's…" I've never told her who Giovanni was to me—or what happened to him. "He's dead."

"Oh," she says, voice quiet. "I'm sorry."

"Look, don't worry about it. Go out with Mr. Bouncer—who has a name, I presume?"

"Probably."

I snort. "Well, have fun with him and his muscles. I'll see you tomorrow night."

When I hang up, I have a smile on my face. It fades as I remember what she said. *He looked like* him, *Clara.* She really has seen a lot of sketches of him. But there are bound to be men who look like him. Dopplegängers. And she saw him in the dark, from one story up. There's no way it's him.

I know this, and yet somehow my fingers are pulling up the Uber app and ordering a car. Then I'm slipping through the crowd, avoiding my sister so she doesn't see me leave.

I'm breathless by the time I reach my building's door and run up the stairs. I throw the door open, but my loft is empty. Of course it is. The window reveals an empty fire escape and an empty sidewalk below.

Disappointment burns in my gut.

I curl my fingers under the wood frame, painted over with swirls of blue, and lift the window.

"Lupo," I call, my voice hushed. The word bounces off the brick walls and echoes back. With a sigh I put out a bowl of dog food in case he comes back later.

Then I shut the window. At least he'll be able to relax better with me gone.

Exhaustion drags at my limbs, the euphoria of the night collapsing into grief. Giovanni is gone. I need to accept that. Sometimes I feel like my life depends on it.

My gaze drifts over to the bare nightstand surface. No oranges. I must have gotten up during the night and eaten them. It's the only thing that makes sense. The only thing left is a full glass of water.

I take a sip, and the liquid feels so refreshing, so calming, that I take another sip. And another.

Soon the glass is half-full. Sleep drags my eyelids down. This is crazy. I'm still dressed in a silver sheathe, still holding my clutch in my hand, makeup on my face and high heels on my feet. I'm not ready for bed at all, but I feel like I'm a breath away from sleep.

The night must have taken more out of me than I thought. I guess it's not that strange for me to be sleepy—I woke up early and then had to deal with Shane. Then there was the unveiling and the impossible hope of seeing Giovanni. Maybe I can take a little nap.

I drink the rest of the glass of water and barely set it down before my hand slips. My eyes are already closed by the time I curl up against the pillow, on top of the blanket.

A little nap.

So strange, though, how quickly I fell asleep. Completely dressed. All of a sudden.

Only as sleep claims me do I remember that the glass was half-full last night. And I didn't refill it today. Someone else did, my mind sleepily fills in. But I'm too tired to care. Sleep pulls me under.

Chapter Seven

Something moves me gently, constant and rhythmic like waves. I'm warm. There's something soft curling around my arms, wrapped inside my fists. Padding beneath my cheek that smells like home.

An unnatural darkness weighs down on me, keeping me from waking up—a demon's whisper in my ear. *You're warm, you're safe. Sleep.*

But something is wrong.

I remember falling asleep, so suddenly, remember drinking water that I hadn't filled. And I remember the phone call from Amy telling me that Giovanni's alive. Impossible.

Awareness pricks my skin like a cold breeze. Wherever I am, I'm not alone.

I blink rapidly, forcing my eyes open. They adjust to the darkness quickly, taking in the tinted windows on either side and the wide leather bench curving beneath me. I'm in a car. A limo, to be exact. And it's moving.

On the opposite side of the long space, a large body reclines. I can see the wide stance of his legs, the pale white of his shirt. A suit jacket tossed beside his hip. His face is hidden in the shadows of the vehicle.

I was raised by the head of the Las Vegas mafia, the capo. I grew up around guns and violence, so I know when a man is armed. It's the way he holds himself, the warning shimmering around him like a dark halo.

This man is armed and extremely dangerous.

Every muscle in my body tenses. My mind still swims in thick water, because I must have been drugged. *He* drugged me, this faceless man. Why did he take me? It won't be anything good, that's for sure.

Even worse, I suspect this has something to do with my past, with my family. It's messed up that I'd rather be taken by some random psycho. But at least then I'd have a chance of getting away.

"Who are you?" I demand, my voice hoarse from whatever drugs they gave me.

There's a long pause, the weight of his regard as heavy as a finger trailing down my neck.

"Have I really changed that much, bella, that you don't recognize me?"

The deep timbre runs over my skin, filling the hollows that have been there for years. Years when I believed he was dead, that he had been killed protecting me. Except he's here.

"How?" I manage, unable to take in any oxygen. The car might as well be a black hole. There's no air here, no light. It's crushing me.

"The water. It had a sleeping pill. Don't worry, it's perfectly safe."

I blink at him, fully awake now. And shocked.

Shocked that he would think I was asking about the water, about the damn drugs, when he's *alive.* After all these years, alive.

It's not enough to hear him. I can't believe my ears. I have to see him. I have to feel him. I'm across the floor of the limo before my limbs have even registered the movement, my hands reaching for him before I can think twice. I'm on my knees in front of him, because somehow sitting on the seat beside him feels presumptuous—but I don't mind. I look like a supplicant. I feel like one. He's some kind of altar, and I'm praying that he's real.

The hard calves beneath my palms feel real enough. Warm. Strong. Muscles flex where my fingers stroke. I can't identify him through legs alone. I didn't even touch Giovanni here before, never had the courage for that.

I'm braver now—and more desperate to know the truth. I slide my palms up his thighs. A slight hitch in his breathing tells me I'm not the only one affected. My hands fall to his hands where they rest on the smooth leather. There's ink there, black and harsh, that wasn't there before.

I run my fingertips over the fine linen of his shirt on either side, up to the open collar, a shadowed V above the white fabric. Coarse hair and rough skin. Rigid bones and tender flesh. The bristle of a jaw that hasn't seen a razor in more than a day.

It could be anyone, I tell myself. Any tall, muscled man in a finely tailored suit.

Except I wouldn't touch any man like this.

I have to lean forward to reach more of him, my hips slipping between his legs. It's an intimate position. Too intimate for strangers. The pads of my fingers brush over his lips, his breath warming me.

I've stared at these lips for enough hours to know the exact place they dip in the middle, the smooth expanse of them at the edge. The rough hair is new, as is the scar bisecting his top lip. I run my fingers over that place, back and forth, as if I can somehow smooth it out, wish away the hurt.

His nose is the same proud shape—a Costas nose, passed down from father to son, inevitably broken more than once by a life of violence. I try to smooth that away too, clay beneath my hands.

He isn't clay, though. He's living, breathing, and letting me explore.

His eyes fall closed when I reach them, eyelashes tickling my fingertips. My hands are trembling now, shaking as I trace the curve of his lashes, then higher, his brows. There's another scar here, something jagged and hard that just missed his eye. So much pain.

It's his hair that breaks me, the way one lock falls over his face no matter how much he pushes it back. My heart clenches. I finger the silky-smooth strands, wondering how something so soft can exist on a man so hardened.

"How is this possible?" I breathe. "How are you alive?"

"The same way you are, I imagine. I survived."

It wasn't the same, because I had my sister to protect me. He had no one. A sob escapes me. "Gio, let me see you."

I pull his neck to bring him forward, out of the shadows, but I might as well pry the seats away from the car. I can't move him at all if he doesn't want to go. "Let me see you," I beg softly.

A slight shake of his head. "Soon enough, bella. I want to look at you like this."

He must have looked at me plenty while I slept on the opposite bench. And it occurs to me he's been watching me for some time—in my loft and outside the club. He was the one who took those orange slices. He's the one who hit Shane.

"Like what?" I ask, almost a whisper.

"With that hope in your eyes, like you know me."

"I do know you, Gio." Sometimes I felt like he was the only person in the whole world I really knew. Not my father and definitely not my mother. Even my sister had an otherworldly grace, a fairy watching over me more than flesh and blood. But Giovanni held my hand, whispered confessions in the dark. He was my first kiss.

He shakes his head slowly. "You don't know who I am now."

The gravity in his voice gives me pause. I was overcome by the realization that he's alive, the pure joy of it. Part of me understood what he's done, what it means. If he grew up in that world, he's become what he was meant to be—a foot soldier for the mafia. I don't know who took over for my father, but they would have a vested interest in taking me. For leverage? A blood debt? Whatever it is will be violent and awful, and Giovanni is helping him do it.

Maybe I should condemn him for that. The severe expression on his face tells me he expects that. Except I know the penalty for disobeying an order. Death. And not a quick one. How can I blame him for surviving? I can't, I won't, not when I'm overjoyed to see it. Whatever he's had to do to survive, whatever he's endured, I'm grateful because it means he's alive.

"We don't have to talk about that now," I say, and I mean it. There will be plenty of time later for fear, for bloodshed. Plenty of time to find out who's orchestrating this. "Tell me how you are. Tell me how you survived. God, Giovanni, tell me the weather report if you want. I just have to hear your voice."

There are tears shimmering in my eyes, so I can't see him clearly, but he swallows hard, leaning forward. He isn't as unaffected as he wants me to believe.

"Clara." His voice is rough. "I'm not the boy I was."

"You think I care about that? You think I care about *any* of that?" I grasp his hands, my smaller fingers curving around his larger ones. There are scars here too, so many of them. They speak of beatings, both given and received.

"So quick to forgive, Clara. That was always your weakness."

He thinks he's changed so much. He's not the only one. "You think you know me?"

His thumb brushes across my palm, one swipe that's quick but no less devastating. "You look just like I remember you. Young and beautiful and innocent."

I've never been quite as innocent as he believed. "Is that why you attacked Shane?"

His expression darkens. "He was hurting you."

"Is that the only reason?" I know I'm challenging him, but this situation is already dangerous.

"He was *touching* you." His hands close around mine, engulfing them, warm and firm. "No one gets to touch you, except…"

We aren't going to be able to escape him, I realize. This looming presence. He's the reason we're in this limo right now, whoever gave the order to have me kidnapped. And I can't even fully regret it, because it brought us back together. "Who is he? The man who took over after my father?"

A coarse laugh. "No one you want to know."

I shiver because I'm sure he's right. There would have been absolute mayhem after my father was killed, a war to determine who would be next in line. Whoever won would have been brutal. "But I'm going to meet him, right?" I glance out the window at the miles of endless desert, low mountains in the distance. We're closer than I thought. "That's where we're going."

He's silent a moment. Then he says, "Do you know why you're valuable, Clara?"

"Because of who my father was. Except…he wasn't really my father. Whoever took over must have heard the rumors." Everyone knew about the gossip, that my mother had slept around. And I looked nothing like my father or my sister.

"Your mother, Clara. She was the daughter of a consigliere in Italy. Whether you are or aren't your father's daughter, you have ties to the homeland."

My stomach drops because I know what he's saying. I'm not being taken somewhere to pay a blood debt, a revenge killing for whatever my father did. That should be a relief, but what he's saying is almost worse. If I'm valuable for my lineage, then the only way to use me is by marriage.

I'm already on my knees in front of him. It's that much easier to beg. "Please, let's run away together. You and me. I love you, Gio. I never stopped—"

"Christ," he says, throwing off my hands. He turns his face away to watch the flatlands race by.

"You must have thought about it." I remember those missing orange slices. Did he hold them in these calloused hands? Did he put them in his mouth, bite into the sweet flesh? "You know what will happen to me there, but it doesn't have to be like that."

"It does," he says roughly. "You don't know what you're saying."

"I know you're loyal to the family." It's the only way he could have survived this long. "But look at what they've done to you. Look at what they've made you."

"A killer?" he says, his voice taunting.

I flinch at the word, at his tone. At the image of my sweet Gio taking a life. He would have taken so many. "You don't have to stay with them."

"Where would we go, bella? Where would we go where they couldn't find us?"

My heart beats faster. He's actually considering it. Hope shudders through my chest. "Anywhere. I'll change my name, dye my hair. No one will know where we came from."

"And will you still make your art?" he asks. "The statues rich people want to put in their gardens?"

I blink, uncertain. How does he know about that? Of course he's been watching me. It hurts, the faint mocking strain of his voice. As if I've done something wrong. And maybe I have. "No," I say slowly. "I couldn't."

"Because there would be newspaper stories. Social media accounts."

My heart sinks. There was already a small newspaper story about the Grand's opening, including a picture of the statue. And then there's my Instagram account. "Is that how you found me?"

Sensual lips curve in a knowing smile. "I found you long before that." He leans forward, the back of his knuckles brushing my cheek. His large hand falls to my neck. He holds me loosely, but the meaning is clear enough. "And I kept you hidden. But you wouldn't have stayed that way for long. Someone else would have taken you if I hadn't."

And so I brought this on myself. The one thing that kept me alive, the one thing that sustained me. And even this I can't regret. Wonder is too sharp and bright to really feel anything else. "Oh, Gio. I thought you had died."

All my grief, all my longing comes out in those words. Torment fills his eyes, a deep pain that mirrors my own. He may think he's changed, but I recognize the boy in those deep wells.

Then his expression flattens. There's no emotion there, only hard lines. "Giovanni Costas did die eight years ago. There was even a funeral for him."

A tear slips down my cheek, unchecked. "I believed you were dead."

He closes his eyes. When he opens them, there's a new glint, almost cruel. "Then you understand. I'm someone else now, someone darker. Someone you don't want to know."

I rock back on my heels, shock and horror rendering me speechless. All I cared about was seeing him alive. Even if he took me captive, he was only following orders.

No one you want to know.

"Who told you to take me?" I whisper.

He shakes his head, and I already know the answer. *No.*

"Who made you do this?" I demand, tears burning the backs of my eyes. "Who's going to use me for their own gains? For power? For blood?"

He swipes my cheek with the rough pad of his

thumb, taking a glistening drop. His lips close around the thumb, sucking the salt of my tears. "No one made me do this, bella. I wanted to."

It shouldn't have been possible. When I left, Giovanni was barely even of age—and they would have known he helped Honor and me escape. He would have been punished somehow. And even without that, he was the son of a foot soldier. He never would have risen this high, not in eight years, not in a hundred.

Except there would have been a war when my father died.

Lineage and money would matter, but only the most brutal would win.

My eyes widen, and I scoot back across the soft limo carpet until my back touches the base of the seat on the opposite side. He's telling me the truth. He really is a different man now, someone I didn't want to know.

He nods, a slight dip of his head. "That's right. You're mine now."

I make one last plea, one direct request. The old Gio would have given me this. "I want to go home. My sister is there, my friends. My school."

"And your boyfriend?"

I look away, ashamed. I don't want to talk about Shane.

An almost feral undercurrent sharpens his voice. "You'll never see him again."

The truth is I hadn't planned on seeing him ever again. That relationship was a mistake. I let it go on too long. But I'm not about to tell Giovanni that, not when he's keeping me against my will. "That's none of your business. You don't control me."

His lip curls into a cruel smile. "Don't I?"

And I finally understand in a soul-deep way: this isn't the old Giovanni, the boy I met in the pool house. That Gio cared about me, about my family. My dreams. This man is a stranger.

CHAPTER EIGHT

MY THROAT ACHES, dry from whatever drugs he gave me. As if he knows, he hands me a bottle of water. The seal is already broken. I give him a long look, full of suspicion and dark dread.

The corner of his lips tilts up. “You’re thirsty.”

“You’re drugging me.”

“It’s a long way,” he says, not sounding apologetic in the least.

Because he’s right, I take a sip. I am thirsty. And it’s a long way. Though most of all, I need those drugs to douse the raging fires in my mind—the joy, the pain. The fear.

When the bottle is half-empty, I hand it back. Then I curl up against the leather, as far away from Giovanni as I can get. He’s the last thing I see before sleep claims me again.

Dreams filter through the drug’s heavy shadows like glimpses of sunlight through the leaves. I remember his smile, sometimes shy, sometimes pleased, in the pool house. Then the picture changes—his face grows harder, darker, scarred. He doesn’t smile, not anymore. Just a tilt of his full lips, an echo of the boy he used to be.

I dream of his hands, once so gentle and sweet. He stroked my hair while I leaned my head against his thigh. He gripped my hips the last time I saw him, during our one and only kiss.

The picture shifts again, and I'm being held down this time, arms raised above my head. I'm fighting him, but he's too strong. Ruthless. His fingers bite into my flesh, and I know they'll leave marks.

Maybe that's what he wants.

I wake with a gasp, body shivering, resounding with remembered pain. Something is draped over me, something warm that smells like him. His jacket, the one that had been beside him. It's now covering me like a blanket.

His fingerprints still bite into me from the dream, and I hold up my wrists, almost surprised to find them pale. No bruises here. It was just a dream, and the real Giovanni sits across the limo, face still shrouded in shadow. I'm still wearing the silver dress from last night, now rumpled.

I push the spaghetti strap back up where it had fallen. "How far are we?"

"We're here."

I peer out the window, eyes widening at the sight of the lush palms and lavish turrets that surround my father's estate. No, not my father's any longer. He's dead.

There hasn't been much time to come to terms with any of this, but if I could have guessed, I'd have assumed that Giovanni moved elsewhere. Maybe some condo in a glass-walled skyscraper off the Strip, something closer to the action. The mansion feels a little too domestic, even if it is surrounded by an electric fence. It's meant for a family, and Giovanni is a lone wolf.

You're mine now.

Though he might not be alone anymore. If he wants me for my lineage, the only way to get it is to marry me. Against my will, if the drugs in the water are any indication. There are enough Catholic priests in the mafia's pocket not to question my consent.

And what about children?

What about love?

It sounds crazy to even think about those things with a man I thought was dead yesterday. I had a million fantasies about marrying him when I was fifteen, but in every one of them, we ran away together. In my fantasies we escaped a life of violence.

The man across from me watches with a stillness I can only describe as lethal. Observing every breath I take, cataloging every point of weakness. Waiting to strike.

The limo slows to a stop in the wide circular drive. Armed guards in suits step forward to open the door, blinding me with the bright Vegas sun. The mansion is thirty minutes from the Strip, technically in a suburb, but my father was the capo of the entire Vegas operation.

Not my father anymore, I remind myself. Giovanni Costas.

If I doubted his words, the deference the men show him proves he told the truth. Giovanni exchanges words with one of them over the black bow of the car door. I've seen orders given enough times to recognize it now. The other man nods and heads into the mansion.

We aren't unguarded though. One man still stands by the door, manning his post. The driver of the limo steps out and waits by the front door. I have no doubt that both of them are armed. I have no doubt that they've killed before and wouldn't hesitate to do so again. My blood runs cold.

But would they kill me if I made a run for it? I'm under Giovanni's protection now.

Under his control.

He stands outside the door and extends his hand. "Clara."

His tone says he expects me to obey. To be the good mafia princess I was raised to be. For a long time I tried to be that person, so it's easy for me to take his hand. Easy to stand with practiced grace. Easy to school my face into one of complacency instead of fear.

Giovanni doesn't release my hand. Dark eyes search my features. Whatever he finds, he doesn't like.

His hand tightens around mine; his expression darkens. "Are you afraid?"

I'm afraid of this mansion, afraid of him. I'm afraid of being the girl I was raised to be. "Are you going to hurt me?"

He cocks his head to the side, considering. Which isn't the most reassuring response. "You'll be my wife."

It hits me then, like a fist to my stomach. This is his proposal, no whispered words in the dark. No sweet promises. It's right that I spent years mourning his death, because the boy I knew is truly gone.

I close my eyes. "You wouldn't be the first capo to raise his hand to his wife."

Giovanni brushes his thumb over my knuckles. In comfort? "I'm not your father."

He knows what my father did to my mother. Everyone does. In fact it was widely believed that he killed her until Honor revealed that she escaped instead. She was still beaten and used by my father.

Maybe that should excuse the fact that she left his daughters, but it doesn't. Bad enough that she left Honor to whatever fate the mafia had in store. But I wasn't even my father's blood daughter. He didn't feel any restraint when it came to me, no loyalty.

Not even Giovanni knows the full extent of the price I paid.

Back then I was afraid to tell him, afraid that he might do something to protect me. Afraid that he might get himself killed. Now I won't tell him because he doesn't deserve to know. The boy I loved is dead. This man is the embodiment of everything I've grown to hate.

I lift my chin. "Are you sure about that? He didn't care what I wanted. He only cared how he could use me. You're no better than him."

Something flickers in those dark depths. Respect? Pride? I don't care because I'm not his pretty little princess to dress up, to parade around. I will *never* be that girl again.

The quirk of his lips offends me, that mocking expression on a face I used to love.

I raise my hand, my intentions clear. I'm going to slap him.

Except he catches my wrist, his expression unforgiving. My breath stutters. His fingers press marks into my skin, just like they did in my dream.

His other hand brushes down my cheek. "I didn't get where I am by being weak."

"No, you got here by killing. By hurting people." My voice breaks because his hand is hurting me. And because maybe I did want to test him, to see if he really is the hard man he claims to be.

He twists my arm behind my back, bending me over the trunk of the car. My breath comes faster. This position. *No.* Black spots dance in front of my eyes. My muscles lock up. "Please. Stop." I barely get the words out.

"Don't push me, bella. You won't like what happens."

His fingers open, releasing me. I stumble away from the car over the smooth slate tiles on the drive. If that was a test, then he passed with flying colors. He really is a ruthless bastard.

He turns his face up, the hot Vegas sun drenching his features in startling light. Then he looks back at me, his eyes flat once again.

"Come inside, bella," he says mildly. "We don't want you to burn."

✧ ✧ ✧

HE GIVES ME a tour of the mansion where I grew up, as if to drive home the point.

The point is that he is in charge here, and I am at his mercy.

Maybe he thinks that will shock me. When I was the daughter of the capo and he was the son of a foot soldier, he had to show me deference. I lived in this mansion, while he lived in a small complex set behind the property.

What he doesn't realize is that I never had any power between these walls. On this antique sofa or in the glass-domed greenhouse. I definitely never had any power in the office.

Most of the rooms look the same. The office too.

Leather armchairs gather around a heavy stone fireplace. It always seemed silly for a place as hot as Vegas. Then again, nights get cold in the desert. My father's desk is ornately carved with naked men and women, arms raised to support the thick slab of wood on top.

The only difference is the leather armchair with wide wings. It's empty.

Every other time I've come here, I was summoned. Escorted here by one of the armed men, usually while my sister was at ballet practice. My father would be waiting in that seat, framed by the tall window at his back. My heart beats faster, muscle memory feeding the same fight-or-flight response I had back then.

The touch of Giovanni's hand snaps me back to reality.

With two fingers, he turns my face to look at him. "You're upset."

"I never expected to see this room again."

"Are you sad that your father is dead?"

His words are blunt, without sympathy. He might as well be made of rock for all he seems to understand grief or pain. "He deserved what happened to him."

"Because he tried to force your sister to marry."

And because he hurt me. That information is too private. It hurts too much to share with stone.

"There's only one way out of the mafia," I say, repeating words I've heard a hundred times. When my father whispered them to me, they were a threat. They still feel like a threat, now that I'm here again.

"Did you think you had escaped?" Giovanni's tone disturbs me, detached and curious. His expression disturbs me too. He looks as if he's inquiring about the timetable of some business takeover, something with a foregone conclusion. Something he will no doubt win.

In the face of his cold regard, tears prick my eyes. "I should have escaped. God, you *helped* me escape. You risked your life to help me, and now you're the one to bring me back? Why, Gio?"

He studies me, his eyes dark and tumultuous. "That newspaper article. I couldn't let anyone else take you."

I won't let him off the hook that easily. "Then why not warn me? I could have run."

His head shakes slowly, almost regretful. "I let you go

once because it was the only choice. The only thing I could do to keep you safe."

"And I'll be safe now?"

Violence flashes across his face. "Anyone who touches you will die. I'll kill them myself."

A shiver racks my body. "Then who will keep me safe from you?"

Chapter Nine

THE TOUR ENDS upstairs, in my old bedroom.

Everything is exactly where I left it, down to the pink ruffles on the bed and haphazard makeup on the cream wood vanity. I wasn't allowed to actually paint the walls, but I had four large canvases hanging that must have twenty coats of paint each.

Giovanni hasn't spoken to me since we left the office. Now he turns to face me in the center of my room. "You'll stay here until I can trust you. The door locks from the outside."

I know very well that the door locks. My father had the key.

There's one way I can leave, though.

Gio's dark eyes flicker with amusement. "The window's bolted shut."

Of course he knows about that. It was the only way I could meet him in the pool house. My eyes narrow. "And what happens when we get married? Am I still going to sleep here?"

His expression is impassive. "I won't force you to sleep with me."

Anger rises up in me at how casually he discusses our

marriage. It should be something sacred, something beautiful. Now it's depraved. "So we'll be husband and wife in name only."

He takes a step toward me, then another. I'm backing up before I can stop myself, shoved flat against the door. Somehow it's closed. We're trapped in here together, and my breath is coming too fast.

His broad shoulders block the light, casting his face in shadows. "We'll consummate this marriage. After that it will be your decision."

My throat tightens. "It should always be my decision."

He runs his hand up my arm, sending shivers over my skin. Inexplicably my nipples tighten beneath the cups of my bra. "You're right, bella. But that isn't the world you grew up in. You were bred for this."

As if I'm a horse. An animal. "You don't own me."

"Ah, but I do." He sounds almost sad. "No one is coming for you. Not your sister. Not your sister's husband. Not even the owner of that club you were at would dare to touch you now."

I shove at him, but he doesn't move an inch. Instead my palms encounter hard-packed muscle covered in thin white fabric. "You can hold me captive, but you'll have to use that lock forever. I'll *never* stay."

"Good," he breathes, his lips inches from my temple. "You shouldn't trust me. You shouldn't let me in."

"I won't," I say, but the moment has shifted, altered. It's intimate when he's this close to me, when my hands are on his body. It feels like I've already let him in. Like I already trust him, even though that's impossible when he's keeping me against my will.

For a breathless, tense moment I think he's going to kiss me. His gaze is on my lips, head bent close. Somehow my chin turns up as if to meet him. This is crazy. This is dangerous…

A sharp bark echoes through the room, and I jump.

Slowly Gio lifts his head and steps back. His eyes are hazy with lust, and as I watch, his focus returns. It should be a relief. I don't want his lust. I don't want his attention in any way.

But I can't shake the feeling of loss when he's back to his stoic self.

"What was that?" I manage, my voice uneven.

He inclines his head toward the door to the bathroom, which is closed. "See for yourself."

My stomach fluttering, I push away from the wall and edge around him, careful not to touch. He's like a flame, hot enough to burn. I open the bathroom door in time to see an orange and brown blur streak by me.

Then he's under the bed. "Lupo!"

Elation lifts my voice and my spirits. Two eyes glare at me from beneath the pink frills. I fall to my knees by the bed and reach out my hand. Lupo sniffs my fingers before backing deeper under the bed. He doesn't trust me any more here than he did on the fire escape. Gio must have had him sent ahead of us. That's why I didn't see him last night before I fell asleep.

At least now I won't have to worry about where he gets his next meal.

My gaze lifts to Gio, a mixture of fear and gratitude in my heart. He must have watched me for a while to see me put food out on the fire escape.

And he's watching me now, a strange expression on his face. "You always wanted a dog."

A clench inside my chest. "Thank you for bringing him."

His eyes flicker with something painful and sweet. It looks like he's going to open up to me. My breath hitches. *Please, please.* Then he pulls back, the walls slamming down again.

"The engagement party is tomorrow night," he says.

Before I can respond, he turns and leaves the room. The lock clicks into place.

Lupo growls at the door from beneath the bed. Apparently he trusts Gio even less than he trusts me.

Gio didn't trust me when I first talked to him either. He was a surly teenage boy, convinced that I would be stuck up. Or that I was toying with him, that I would tell my father that we had talked and get him in trouble. It took time for him to open up to me, for him to trust me.

I claimed he's just like my father, and in some ways that's true.

My father would never have brought this dog along.

The soldier or the boy. The monster or the lover. Which one is he? I think he might be a little of both, but the two can't exist side by side. They're fighting each other, battling within him. It remains to be seen which side will win.

✧ ✧ ✧

I DON'T SEE Giovanni the rest of the night, which is a relief. I need time to think about what he's become—and what he wants to turn me into. A mafia princess. No, that's what I was. He wants to make me his queen. A dubious honor when I don't have a choice.

The shower holds the same kind of soap I use now. The closet has all my old clothes. This place is a curious mixture of old and new, a rabbit hole I've fallen into—everything too large or too small, upside down and color-bright.

My sheets are the same pale-pink paisley that I slept in as a child. The same sheets I slept between when I dreamed of Giovanni. The same sheets where I first touched myself, tentative and curious.

When I pull back the knit white blanket, only the faint smell of flowers rises up. No dust.

He prepared for this.

Of course I know he did. The way he had Lupo transported here ahead of us proves that much. As do the toiletries in the bathroom. He was watching me, *stalking* me.

He protected me too.

I rest my head on the pillow, gaze trained on the locked door. Waiting for his return, dreading it—wanting it. Lupo stays under the bed, in much the same position, I'm guessing.

How is it possible I can sleep this way? In a place I thought I'd never come back to, held captive by a man I thought was dead? Maybe the drugs are still in my system, because the room narrows and then goes black.

When I open my eyes my stomach growls with hunger.

Or maybe that's the sound of Lupo growling.

I sit up in bed just as a lock turns in the door. I'm wearing a nightgown with a scoop neck and cap sleeves—modest enough, but I still hold the pink sheet up to my chest as the door swings open.

It's not Giovanni.

That knowledge sets off a firestorm inside me, relief an inky fuel, anger a lit match. I don't really want to see him or his cold eyes. I don't want to find out all the horrible ways he's changed. But I don't really want him to ignore me either.

And I'm cold. So incredibly cold in these old clothes and old blankets. I still remember the heat of his gaze, the hot brand of his fingers around my wrist.

If he's going to hold me captive, the least he can do is hold me.

The man who enters the room has dirty blonde hair and a sharp suit. The effect is ruined by a blue dog leash in his hand. "Where's the mutt?" he says, clearly annoyed to be assigned this task.

Romero. I think that's his name. I was never really invited to the parties where I might have learned their ranks, the way my sister, Honor, was. Supposedly it was because I was younger, but everyone knew the real reason. Because I wasn't really blood.

I hold my hand out. "I can walk him."

His eyes are pale and almost dead. "Put the dog on the leash if you want him to go outside. Either that or he can piss in your room."

I'm not willing to test that theory, so I hop out of bed and grab the leash. Lupo rumbles as I reach for him under the bed. I've never forced myself that near to him, so I'm half expecting him to bite me. Instead he freezes as soon as my hand touches his wiry fur.

"That's right," I croon softly. "I'm not going to hurt you."

I snap the blue leash to a matching blue collar nestled in his fur. That means someone else has gotten close to him. They must have in order to get him here. I hope they didn't hurt him. For that matter, I hope he didn't hurt anyone else. Even if they might have deserved it. I don't know how far Giovanni's leniency will go.

"Be a good dog," I whisper as I tug him out from under the bed.

He yanks his head against the collar as if testing how far he can go. His eyes are suspicious when I hand the lead over to Romero.

"He's nervous," I say, hoping he won't push the dog too far and too fast.

Romero gives me a hard look and turns, yanking on the leash. I hold my breath because the last thing I need is a made man losing his temper on a stray dog. Giovanni may have me under his protection right now, but I doubt that extends to my dog.

Lupo follows the man outside, body sunk low, tail between his legs.

Only then can I breathe out a sigh of relief. And inhale the scent of bacon.

A young woman enters the room and closes the door with her hip. She's carrying a tray laden with plates of eggs and toast and fruit. There's a small silver pot that must have coffee.

She sets the tray down on the small round table. There are two antique white chairs around it, but I doubt she's planning on staying. I've never seen her before, but I can't waste this opportunity.

"What's your name?"

She doesn't look up from where she's setting out silverware.

"Please," I say, approaching her. "I'm being held against my will."

She pours a cup of steaming coffee. "Cream?"

There's a faint accent in her voice, but I can't place it. "Please help me."

She pauses, and I feel her distress vibrate in the air. At least she's considering it. "I can't."

"Can't or won't?"

"Does it matter?" She stands back. "Eat now. I have until he returns with the dog to take the tray."

"At least sit with me."

Her lips purse. She doesn't want to, but there's not really anywhere else to sit. "It's not right."

"None of this is right. He drugged me. He—"

"Mr. Costas is a good man."

Her loyalty hits me hard—not only because it means she won't help me. Also because I used to have that kind of unadulterated trust in Giovanni. Not anymore. "He's forcing me to marry him. He's going to force me to…" I can't even speak the words, not where he's concerned. Force me to have sex with him. As much as I know he's changed, it's still impossible to believe he'd do that.

She looks pained, and I have to wonder at the exact nature of her loyalty to him. Giovanni wouldn't be the first man to use the household staff to meet his needs. My father certainly did.

A pang of jealousy hits my breastbone. I ignore it because that doesn't matter.

He's probably been with a hundred women.

And now it's hard to breathe.

"Senorita, are you okay?" Her voice sounds far away.

I feel her guide me to the chair, and I'm grateful for that. My hands grasp her, keeping her close. I meet her dark gaze, pleading. "Just a message, so my sister knows where I am. So she knows I'm not dead."

Her lips part, and I'm praying, hoping. Nothing comes out. Her brow furrows. Genuine worry shades her brown eyes, and I think she might actually do this for me.

A sharp yip comes from the hallway, and she jerks

back.

Seconds later Lupo dives into the room and under the bed. Romero appears, looking disgruntled, his suit askew. “Let’s go,” he says, not waiting until the girl complies.

She gives me one last worried look before hurrying out.

The door closes. The lock turns.

She didn’t agree to send a message, but she didn’t say no either. I’ll ask her again when I see her. I’ll get down on my knees and beg her. I really do want my sister to know I’m okay. Maybe she can help me escape, but even if she couldn’t, I know she’ll rest easier if she hears from me.

And I am desperate to break free. I don’t want to think that Giovanni will do what he says. He wouldn’t. I’m sure he wouldn’t force me to have sex.

Don’t push me, bella. You won’t like what happens.

I want to believe he wouldn’t, but I’m terrified to find out for sure.

CHAPTER TEN

THE LOW MURMUR of male voices bleeds through the door.

Lupo's ears perk up, and his growl fills the room. He had another walk at lunchtime. I had a bowl of soup and thick focaccia bread, but the girl wouldn't talk to me again. She wouldn't even meet my eyes. I may be captive here, but at least they're keeping me well-fed.

I'm expecting Romero again or maybe the girl with a late afternoon snack.

So it's a shock when Giovanni walks into the room.

I saw him yesterday, so I should be used to the way he's changed, his expression harder, shoulders somehow more broad. Is it possible for him to be taller than he was at eighteen? He definitely seems that way. He may as well be a giant the way he fills the room.

And he's carrying something. Not a tray of food or a leash, though.

A dress.

Something shimmery and glittery gold is draped over his arm. He sets it on the bedspread in front of me. "For tomorrow night."

Lupo growls, but he ruins the effect by backing up

until he's underneath the bed.

I narrow my eyes. "How do you know it fits?"

His gaze flickers over my body, and suddenly the tank top and jeans I'm wearing may as well be see-through lace. It's like he can see all of me, every inch of my skin, every shadow and curve. My body responds with inappropriate heat, starting in my core and spreading outward to harden my nipples.

His eyes darken. "Try it on."

He makes no move to leave, and I have no desire to undress in front of him. "I'm sure it fits."

"Do you have everything you need?"

The amusement in his voice turns my stomach. How dare he find this funny. I could be in chains, could be beaten and starved, but it's hard for me to be grateful. I'm a captive just the same. "Oh, let's see. Food, check. Water, check. Freedom? Not so much."

His amusement evaporates like a drop of water on hot concrete. "Freedom is for other people. People who aren't born the daughter of mafia royalty."

"They're dead," I mutter through gritted teeth. My mother didn't care enough to stick around. My father…well, let's just say I would have preferred for him to care a little less.

"Which makes you their heir. But you know this."

"I know there are people who would use me. I just don't understand why you are one of them. Where is the boy who held me in his arms when I cried? What happened to the boy I loved?"

A moment passes in utter stillness. I didn't mean to let out so much frustration. And I don't expect a real answer, because he hasn't given me one before. He shifts, and I push up from the bed, backing into the wall. No, I don't expect a real answer—but he might do something worse. He might punish me. He might prove just how bad captivity can be.

He turns just enough to shut the door. It closes with a quiet, painful *click.*

A shrug of his large shoulders drops his jacket to his hand. He tosses it on top of the dress, and it's a strange intimacy, seeing our clothes mingled together. Next his fingers work at the buttons of his white shirt.

My breath strangles in my throat. "Giovanni. What are you doing?"

He doesn't answer except to continue working the buttons, exposing more deep bronze skin and sculpted muscle. Down, down, to the sprinkle of dark hair in a sharp V.

I've seen naked bodies before, many of them. Amateur models undress almost daily in the art building for classes to draw. I've shaded that line down the middle, sketched those indentations arrowing down. I have run the tip of my pencil over a hundred different bodies, but never have I see one as hard and as strong as his. He's all muscle, no fat—not even the kind of padding that makes a body warm and comforting. There's nothing comforting about the way his abs ripple as he takes off the shirt.

"Gio," I whisper.

I thought I had more time before he forced me. I thought he'd wait until we were married, even if that's only days away. God, I thought he wouldn't really do this to me.

His expression is flat, barely human. "You wanted to know, bella. You asked."

It takes me a moment to register the question. *What happened to the boy I loved?*

He turns to face the door, and my breath sucks in. This is his answer. There are crisscrossed scars on his back, wounds shaped like talons, skin that healed in thick ropes piled over each other. He wasn't just beaten. He was tortured.

"Who did this to you?" I choke out.

He turns enough that I can see his face. The complete lack of pain there is almost more disturbing than the scars on his back. Whatever they did to him changed him, turned something off inside him. And I understand why he's showing me this.

The boy I loved really did die years ago.

He lifts one broad shoulder, a shrug casual enough to break my heart. "The place was swarming with security for the big party. They were prepared for an attack against the Russians, considering your sister's engagement would have been bad for them. You wouldn't have made it out undetected."

A knot has formed in my throat, so hard and so big I'm not sure I'll ever be able to breathe normally again. I knew that he helped us escape. I suspected that he paid a price. Seeing the proof of that is almost too much to stand. "So you distracted them?"

"They were looking for an attack. I gave them one."

"And they realized it was you?"

"Not right away." Something cold flickers over his expression. "When they connected me to the explosion, they figured out why I'd done it. Nunzio told them we had been meeting in secret."

I gasp because they were family. Cousins, technically, but like brothers. Giovanni had told Nunzio about meeting me in the pool house, had used his help to do it. "How could he do that to you?"

"They probably threatened him. Threatened his parents." A pause. "Or maybe he didn't want to get strung up in the basement like I was."

Without meaning to, I take a step forward. A step toward him.

He puts his hand up to stop me. "I don't need your pity, bella. Don't waste it on me. I show you this so you'll understand. So you don't look to me for mercy. I have none."

I swallow hard. He's right. How can I beg him for freedom when he was tortured to try and save me? Those are not his scars. They're mine. He took them for me. Grief shudders through me for the boy who died that night, in spirit if not in body. I may have believed him gone all this time, but now I know exactly how it happened. It broke something in him, and God, just the knowledge is breaking something inside me.

"You want me to wear that dress tomorrow night? Fine. I owe you that." I force myself to take a breath. "I owe you more than I can ever repay. You want me to stand up in front of a priest and say the words *I do* for whatever power it will bring you? Fine."

If I expected to see satisfaction, I would have been disappointed. I'm giving up everything I have to a statue made of stone. He doesn't move, still naked from the waist up, still impenetrable.

I do take a step closer then, because I'm not completely defenseless here. At least, I hope I'm not. "But you can't force me to consummate this marriage. I'm asking—" I'm more than asking. I'm begging. "Please, Gio. I may not love the man you are now, but don't make me hate you."

His head cocks to the side, his eyes incisive, like he's trying to figure me out. "Do my scars disgust you that much?"

The crack that formed inside me at the sight of them breaks into a thousand pieces. "No, Gio—how could you think that? Your body doesn't disgust me." His body is beautiful and strong, a temple of masculine power. The scars don't detract from that. He's been forged in fire.

"Then what?"

"I don't want to be forced, Giovanni. Not about that."

He takes a step close, and his legs are long enough that we're only inches apart. The air fills with the salt and spice of him. My heart races. His eyes are dark pools that I can sink into, quicksand, pulling me down faster the harder I struggle.

"Then don't make me force you, bella. Don't fight."

My mouth opens, but nothing comes out. I can't agree to this. It would be the same, whether I lashed out at him with my fists or whether I lay still and accepted him. Either way, it would be force. Because I have no choice. I can have no real choice as long as he holds me here.

"One more thing," he murmurs. "Don't ask Maria for help again. It won't work."

My breath catches in my chest. I hadn't been sure she would help me, but I'd hoped she wouldn't tell on me. Apparently her loyalty to Giovanni runs deeper than I thought. Certainly deeper than any of the household help felt for my father.

Before I can respond, he turns and strides from the room, his shirt and suit jacket still draped over the gold fabric of my dress, a symbol of his command over me even when he's gone.

Chapter Eleven

I told Giovanni I would stay and do what he needed. I think I might owe him that, not that I have much choice at the moment. But I'm not going to stay forever. Whatever power play he's working on will end eventually. My mother escaped my father. I'll find a way to leave too.

For right now, I'm focused on getting a message to Honor. She'll be crazy with worry. She would have tried to call me the night of the party at the Grand and expected me to meet her for a spa day the next morning. For that matter, Amy will worry too. I have to at least let them know I'm alive, that I'm safe.

As safe as you can be with a mafia capo holding you captive.

The next morning I'm determined to find a crack in the walls. Clearly the girl, Maria, told Giovanni about me asking for help. Asking again won't do any good and, more than likely, would just piss off Gio once he heard. Instead I focus on trying to get information. Maybe she can tell me something useful.

The tray she brings in this morning is piled with thick French toast and sliced fruit. She sets it down while

Romero takes a snarling Lupo downstairs. Worry tugs at me as I watch the gray mop of fur disappear through the door, tail between his legs, body low to the ground. He doesn't trust Romero, which is understandable. I don't either. But he doesn't trust me, doesn't trust anyone.

That's no way to live.

Maria looks like she's about to leave once she sets the food out.

"I'm sorry," I say quickly.

She doesn't say anything, her eyes wary.

"I'm sorry I put you in that position. I know it would have been risky for you to do anything to help me. You could have gotten in trouble."

Her dark brows lower, and I sense her indecision. Some part of her did want to help. Then her lips firm. "Mr. Costas is a good man."

Forcing myself to look casual, I take a seat at the small table. The orange juice is freshly squeezed, like drinking sunshine—sunshine I desperately need after being indoors for two days now. I wonder if he'll let me walk Lupo if I ask him.

He'd have to trust me for that.

"You seem very loyal to him," I say. "I'm not sure anyone was that loyal to my father, even his men."

"Loyalty is the only thing holding us together," she says, her tone fierce.

My father said something similar, except he used the word *blood.* Blood was the only thing holding us together. It's interesting to hear how things changed now that a man who wasn't in line has the helm.

Although once we're married, he'll at least be related by marriage.

"Are you married?" I ask softly.

Her eyes flicker with something. Fear? Shame? "No."

Giovanni would only have sent someone in here if he was sure of them. And she does seem fierce in her loyalty. Definitely too fierce for someone who cleans rooms. Does she do more than that for him? The way the maids had to serve my father? He was a cruel man with dark tastes. They hadn't liked what he did to them. But maybe Giovanni is different. Maybe he's convinced her there is something romantic between them.

Or maybe there really is something romantic between them. My stomach turns over. If that were true, she wouldn't be okay with him marrying me, would she? Then again, sometimes we do hard things for the sake of love. And maybe *that's* why he only wanted to consummate the marriage, nothing more.

Information, I remind myself. *Find the cracks in the wall.*

"How long have you worked for Giovanni?" It can't be longer than a couple years. I've only been gone eight, and he would have needed time to rise to power. There's a huge gap in my knowledge, though.

She definitely looks nervous now. "Almost a year."

My stomach churns. I don't want to imagine her with Giovanni, but it's hard not to. Her loyalty, her nervousness. All of it combines to paint a picture my mind would rather not see.

She's definitely pretty, with black hair and dark eyes, her slender body a sharp contrast to mine. The clothes in the closet fit perfectly except for the bust. Some of them are tight, including the tank top I'm wearing now. Giovanni used to like my body, but he's changed in many ways.

I'm the one too scared to push for answers, to find out if he's been with her. "There's a party tonight," I say instead. "Does he have parties often?"

"This will be the first one," she says, sounding relieved that I changed the topic. I'm not sure whether he told her she could speak to me or not, but she has to stay until Romero returns and unlocks the door.

"Oh." My father had parties regularly. I watched a few of them between the balcony rails, wearing my nightgown. Before my father found out and started locking me in my room. Only my sister was required to attend, wearing Versace and Gucci, the first daughter, the real one.

My gaze sweeps to the glittering dress where I hung it on the closet door. Even from here I can see the fine stitching and needlework with the gold pieces. I have no doubt that it's a designer gown, that it's expensive, but that says more about Giovanni's status than it does about mine.

"Do you…" Maria pauses, looking uncertain. "Do you want me to do your hair? I practice with my sister sometimes. I can put it up for you."

"Oh, that would be really nice." I tell myself I only care because it gives me more time to get close to Maria, to get information from her. Not because I want to look pretty for Giovanni.

She gives me a small smile. "I can do it after lunch."

"Thank you."

Worry passes over her eyes. "He does not… Mr. Costas. He does not want you hurt. He's said that you're under his protection. He's a good man."

Anyone who touches you will die. I'll kill them myself.

That's possessiveness, not necessarily protection. He could hurt me. He probably will.

My doubt must show on my face, because Maria continues. "He does not…" In her pause I see her struggle for the words. I wonder if it's a language barrier. Her accent is slight but discernable. "He does not hurt women."

The tone in her voice reminds me of the girls who dance at the Grand, girls who were hurt by men too many times. My heart cracks against that hurt, even for this stranger, even for this woman who's helping keep me here. "Who hurt you, Maria?"

Fear floods her eyes, and her lips press together. "I can't help you."

I've lost her again, and I'm desperate. "Please. This isn't for me. It's for my sister. She's worried about me." And if Maria knows what it's like to be hurt by men, she'll also understand my sister's fear. After what Honor has been through, she'll think the worst. "You don't have to tell her where I am. If you just—"

"No," she says, hardening her voice. "I owe Mr. Costas my life. I will do nothing to harm him."

"Even if he hurts me?" My voice cracks. I didn't mean to say that. Didn't mean to beg for help, at least not to escape. I keep trying to convince myself that it doesn't matter if he forces me to have sex. He's already keeping me here. It's just one more thing.

But that's a lie. It would break something inside me, something that could never be repaired. Not just for a man to force himself on me, but for Giovanni to do it.

Her nostrils flare. "He wouldn't."

God. I need to get myself together. It feels like I'm breaking apart, looking at this woman who would defend Giovanni, even against himself. He's already said what he's going to do to me. I need to find some way to accept it. And she isn't the answer I need.

"Thanks," I say, swallowing hard. "I think I'll just do my own hair."

I hate that she looks hurt, but I just couldn't. It would be too creepy for her to dress me up, make me pretty just so Giovanni can rape me. Too wrong.

She nods stiffly as the sound of a growling dog comes through the door. Then it's open, and she leaves without another word, brushing past Romero on her way out. He barely spares her a glance, frowning at the dog as he unhooks the leash.

My gaze focuses on him. I thought Maria was my best chance for help, but I was wrong. She's sympathetic toward me, yes. And way too loyal to Giovanni. Romero, on the other hand, is stuck doing dog-walking duty. He must have fucked something up to be given such a crappy task.

"Romero," I say, questioning.

He looks up in surprise. He hadn't thought I would remember him. The sound he makes is more of a grunt than a word, but I take it as encouragement.

"You worked for my father." I need to feel him out, find out if he's as fanatically loyal to Giovanni as Maria is. And judging from the zealous flash in his eyes at the mention of my father, I'm guessing not.

"Your father was a good man," he says gruffly.

No, he was a horrible man. "I miss him," I lie, because I'm running out of time. Tonight is the engagement party. I'm guessing the wedding will be soon after. There's no need to waste time on propriety when the bride is being forced. "I didn't want to leave before, but now I do."

His eyes flash again, this time with jealousy. "Everything is different now."

"I know." I pretend to be sad about that as I round the table, moving slowly, letting his eyes roam my body. "But you know the old ways. You were the kind of man I looked up to."

His gaze is locked on my breasts, which are barely contained by the tank top. I don't know whether Giovanni likes my curves, but Romero apparently does. I move closer to him, letting my hips sway. My stomach ties into knots. I don't know how far I'll have to go to get him to help me, but I have to try.

"You didn't look at me twice when you were here before," he says, his voice rough. With desire? Or with anger? This is a man I wouldn't want to see angry. Not the cold fury that Giovanni would have. This man would be wild in his anger, like Shane.

"I was young," I say honestly. "I didn't understand how things worked. And…I was afraid of you. Because you're strong." And violent. And probably sociopathic. "I'm grown now."

"Yes, you are," he mutters, daring to place his hand on my hip.

I hold back my flinch. "It isn't right, him having me. Daddy wouldn't have wanted that."

That much isn't a lie. He would be furious to know that Giovanni, the son of a foot soldier, had somehow usurped his position. It bothered him deeply that he never had a son. So he'd done the next best thing and chosen his successor, who was to marry Honor. Now all his plans are ruined.

Romero looks just as pissed as my father would be. "There's a natural order."

"I know," I say, placing my hand on his suit lapel. "But I can't do anything about it now. I'm trapped in here. He's going to take what he wants from me. What he doesn't deserve."

I may not want to be a princess, but that's how I was born.

There's a girl in my Advanced Sculpture class who said that fairy tales are stupid, that she didn't need a prince to save her. But she doesn't understand.

Fairy tales aren't for the girls who have a choice. They're for the girls shoved into corners, trapped in darkness, bent over desks. Places where hope is an act of bravery. Where believing in love is an act of rebellion.

Fairy tales are for girls who dream of happy endings, knowing they might not live to see tomorrow.

Romero is far from a white knight, but he rises to the occasion. "You don't belong with him. Fuck, I was higher on the food chain than his father. If anyone gets you, it should be me."

Not the most heroic of speeches, but I'll take it. I look down, stroking the silky fabric of his tie with one finger. "If only things had been different."

I'm waiting for the magic words, praying he'll promise to carry me away, when I see a flash of gray streak past me, between our legs, and out the door. *Lupo.*

CHAPTER TWELVE

I'M OUT THE door before Romero even knows what's happening. He shouts, and I know he's on my heels. There's no chance I can actually escape like this, not with him this close and more men walking the grounds. I'm just focused on catching Lupo before he actually leaves the grounds. Or worse, attacks someone. I don't think he's a dangerous dog, but he's trapped just like me. He'll fight if he needs to, but the men he'll be fighting have guns.

If we were in some other mansion, or even a hotel kind of place, I would be slower. Wouldn't know which way to go. But I grew up here, barefoot on this same overlong oriental rug. A childhood of racing through these halls with my sister with a child's exuberance gives me the burst of speed I need. I hear the clatter of Lupo's nails on the stairs a second before I swing around the balcony. Then I'm racing down the steps after him.

He pauses at the bottom, unsure which way to go. The front of the mansion is closed off by wide double doors and thick stained glass. The back has large paned windows to show off the double-level pool and courtyards, which means Vegas's sunlight pours in. Lupo heads for the back, not knowing he'll be locked in that way just as much as the first, but then a man in a suit rounds the corner from the opposite direction.

There's a horrible grinding sound as Lupo's nails dig into the hardwood floors to stop his slide. He's caught between me behind him and this unknown man in front of him. Before I can call his name, he darts through a one-foot opening in the door to the side. My heart pounds. The office.

I don't recognize the man opposite me, but I know his type. He's armed and dangerous and at least mildly sociopathic to even be in this job. His eyes narrow as if he's trying to figure out who the hell I am or what I'm doing. Then he reaches into his jacket to draw his weapon. I don't wait to find out if he's going to threaten me or just open fire. I dart into the office after Lupo and stumble to a halt.

It's dark, because the office is one of the only rooms in the mansion with no windows. Therefore it's the most secure if it were to fall under attack.

But it's not filled with cigar smoke or that clove spice I sometimes smell in my nightmares. I suppose there are some habits Giovanni chose not to pick up.

"Lupo," I whisper.

I need to get ahold of him before that guy comes in, before Romero catches up to us. Hopefully we'll both be escorted back to the room without anyone getting hurt. And without involving Giovanni.

I raise my voice to a hushed demand. "Lupo, come

here right now. *Please.*"

The door swings open behind me, sunlight bouncing off the glossy wood and spilling onto the rug in the office. Romero looks rumpled from the short run and pissed off. So much for getting on his good side.

"I'll find him," I say, praying he lets me handle this. Lupo has already been grumpy dealing with the walks. He'll be even more defensive after getting cornered in here.

Romero reaches for me. "I'm putting you back in the room. Then I'll deal with the mutt."

Shit, this is what I was afraid of. I back up. "Wait. No."

His eyes flash. "I have authorization to keep you in that room with force. Don't make me use it."

I shiver because I don't want to imagine Giovanni giving that order. But it's not like the locked door or the armed guard outside are particularly subtle. I'm his prisoner.

"Please," I whisper. "I'll get Lupo. We won't cause trouble. Don't tell Giovanni what happened."

A drop of orange-yellow pierces the darkness. Giovanni is sitting in an armchair, large body reclined, one ankle slung over his leg, a lighter in his hand. The flame dances from the silver cylinder, casting eerie shadows on his face. "What shouldn't he tell me about?"

My pulse pounds in my ears. "God, you could give a girl a heart attack."

"I'm sorry," Romero says, his voice clipped. "The

dog got out."

"And the girl?" Giovanni says, his voice low and liquid.

I plant a hand on my hip. "The girl is grown up. And she got out too."

A smile in the dark, the flash of white teeth. The Cheshire cat's smile. "Careless," he says.

Romero swears under his breath. "It won't happen again."

"Leave."

"But—"

"Now."

Romero's embarrassment and anger bubbles in the air behind me, and I know I'll have to deal with him later. For now I have to deal with the man in front of me. As my eyes adjust to the dark, I see a small and trembling figure in the corner, behind an antique globe. Footsteps recede as Romero follows orders.

"I'll just get Lupo and go." Whatever courage I felt when I corrected Giovanni left with Romero. Now I'm alone in a room—in *the* room—and all I want is to leave.

"Wait." The word is soft but clearly a command.

I wait.

He stands, still holding the lighter up. One step closer. Without thinking it through, I take a step back. We move that way, one forward, one back, until the wall stops me. This was a bad idea. Everything about this is bad, from the fact that I just moved into the shadows to the way he's looking at me. Hungry. Starving, like he needs to devour me just to survive.

"Giovanni," I whisper. "Let me get Lupo. We'll leave you alone."

His dark gaze flicks down to where my camisole doesn't cover enough of my breasts, the orange-yellow light warming my curves. "Careless," he says again. "What had Romero so distracted?"

The way he says it, he knows. He may not know that I was teasing Romero deliberately, trying to soften him up so he'd help me. But he knows exactly what Romero was looking at when Lupo escaped.

They're a distraction, but I need a different kind of distraction right now. "What did Romero do wrong that you assigned him to dog walking?"

"It's more what he didn't do."

I can't forget how quickly Romero spoke out against Giovanni. It's something I might be able to use to my advantage, but it's also dangerous for Giovanni. I suspect he knows that. It's a little hard for Romero to plan a coup if he never leaves the mansion. "Friends close and enemies closer, is that it?"

He makes an approving sound. "You understand the life."

Anger flashes inside me. "I understand it, but I don't want it. You have no right to force it on me."

"That's just it, bella. Force gives me the right to do anything I want."

Fear quickens my heartbeat—fear and something else. Something like anticipation. It must be muscle memory, except the muscle in question is my heart. It remembers that it loves him, even if it shouldn't. That's the only explanation for how I can still want a man who holds me against my will.

A flick of his thumb and the lighter shuts off, plunging us into darkness. The door is still open, drawing a prism of saturated light, but backed into the wall, it's completely black.

"It gives me the right to keep you here," he says, his breath soft against my forehead. Then his hands are closing around my wrists, lifting them above my head.

My breath catches. "Stop."

"It gives me the right to touch you."

"No."

He places one of my wrists on top of the other, holding them both easily with one hand. His other hand lands on the curve of my hip—and it burns. I shut my eyes tight as if I can deny what's happening that way. That only sharpens my other senses, the feel of him, the heat.

"Clara," he murmurs. "It gives me the right to kiss you."

My lips are trembling, and I can't deny that I want it. And that I hate it, this wanting.

He kissed me only once before, only minutes before I left. I was breathless, a mixture of young desire and fear. Part of me believed that my love for him would conquer what we faced. The other part of me knew that I would never see him again. It turns out that I was wrong on both counts.

His lips are surprisingly soft and achingly sure. They touch mine with a deliberation that can only be possessive. He can take this much time because he owns me. Because I'm his to do whatever he wants with—and he wants my lips, over and over again. He presses his mouth over mine in a way that would almost be chaste if it weren't for his hand on my hip or his hot length against my stomach.

His tongue swipes across my lip, sending sparks through my body. I shiver, and he does it again.

It feels like I'm on fire from the inside out, flames of need licking my body on the inside, the heat and pressure of him on the outside. And the worst part is how I want to give in, to let him scorch me. I would never be the same again. I would never recover, but God, how sweet the pain.

Want and need war within me, and I let out a sigh. He uses the opportunity to slip inside my mouth, to spread me wider for his invasion. I imagine him saying, *It gives me the right to use your mouth.* I should hate him, but somehow it only makes me hotter.

He explores my secret places with terrible patience. I'm the one straining for more, faster, deeper. His tongue slides against mine, a sensual swipe that makes me moan. On the next glide his body rocks into me—only once. Once is enough. Now I know how it will be when we're together, his body moving against me, invading me, a rhythm I'll never forget.

My breasts feel heavier than they've ever been, the fabric constraining them too tight and harsh. The cami is thick around my breasts, but even so my nipples harden and press against the restraints. It might as well be lace holding me, whisper thin but textured. When Giovanni's body shifts in front of me, the fabric of his suit rubs against them. My breath catches, and without meaning to, I roll my body, pressing my breasts into him.

He groans into my mouth. "Christ, bella. What you do to me."

At least I'm not the only one breaking apart. I'm floating, flying. I'm breathing hard, but he is too. It's like we've run a marathon instead of kissing for a moment. He's too close, too large. Too sensual. I have no defenses against him, especially when his thumb slides under the hem of my cami, a lone and soft slide against my bare skin.

A shudder racks my body. "Gio, I don't know—I feel strange."

His laugh is unsteady. "You need to go."

"I…what?"

He turns just enough to rest his palm on the wall beside my head. His other hand falls away from my hip. I feel the loss acutely, the air almost freezing in comparison to his touch. "You need to take your dog and leave this room."

My body aches for something only he can give me. I lean toward him instinctively, knowing he can assuage me. It actually hurts, these knots he's tied inside.

"Go," he says roughly. "Unless you want me to fuck you on this rug right now. Leave."

The word *fuck* jars me out of whatever trance I've been in.

Oh God, no. No no no. This is all wrong. Why did I let him touch me like that? Except that's not the question I need to be asking. Why did I like it so much?

And even fully aware, I still want him to touch me again.

The only thing stopping me is the room. The rug. The office and all the things I've never told a living soul. I'm not about to start by telling my captor, even if he does make my body yearn.

It takes me longer than I want to coax the dog out from behind the globe. The entire time, Giovanni stands against the wall, silent and still. I wrap a shivering Lupo in my arms and hurry up the stairs, where Romero waits outside the door to lock me inside.

CHAPTER THIRTEEN

I THINK ABOUT the way his lips felt against mine—hot and sweet, sensual and somehow comforting. Sharp desire mixed with an ethereal relaxation. I could have stayed like that for hours, for days. I could have kissed him forever.

Which is really messed up, all things considered.

It's also messed up that I regret not letting Maria help with my hair. What should it matter whether I'm pretty? I'm a prisoner here, no matter how good the food or how sexy my captor.

Only with Amy's help could I ever do anything fancy with my hair. It's too thick and unruly, tied up in wavy knots no matter how recently I've brushed it. Princess hair, that's what Honor called it. The kind Rapunzel let down from her window. I'm looking out my window now, but there's no prince at the bottom.

A knock comes at the door.

I turn and pad across the room barefoot. It felt strange to wear heels alone in my room, but it feels stranger to open the door to Giovanni like this—intimate. The air in the room evaporates when I see him in his tux, so dignified and solemn. He's dressed the opposite of when I knew him before, in well-washed jeans and plain T-shirts. Except he reminds me more of that boy in this moment than since I first woke up in that limo. He looks both expectant and resigned, as if he knows something bad will happen but he's determined to withstand it. Back then I thought the horrible thing was his family or maybe mine. Now I'm not so sure what tests him. Maybe it's me.

His dark gaze lingers over my body. I saw myself in the mirror so I know what he sees. Ample curves wrapped in gold so formfitting it could have been painted onto me. It looks like the individual shimmering beads adorn my skin. It's ridiculously sexy but, considering that most of my skin is covered, classy too. I feel like a complete stranger.

His voice is stiff. "You look…beautiful."

I make a face. "You don't have to say that."

He gives a rough laugh, a little unsteady. "Jesus, Clara."

"It's not like this is a real date."

His amusement evaporates. "No, this isn't a real date. This isn't how I imagined taking you out when I let myself think about it."

My curiosity sparks despite myself. I don't want to be interested in him, this ghost of the boy I loved, this imposter. "What did you imagine?"

"A drive to some high spot where we could look at the city lights and be alone. We'd lie down on the hood of my car while it was still warm." He gives me a small smile. "We'd talk about our plans, because when I thought about it, we had a future."

My chest constricts. That would have been paradise. There's a part of me that wants to say, *We can have a future now.* Except kidnapping isn't a real foundation for a relationship. And he's a violent man, ruling a world I've wanted to escape my entire life.

"That would have been nice," I say instead.

The gravity in his eyes tells me he understands the difference. It would have been nice before. Now we're just a mafia capo and his stolen bride, preparing to attend our fake engagement party.

He holds up a velvet box. "For you."

"Oh." It's stupid to feel grateful that he's gotten me a present. Like the dress, it's more about his status than doing something nice for me. Still, my heart pounds as I reach for the lid.

A sapphire pendant takes my breath away, its many facets catching the faint light in the room and sparkling even brighter. The dainty gold chain emphasizes the weight of the gem.

"I can't," I manage to say. It's too much, too beautiful. Too expensive.

He raises an eyebrow. "Why not?"

"What if I lose it?"

"Then it will have served its purpose."

I can't breathe, watching him. Wanting him. "What purpose?"

He takes my hand and leads me to the mirror. A

woman I don't recognize stares back at me. She does actually look beautiful—and confident and sensual. This is some dress. Giovanni stands behind me, his broad shoulders dwarfing mine, his eyes fathomless where they meet mine.

His large hand sweeps my hair to the side, achingly gentle, exposing my neck.

He holds the delicate strands of gold and rests the sapphire against my breastbone. It's cool and heavy, glinting in the mirror. With quiet concentration he fastens the necklace behind me and smooths my hair back into place. The entire time, he doesn't touch my skin. My senses heighten as if reaching for the feel of him, begging.

By the time he's finished, I'm breathing harder, making the stone rise and fall.

"Beautiful," he murmurs. "Whether it's a real date or not, you're the most beautiful woman I've ever seen."

"Don't," I say, my voice thick with tears. I don't want to soften toward him, but God, I already have. I could never really be hard toward him. He's dragged me back into my worst nightmare and somehow made me want it.

"This is all I imagined," he continues, his voice harsh. "I bought this a week after I took over, because it reminded me of your eyes. I never thought I'd see it on you, but I wanted to. I want to dress you in diamonds and lace. I want to give you everything."

The sapphire hangs at the perfect height for a pendant, an inch above the top of my breasts. But somehow it feels constricting, like a collar. A leash. "Everything but my freedom."

"I can't let you go, but I can make this good for you. Let me, bella."

Something inside me unfurls. The temptation is too strong, my love for him still burning too bright. As wrong as it is, I want him to soothe me, to make me want this cage.

The look I give him is all the acquiescence he needs.

With a low groan he presses his face into my hair. Gentle hands push it aside, baring my neck once again. His lips meet the angle of my jaw. He forges a trail down my neck, branding me with every soft kiss. But while his lips are soft, his hands on my hips are not. They hold me still as if he's afraid I might bolt. His body is as hard as a brick wall behind me, unforgiving. A rock of his hips and I feel the column of his arousal.

"I don't want to take you downstairs," he mutters. "Don't want to share you with them."

Except those people are the reason he kidnapped me. Because of the blood that runs through my veins. Because of the birthright that feels more like a curse.

Tension wraps around me, so tight I can't help but speak. "Then let's leave them, Gio. We can run away together, like we always dreamed about. Just you and me."

He pauses, his face pressed into my neck, and it feels like a refuge.

Then he steps back, and the cool air between us might as well be a desert. "It's not that simple," he says, voice dark enough to ward off any more intimacy.

THE PARTY IS in full swing by the time we reach the staircase, the foyer and parlor room packed with custom-made tuxes and designer gowns. Heads turn when we make our descent, watching us with blatant avarice. Giovanni's arm is solid, steady, which is good because I'm clinging to him. He might be my kidnapper, but tonight he's also my shield.

"There you are," exclaims a voice I haven't heard in years. Both of us turn to greet the gray-haired matron, Ada, a force of nature in this social circle. Her hair shines the same silver as before, her eyes just as shrewd. "Haven't you grown into a fine young woman."

I give her a real smile, if somewhat nervous. She was always nice to me, even knowing about my parentage. "Ada. So nice to see you again."

Her expression is knowing. "It's good to have you back."

My mouth opens and then closes. I'm not prepared for faking it through all these people. And we'll have to meet with all of them. Some I recognize, some I don't. And the entire time I'll have to pretend I actually want to be here.

Ada pulls me close, suffusing me with the fresh smell of gerberas. "Chin up, darling. The vultures only circle when you bleed."

I glance at Giovanni and see he's watching me with an unreadable expression. He's certainly not anywhere close to bleeding, his posture both confident and relaxed, as if he belongs here. And he does, if the glances of respect and jealousy are anything to judge by. He belongs here more than I ever did.

"Thank you," I whisper to Ada.

She nods and turns away, leaving me to greet another old family friend.

At least, that's what I would have called them before. Now I know they're hardly friends. They're vultures; Ada was right about that. I lift my chin and meet their gazes, determined not to bleed.

A hundred people later—or maybe only ten—I'm close to falling down. This is no different from the nights on Party Row. Oh, the jewels shine brighter here, but it's the same. Posturing and smiling. Pretending and judging.

No one dares to whisper about me when I'm nearby, not with Giovanni at my side.

I know they'll talk, though. I feel their looks burning into my back.

"Dance with me," Giovanni murmurs.

He's been an utter gentleman the entire night. He was always kind to me, but I never knew he had polite manners for such a formal social situation. Actually, he probably didn't. He must have learned them since ascending to his title. And I don't want to imagine another woman on his arm while he did.

"All right," I say because anything that will take me out of the spotlight sounds good.

Except that the small crowd of dancers part when we step into the ballroom.

Giovanni turns back and holds out his hand.

It feels momentous somehow, as if he's offering more than just a dance. Although what, I can't imagine. Certainly not a real life together. Not love. This entire thing is a charade, the same way it was with Shane. He may as well be groping me at a cocktail table while someone brings around test-tube shots.

I place my hand in his, and heat shoots up my arm to settle low in my stomach.

That much is different, though. That much has always been different.

And then he brings me into his arms, moving me around the dance floor with such casual grace that my breath catches. Who is this man of elegance and power? I used to lie with him, sharing my headphones as we both listened to the music on my iPod. Now we're dancing to a six-string orchestra.

His gaze is dark as he watches me, his grip sure.

"Where did you learn to do this?" I murmur, uncertain if I really want to know.

"To dance?"

"All of it. To smile and charm people."

"I wasn't charming before?"

"Not like this. That was real. This is…something

else." This is the life, the life my father lived, the one he groomed Honor and me to live. The one I thought I had escaped.

He considers this as we take another turn around the ballroom. It's not quite a waltz but not quite modern either. It's more that he's turning my body in time with the music. It's innate, I realize. A deep and sensual connection to the music that he wouldn't have learned in lessons.

I half expect him to ignore my question or pretend not to know what I mean. To turn away from the elephant in the room, that neither of us were meant to wear these invisible crowns. Instead he says, "I learned by necessity."

That tells me nothing. "Someone must have helped you."

"Ada taught me some of it," he says finally. "About the parties. The social rules."

"Then she supported you." I'm moving dangerously close to the topic we haven't yet touched—how he was able to take over after my father died. And what happened to him when I left.

He's silent as we take another turn, the faces around us blurring together.

"She likes you," he says.

"Did she know you were going to get me?"

"Yes."

I shouldn't feel betrayed by that. Ada has always been nice to me, but obviously she felt no loyalty for me if she supported Giovanni kidnapping me. "I see."

"Clara."

Tears sting my eyes, and I focus on the crisp white of his shirt. I wish he would go away. No, I want to be the one to go, for the smooth blonde floor to open wide and swallow me whole.

"Clara, look at me."

He waits patiently while we dance until I gather myself and lift my chin. *Don't let them see you bleed.* I realize then that she may not have only been talking about other people. Giovanni is coming for me like a bird of prey. I force the tears back.

"You asked why we couldn't just leave. There are many reasons, but one of them is Honor."

"What does she have to do with this?"

"I told you they would find you. Your sculpture at the Grand. Your art. It was only a matter of time."

"You said that already. Except you could have warned me there. I would have run."

"And your sister? Should she uproot her life? Her husband?"

I press my lips together, obstinate. I'm aware that it would have been awful for her, that whatever he does to me is probably worth sparing her, but I would have liked the choice.

"Her baby?"

I stumble at the word, only saved from tripping by his strong arms. "What?"

"She didn't tell you?"

"No, I—" I had been distracted lately, though. Distancing myself so she wouldn't find out about Shane and worry. "God, how do you know?"

He lifts a shoulder. "My people are thorough. Other people are thorough too. She wouldn't have been safe there. Those people wouldn't care that she's married to someone else, not if they could use her."

Panic claws at my throat. "Then she won't be safe there now. You have to let me warn her."

"You're here now. We've announced our engagement in public. If anyone were to try anything, they'd go after you."

I shiver at his words. "That's not very reassuring."

"I already told you, I won't let anyone else touch you."

Except you'll touch me, even if I say no. "You don't know for sure she'll be safe. I have to warn her."

He says nothing.

"And she'll be so worried about me. I need to at least let her know that I'm okay. Please." I'm begging, which is a bad position to be in. Of course, I'm already completely under his control.

He shakes his head. "There's more going on than I can tell you. Warning your sister would put everything at risk."

"Not warning her is already putting her at risk."

His hold tightens on me. "I'm going to keep you safe, I promise you that. And I'm doing my best to leave her out of this. That has to be enough for you, bella. Don't ask me for more. Not now."

CHAPTER FOURTEEN

"CLARA?"

I look up from where I'm rubbing my feet, flushed with guilt and embarrassment. At least until I see who it is. Juliette looks genuinely excited to see me, her brown eyes warm. I need a friendly face after the coldness of Giovanni's words and the sordid curiosity of the other guests.

I stand without my shoes and give her a hug. "Oh my gosh, it's so good to see you."

She squeezes back. "So grown up, little Clara."

Making a face, I point to the shoes. "Not grown up enough for those. My feet are on fire."

Her laugh lightens my mood. She was always more Honor's friend than mine, being two years older than me. But she was always kind. Her father was the consigliere before his death, which gave her and her mother enough status to remain in the family, despite their poverty due to his gambling debts.

"Well, let's sit down," she says kindly. "You can tell me where you've been, all the things you've seen. I still haven't left Nevada."

"Oh, we didn't do much traveling." And I'm not

sure how much I should really share. Talking about where I've been and what I've been doing just leads to the fact that I didn't want to leave.

"And what about Honor? Is she okay?" Concern shines in Juliette's eyes.

"She's fine," I assure her. And apparently pregnant. I ache to hug my sister, to ask how she's doing, to offer her a shoulder rub or whatever it is pregnant women need.

Instead I'm just adding to her stress by disappearing.

And despite what Giovanni said, I'm not content to do nothing and hope she's okay. Maybe kidnapping me has diverted the attention, but what if it hasn't? It's not a risk I can live with. I know that her husband, Kip, will keep her safe—he's a force to be reckoned with in his own right. He protected her when our father found us once. And he takes security measures more than most men would.

But he doesn't know about the imminent potential threat to her. He'll know I'm missing but not who took me. And the ease with which Giovanni found me, stalked me, and kidnapped me from my own bed proves the danger is real.

"Juliette, I need your help."

Her dark brows lower. "What's wrong?"

I drop my voice, glancing behind me. The corridor is empty. I left Giovanni's side under the guise of using the restroom, but I turned left instead of right. There are some benefits to having grown up in this mansion. So I've been hiding on a plush bench that sits right outside the conservatory. Luckily it's also far enough away from the party to make this request.

"I need you to get a message to Honor."

She looks around, understanding the covert nature of my request. "I'm guessing she's not coming to the wedding tomorrow?"

I huffed a laugh. "Not hardly. Wait…did you say tomorrow?"

She bites her lip, looking conflicted. "Oh no. I worried it was something like this."

"The wedding is *tomorrow?*"

Worry floods her brown eyes. "I mean, I knew you wanted to get away from all this, but I remembered you had a thing with Giovanni. I'd hoped that meant this marriage was…"—her voice falls to a whisper—"real."

"He drugged me while I was sleeping. I woke up in the back of a limo."

Pain washes over her expression, but not surprise. The family is too messed up to be shocked that something like this happens. "Oh my God, Clara. Do you need to get out?"

"Unless you have a small army I don't know about, you can't get me out." And it would be dangerous for her to try, considering how heavily guarded this place is. Her position in the family is already tenuous without a protector. "But if you can get a message to Honor, at least she'll know I'm alive."

She doesn't hesitate. "Of course I will. Tell me how."

I open my mouth to rattle off her cell phone number,

the first number on the tip of my tongue. Except what if someone is looking for Honor, and Juliette tells them how to find her? They were friends, but a lot can change in eight years. Giovanni is living proof of that.

Even if she wanted to remain loyal, she might not have much choice. I have to tread carefully here.

Instead I give her Candy's phone number. She'll relay the message to Honor, but it won't be trackable. And unlike the sweet bungalow my sister and her husband live in, Candy lives in an upscale fortified townhome with 24-7 security guards already in place. As soon as she gets the call, she'll tell her husband, Ivan, who will lock the place down tighter than Fort Knox.

"Honor doesn't have a phone," I lie. I feel a little guilty about that, about not trusting a friend, but I've been burned too badly. This place is toxic. The family changes people. We may not be born evil, but we turn that way if we stay.

Juliette types the number into her phone, then tucks it away. "I'll do it tonight."

"Thank you," I tell her, meaning it. I'm still hoping she's being honest. And this way Honor will know what happened to me. She'll still worry, but at least she'll know to protect herself too.

A slight sound makes me jump.

Giovanni turns the corner, his expression severe. *Shit.* Did he hear me? I scan his eyes, trying to find some hint of what he's thinking. But he's like a monolith, dark and forbidding and completely inscrutable. He comes closer.

His broad shoulders block the light, and I blink at the contrast.

"Hello, Juliette." His tone is cordial but the meaning plain. It's a dismissal.

She gives him a nervous smile, already standing to leave. "Hello. And congratulations." He nods, but she's already making her excuses. "I think I should find my mother. But it was great to see you again, Clara."

Then she's gone.

Giovanni's tone doesn't change as he asks, "What is she doing tonight?"

Shit shit shit. "Something blue," I blurt out. "For the wedding. Which is *tomorrow,* by the way. Why didn't you tell me?"

"Something blue?"

"You know, something borrowed, something blue. It's for good luck." And this marriage will need all the help it can get. He looks dubious, so I move to distract him. "Take a walk with me?"

He glances into the dark opening of the conservatory. "At night."

I really don't need him thinking too hard about what I said to Juliette. "It could be romantic."

His eyes narrow. "You seem awfully comfortable with the wedding."

This is the problem with your kidnapper being your first love. He knows me too well. "Of course I'm not comfortable. I'm getting married tomorrow. *Against my will.* Who would be comfortable with that?" *Stop bab-*

bling, Clara. "I'm actually really pissed at you."

My face flames with embarrassment, fear tinged with affection. I used to get this way around him, talking too much because I had a crush. Now I'm talking too much for an entirely different reason. It feels a little bit the same, though. Enough that I head straight to the center of the conservatory where it's dark and quiet, hoping he doesn't follow me. I leave my shoes in a sad pile beside the bench, running barefoot.

He does follow me, of course.

I hear his footsteps behind me and speed up.

There are short walls built into the space with ivy and moss grown around them. The air is thick with moisture and sweetness and earth. I breathe it in deeply, take the earth into my body. Being locked up in a room without access to sunlight, to dirt. I've always hated it. Always fought it.

And here I am again, grateful for even the taste of freedom.

CHAPTER FIFTEEN

ALL THE PATHS lead to the middle of the space, where a three-tiered fountain pours water from a pineapple at the top. Except when I reach the middle, it's gone. As far as I can tell, the walls and the plants are exactly how I left them. But the fountain is missing. In its place is a large plot of bare ground.

The heat of Giovanni's body is a gentle caress at my back, letting me know I'm caught.

I could keep running, but I'm mesmerized by the flat circle of dirt. So much about this mansion remained the same. Even things I would think a man would prefer to change, to make himself more comfortable, to decorate to his tastes. It's almost as if it's been preserved like a museum.

Except for this. "Where did it go?"

He doesn't pretend not to know. "I didn't like it."

My room, the same. My father's office, the same. The ballroom with its parquet floor and orchestral booth, the same. "Not a fan of pineapples?"

"Maybe you can sculpt something for it."

The soft, almost diffident way he offers it makes my voice catch. This is real. The wedding tomorrow that I still can't quite comprehend. Giovanni standing behind me. This life he thinks we'll build together. All of it is made real by his hesitant offer to let me sculpt something for the mansion. In this he is totally unlike my father, who dismissed my work as a child's scribbles.

"You would let me?"

"I would love it," he says, his voice hoarse.

A shiver runs over my skin. Could I really make a marriage out of this? Could I really accept the life I'd always fought because I had no other choice? Part of me wants to forget about the drugs and the limo. To pretend like I'm here because I want to be here. The other part of me knows that a man holding power over a woman can never be a partnership. I would always be his prisoner.

I take a small step to the side, skirting the patch of empty earth. The brick walkway is cold under my feet. "What would I sculpt?"

The beads on my dress catch the faint light, shimmering like the drops of water on leaves. I feel a little bit unearthly, the way I'm shining in the dark. A little bit beautiful, the way he can't seem to stop looking at me.

He remains where I left him. "Anything."

Something gnaws at me, the question of why that one random thing offended him enough to remove it. "But not a pineapple?"

A pause. "If you like."

"On top of a fountain?"

"No." His tone doesn't invite more questions.

I continue walking the circle, considering the space,

considering *him.* They're not so different. I want to figure out what to sculpt for the space. The process feels less like creating and more like whittling away, taking away bits of air in my mind until the right shape forms. I'd never actually have sculpted a pineapple on top of a fountain, but it's curious that he doesn't want me to.

Giovanni is another puzzle I have to chip away at until I find the shape of him, whittle away at this cold, powerful exterior to find what's underneath.

"I found your obituary."

He blinks, faintly startled. "You looked?"

"I loved you, remember?"

The shadows at his neck move as he swallows. "You shouldn't have seen that."

"Or I guess it shouldn't have been written. It wasn't true." I've come full circle around the plot of dirt. There are paths leading away in multiple directions, walls of black alternating with walls of ivy. It creates a kind of intimacy between us, something even more private than when we're alone in my room.

"It was true enough for my mother. She wrote it."

I come to a stop in front of him, heart aching. I never spent much time with his mother, but he talked about her. She was pious and dutiful, the way a good Italian wife should be. Very religious. "She thought you were dead?"

"I was gone for a long time. She didn't know where."

I hear the pain in those words, and anger rushes up. "But you would have me disappear from Honor without a trace? So she can put my obituary in the newspaper?"

"It's better that way," he says sharply. "Dying is the easy part. Coming back…it hurt her."

I think she wasn't the only one hurt. "What about you?"

"What about me?"

"You were gone for a long time."

He laughed shortly. "I didn't go far."

I put my hand on his chest, feeling his heartbeat. So steady, so sure. Such a miracle, after believing he was dead. It still feels miraculous, even if I'm not sure I like who survived. "They hurt you."

The sight of those whip marks are burned into my brain.

"Do you feel sorry for me?" His question is harsh, angry.

Yes, but he wouldn't want to hear that. "How long?"

"Does it matter?"

"You were gone long enough that your mother believed you were dead. She loved you. She wouldn't give up in a day. A week. Not without a body to prove it."

"Three months."

Everything in me comes to a halt, the world slowing down around me. Three months. I saw those whip marks. They beat him for *three months.* My stomach clenches, and it takes everything in me not to turn my face to the dirt and throw up. No wonder he's changed.

With trembling fingers I reach up to trace the shape of his face, to run my fingertips along his clenched jaw. A miracle, not only because he's alive. He survived three months of torture. God.

And then I don't care if this makes me weak. For this one moment, I don't care if he's my kidnapper. I have to be close to him. I have to touch him.

I push up on my toes, but it's still not far enough. I have to wind my arms up to pull him down. He comes, barely, lowering enough that I can press my lips to his.

He lets me kiss him, moving my lips over his, the gentlest caress.

A low rumble runs through him. "Don't," he says, his lips moving against mine.

I pull back enough to meet his dark, turbulent gaze. "Why not?"

He grasps my arms and gives me a little shake, more meaning than violence. "I'd rather have your hate than your pity."

I want to hate him. I want to pity him. But I'm afraid that I love him instead, that I never stopped loving him, not even when he died, not even when he came back to life. No matter what happens tomorrow or in the days after, he deserves a kiss from me—a real kiss, as a woman who knows what she wants. Maybe I deserve that too.

So I shake off his hold and reach for him again, pressing my lips to his in unschooled abandoned. As if unable to resist any longer, he groans a refusal before kissing me back. His lips move over mine as if he were part of the shadows around us, reaching every part of me, velvet and sure.

His body pushes against me, insistent, backing me up. Soft dirt cushions my feet, and I know I've stepped off the path. A wall curves behind my back, ivy tickling my neck, and I know I'm well and truly trapped. I'm breathing harder now, taking in more of that earth-dampened air.

He looks down at me, his face a mask of shadows. "So beautiful," he says roughly. "I dreamed of you like this. Dreamed of touching you, tasting you."

So did I. "Is it like you dreamed it would be?"

Slowly his head shakes. "I haven't tasted you yet."

I would ask what he meant, but he shows me instead. He bends his head to nip at my neck. I squirm away from the sting before pressing back for more. He doesn't give it to me, though. Instead he works his way down my neck with too-light kisses, a brush like the leaves of ivy. It inflames me, making my body burn hotter than I knew it could. For all that I felt grown up at age fifteen, I was still a girl. I'm a woman now, with all the strength and desire that comes with it.

His mouth opens over the exposed skin of my breasts, the soft slope left bare by the dress. Without thought, without intention, I press myself toward him, offering myself, begging. As if to torment me, he pulls away. I moan with frustration, with unsated arousal.

Then he drops to his knees in front of me.

I haven't tasted you yet.

"Gio?"

"Let me," he says darkly. "Don't fight me now, bella. Not about this."

And it seems he understands about tonight, about this gift I'm giving him, giving myself. It's a white flag, a temporary truce. We might take up the fight again tomorrow, but for now I won't fight.

It's a good thing, because I'm not sure I have the strength to fight this. Not when I've wondered for so long. When I've wanted for so long. Desire has made my limbs heavy. I let the wall hold me up as he lifts the hem of my skirt. His hands stroke my ankles, my calves. He caresses me everywhere, appreciation in every brush of calloused palms. There's no time to feel self-conscious, not when every inch of skin seems to entrance him.

"Hold this." His soft voice is laced with command as he presses the beaded fabric into my hands.

I clench my fingers tight, so tight, until the beads dig into my palm.

And then wait, while he runs his hands up the outsides of my legs. Then down over the fronts, his thumbs brushing the insides. My knees are weak, legs shaking. I must waver, because he holds my hips with a firmer grip, looking up. His eyes hold mine as he drags my panties down to the ground.

"Tell me you want this." His voice wraps around me like stone and dirt and ivy, textured with need, a command and a plea.

"Tonight," I whisper.

He nods, once.

Then he shrugs off his jacket and tosses it to the side. It lands in a dark heap on the stone path. “My dress,” I say faintly. “It’ll get stained.”

“I don’t care.”

He presses a kiss to the top of my mound, almost chaste. I shiver from that soft touch, anticipation like a light inside me, blinding even in the dark space.

Rough hands push my legs farther apart, my feet pressing farther into the dirt.

Then his mouth is on me *there*, his lips slick with my moisture, his tongue sliding into the secret space between. A sharp cry escapes me, shock and want and denial all at once. I’ve never had this done before, but I’ve imagined it. And every time it’s been him.

I could never have imagined the way he would eat at me, the ferocious intensity of it, the sharp almost pain of it. The desperation makes him clumsy, exploring one part of me, moving to the next, and then back again. It’s like he wants to devour all of me at once. My body can’t distinguish between the sensations, aching and overloaded. I gasp, trembling, holding on to the crush of my dress.

The first swipe of his tongue against my clit makes me sob. “Gio!”

His growl is pure triumph. He does it again and again, relentless in the way he gives it to me, merciless with the pressure and the pleasure of it. It’s too much, and I arch away, but his hands hold my hips in place. It’s cruel, the way he forces me to accept this, to *feel* this.

Climax slams into me, hard and sudden. I make a choked sound as pleasure rockets through me. Every muscle in my body clenches hard. Even then he doesn't release me, doesn't give me a break from his wicked tongue on my slit. He drinks up all the wetness he can find, lapping at me while I rock over his face.

"Stop," I say, breathless. "Stop. Stop."

His voice is unforgiving. "You gave me tonight."

That's the only thing he says before pressing his face into my sex again. I push up on my toes, trying to escape the aching brush of his tongue on my oversensitive flesh, but I just sink deeper into the earth. He mouths at my clit while his fingers play with my folds, teasing the entrance with maddening patience. I think I liked him better out-of-control and clumsy, almost careless. But that first orgasm seems to have taken the edge off, even though it was mine. He's more leisurely now, taking his time. I'm the one who's worked up beyond understanding, the climax doing nothing to sate me.

The second orgasm rises up like a wave. I can see it coming, but I can do nothing to stop it, nothing but hold my breath as it crashes over me. He licks me through my climax, using his hands and mouth to make it last even longer. At the end of it, I'm panting and begging.

"It's too much," I tell him.

In answer he lifts one of my legs over his shoulder, opening me to him. I'm wet enough that two fingers can slip inside me with ease. He curls them until I whimper.

"Please," I say, tears leaking from the corners of my eyes.

"Please what?" he says, voice dark and knowing. "Do you want me to stop?"

I do want him to stop, because then I could breathe again. Then I could go back to thinking of him as my enemy. My body overrules logic, overrides thought. All I can think about is the way his tongue feels. It's my hips that answer him, rocking forward in silent plea.

He laughs softly. "I thought so."

The arrogance should be frustrating, but I don't feel anything but pleasure when he teases my clit. Don't feel anything but desire when he uses his fingers in that timeless rhythm. I want more of him, *all* of him, and the words are on the tip of my tongue. His naked body against mine. Something other than his tongue and fingers inside me.

Imagining him, hard and thick, pushes me over the edge. He laves my clit with rough, brutal strokes while I shudder and cry out in his arms. He makes me come over and over again, until I'm crying, wordless, incoherent—until I'm sliding down the wall of ivy.

He catches me with gentle arms, using his jacket to create a dry nest for me, laying me down in the cradle of his arm. I think it must be over then, and part of me is sad for that, even though I have nothing left to give. He could do anything to me like this and I would be helpless to stop him, unable to speak.

His fingers toy gently with my folds, exploring the

wet skin.

I let him touch me because I can't do anything else. The darkness covers us like a cocoon, keeping me safe even though my legs are spread open, one hooked over his legs. Then his fingers find my clit, drawing circles, faster, faster.

Weakly I push at his hand.

I couldn't possibly move him like this, but he stops anyway. "No?"

I swallow, struggling to find my voice. "Can't."

My body can't possibly come again, whether I've given him tonight or not. I'm wrung out. Finished.

His expression is stark with tension. "I didn't get to see your face."

My breath hitches in my chest. But it doesn't matter that he didn't see my face, doesn't matter how sweet it sounds that he wants to see me come that way. I'm used up, the sparks of pleasure almost painful now.

Except then he begins to whisper to me in Italian. I never learned, so I don't know what he's saying. The words blend together, a harmony of sex and love, the tenor of his voice shifting somehow. My hips rise up to meet his hand, drawing the strength from him, from the words I can't understand but somehow do.

His fingers play with me, knowing, inexorable, working my body until I'm rocking, needing. The orgasm comes in deep, rhythmic pulses, shutting down every part of my body except there, making the world dark except for the blinding pleasure, stealing my breath except for his name. *Gio, Gio, Gio.*

It will never be enough. The thought comes to me in a flash of terrifying clarity. As much pleasure as he's given me, more than I knew I could take, I want even more than this. I want forever.

A scuffing sound comes from the pathway.

In a flash Giovanni has covered me with my dress. He stands and blocks me with his body.

Someone appears in the center pathway just as I stand up, wrapping Giovanni's coat around me.

Romero's expression is grim in the faint light. "I'm sorry to disturb you. We found someone coming through the fence. We took him—"

In a matter of seconds, Giovanni is back to being a statue. Gone is the man who licked me with passion. He feels cold and distant. Violent. "Take Clara back to her room first. Meet me in the pool house after."

"What's happening?" I hate that I sound so scared in the face of his stoic confidence.

He turns to me, expression hard. "Business."

Fear rises up, sharp and sudden. This is why I wanted to escape the life, this wrenching ache. The knowledge that he might be hurt. Or the more likely scenario that he's going to hurt someone else. The tongue that licked me tonight might give the order to have a man killed. The hands that touched me so tenderly might pull the trigger.

I lower my voice so that Romero can't hear me. "Why don't you want a fountain there?"

He glances at the wide-open space and then back at me. His eyes are soulless, empty. The eyes of a killer. "I don't like the sound of running water." His voice is just as hollow. "Go, Clara. This isn't for you to see."

Then he's gone, leaving me with Romero, barefoot in the dirt.

Chapter Sixteen

ROMERO SEEMS DISTRACTED by whatever happened. That means I can't flirt to get close to him again, but I couldn't have anyway. Not with my sex still ringing from Giovanni's touch. My body isn't the only thing affected. It feels like I'm floating more than walking. I don't even feel any pain from the heels I put on outside the conservatory.

Except something sharp keeps trying to pierce through the orgasmic haze.

Something urgent.

Then I realize. Romero is distracted, hardly looking at me. Giovanni is definitely busy with whatever intruder they found. The party will make it easier for me to blend in. This is exactly how Honor and I escaped the first time.

Of course then she had money saved for us.

And we took Giovanni's car.

I don't have money or a car right now, but I have my determination and a deeper knowledge of this mansion than Romero. This is my best chance, now, before I get locked back in that room with the reinforced window. And if I can get to a phone once I'm out, I can contact

Honor for help.

Lupo. Tears prick my eyes. There's no way I can go back for him first. If I make a run for it now, I can't bring him with me. The best chance I have is to leave now…to leave him behind.

My heartbeat races with anticipation, but I force myself to walk at a regular pace, to keep my expression sex dazed. Because of the party, he's avoiding the front staircase. Doesn't want people to see me escorted to my room under armed guard, I suppose.

Instead we take the back way, the servants' stairs. *Perfect.*

I spy the hidden door as we move up the narrow stairs. I'm still close enough that I couldn't get in before he reached me. I can hear him breathing, his steps loud and ominous. Then someone comes down the stairs from the top, holding a tray. That's all I need.

I pause and press against the hallway as if being courteous. I feel Romero's frustration behind me, but he doesn't say anything.

The maid doesn't meet my eyes. "Excuse me," she murmurs.

I feel bad for involving her in this, even in a small way. I hope she doesn't get in trouble. But I can't waste my one chance for freedom. She takes the steps in front of me. Then another. Another.

Her body blocks Romero's view of me for half a second.

With a sudden burst, I press down the wooden lever

that's hidden in the wall. The panel swings open, revealing the dark tunnel. As I dive inside, I hear Romero's confused shouts, "Hey! What the fuck?"

This is the most important part, locking it closed before he comes in after me.

I slam the panel shut and fumble in the dark for the small metal chain Honor and I added. The tunnels were already here—we found them painstakingly, over years. We added the locks so that if we were inside, we couldn't be found. A sharp pain stabs my fingertip, and I let out a whimper. *Shit.* It's like the metal is a needle and thread, my hands thick and clumsy.

A kick slams into the panel, jarring me to the side. I fall back but scramble up again, pushing against the panel with my body. Finally the metal hook finds the small hole, and it's done.

That lock won't hold for long, not with him kicking it. Especially not if he shoots it.

That means I have to get out of here as quickly as possible. I'm sure I can move faster than him in this small space. And once I get forward about twenty feet, the tunnel splits. He won't know which way I've gone.

The cut on my finger smarts, especially when I have to put it on the dusty ground to crawl along the shaft. That would be just my luck, to catch some horrible disease while making my escape. I don't let it slow me down, not even when my knees feel bruised, not even when I bump my head twice. This was a lot easier as a kid.

Something furry brushes my hand, and I yelp. Cautiously, I push forward again and feel something plastic. A Barbie doll, I realize with a sigh of relief.

I reach the fork in the tunnel and turn left. If I remember correctly, this will eventually lead to a pantry on the east side of the house, where I'm hoping I can sneak outside and hop the fence. It feels like hours that I'm crawling through here, but I know it's no longer than fifteen minutes. I have a thousand tiny cuts on my palms and my knees, a pile of dust in my hair.

My strappy heels keep sliding off, and eventually I let them go, leaving bread crumbs that will be found too late—or not at all. Artifacts, like the Barbie doll, of girls who once lived here. Girls who once escaped.

I emerge into the dark pantry like a wild forest woman, a little out of breath and frantic. I know I've successfully shaken Romero, but there are still guards everywhere. And with dust and spiderwebs adorning the gold beads of my dress, I'll be conspicuous if any of the guests see me.

Pushing open the pantry door, I hear the sound of shoes squeaking on the floor.

Quickly I back inside the dark room, praying they aren't coming in.

There are two people, I realize as hushed voices filter through the thin crack.

"Where did he come from?"

"The south gate. He was dressed up like a guest, trying to blend in."

Not security, I'm guessing. Household gossip. Who's trying to sneak inside? Is it some rival criminal organization, the same one my father was worried about years ago? Or is it different, something related to why Giovanni had taken me? He already has power, but he took me. He must need more for some reason. I supposed I could just assume he's power hungry like my father, but he's shown himself to be just different enough… or maybe I want to believe he's different.

God, a part of me regrets being this close to escaping. How messed up is that? I loved Giovanni for so long, most of my life, that being with him still feels like something I want.

Could it work? A real marriage.

No, normal people go on dates. They didn't drug the glass of water beside your bed. Except what if it *did* work? What if the boy I loved was still underneath all that armor?

No, not armor. Scar tissue. *Three months.*

I slip out the side door into the darkness of the night, more conflicted than I've ever been. Running with my sister was an easy decision—not even a choice, really. She's my only true family. And she was the one in the most imminent danger from the fiancé our father had chosen for her. Technically I was in danger too, but no one knew about that.

If I survived that, I can survive whatever Giovanni does to me tomorrow night.

And stay with him for the rest of my life?

God, I'm going crazy—torn between what I want most and what I fear the most.

In the end, I can't walk away. Enough of me still believes in Giovanni, enough of me still wants desperately to believe, that I can't leave without knowing. Of course there's no litmus test to find out if a man is a monster. Tomorrow night, our wedding night, I'll find out for sure if he'll truly force me. But if I stay to find out, it will be too late to escape. I need to find out now.

Meet me in the pool house after. I know where he is right now.

CHAPTER SEVENTEEN

I WAS FIFTEEN with the biggest crush imaginable. The boy was older and so cute I flushed every time he met my eyes. I did every silly, hopeful thing a teen girl can do—writing our names in my notebooks with little hearts, making excuses to see him.

In fact the first time he met me in the pool house, he was supposed to tutor me in algebra. It wasn't even that hard to play dumb, because I felt completely clueless whenever he was near me. Of course he figured out that I was actually already doing math at a college level. Benefits of a personal instructor and lots of free time.

For whatever reason he continued to meet me in the pool house after dark. I would climb down using the trellis under my window and cross the plush grass, so out of place in the desert, dampened by hours of sprinklers.

This time I'm coming from a slightly different direction, but it feels just the same.

I know all the shadows to duck into while I wait to see if the guards are patrolling this area. The schedule may have changed, but the mansion has not. The pool house was usually dark, with Giovanni waiting. This time there was only the faintest glow from somewhere deep inside, a light on somewhere but not the front room.

The ball of my foot sinks into a dip in the ground, almost marshy after being freshly watered. I suck in a breath as the cold liquid stings the cuts on my feet. Two dark silhouettes appear in the windowed doors, and I dart to the side.

The doors open and close quietly.

I watch with bated breath while someone in a suit walks back to the house, too stocky to be Gio.

Due to a recent sandstorm, the air smells particularly sharp with ozone. That's probably why the patio doors were closed, keeping the party inside. Or maybe he somehow predicted that the pool house would be needed for some dark purpose. Maybe they always use this place to hold enemies, the way my father used the basement. It makes me feel sick that he would use the place we'd met into an instrument of torture.

The basement is soundproof. I have never been there, but everyone knew. Why isn't he using that? I'm afraid I know the answer. That's where he was kept. *Three months.*

My stomach turns over.

The door we always used was technically a side entrance to the pool house, opening directly onto the patio. There's a separate front door to the house with a driveway that left the grounds via a different exit than the main entrance. As I skirt the corner, I see light flooding onto the lawn from the window, slatted by thick palm plants.

The thorns cut into my arms and back, but I'm grateful for the relative cover they provide. Especially when I stand frozen, sickened by the sight inside.

A man stands in the center of the room, his broad shoulders turned away, his gaze on the ground, a gun in his hand. I would recognize him anywhere. *Giovanni.* His name catches in my throat. I want to call out to him through the glass, to deny that this is happening, to somehow turn back the clock so a man isn't bleeding out in front of him.

The man on the ground is wearing a tux, like the maids said. His knees are a mess of flesh and blood, so mangled my mind doesn't even know how to reconcile them as legs. He's sobbing. Sobbing.

My breath won't come at all. I hadn't thought there was a litmus test, but God. Only a monster could watch impassively as someone pleads for their life, desperate, clinging to impossible hope in the face of death.

Giovanni turns enough that I can see his profile. He says something. Asks a question?

The man on the floor shakes his head, frantic. Hands clasped. Begging or praying or both.

I can't watch this.

I can't turn away and escape, knowing this is happening.

The only thing I can do is bang on the glass with my fists, exposing myself, stopping Giovanni. Even for one more second, stopping him from committing this sin.

Murder in cold blood. He must have done it before, and he'll do it again, but I don't care. I can't save those people. I probably can't save this man either, but I have to try.

And maybe somehow I can save Giovanni, too.

This place makes you evil. I figured that out a long time ago, but I refuse to succumb. No matter how much violence I see, no matter how much is visited upon me, I will never accept this as normal, as right. Power doesn't make this okay.

Giovanni's expression darkens when he sees me through the window.

I expect him to send out one of the men standing by the door inside to get me, but he comes himself. His grip on my arm presses deep enough to bruise. "What the fuck are you doing?"

"I don't know," I cry brokenly. I didn't realize how much hope I held that he was still good inside until it was crushed. I'm like the man on the ground in there, knees broken, destined for death but somehow begging—hoping anyway. "I don't know. I don't know."

I don't know why I interrupted him. I want to blame it on my upbringing, but I think it's worse than that. Despite everything I loved him too much to leave.

Giovanni looks terrifying in the slash of light across half his face, like a gargoyle or some other night creature. "I told you this wasn't for you to see."

"So that makes it okay? You can kill someone as long as you lock me in my room first? You can *torture* someone?"

He gestures into the room. "Torture? This isn't torture."

"You shot his knees!"

A rough sound. "He doesn't deserve your sympathy."

"What did he do that was so bad?" I ask, incredulous and tearful. "He crashed your party? For that he should be killed?"

"Don't be foolish," he says, his voice as harsh as I've ever heard him. "He came for you."

That makes me stop. I swallow hard, tears cold lines down my cheeks. "What?"

"Christ, bella. He took her, he'll take you too."

"He took…he took who?" I never imagined he was a monk in the years I was gone, but I didn't think he found someone else. Someone he got close to, someone to love. Was he engaged to someone else? Married? Was she kidnapped?

Then I'm more of a pawn than I even knew.

Giovanni turns away with a low growl, running a hand through his hair. "You shouldn't have come here."

"You're right." I wrap my arms around myself as if that can control the shaking. My throat sounds like it's been cut with broken glass. "I should have just left. That's what I was trying to do. I got away from Romero. I was going to escape."

"Then why didn't you?"

"Because I wanted to be wrong about you." I lose my tenuous grip on the tears, and they fall freely now. "I wanted you to be the Giovanni I loved. And God help me, I wanted to marry him."

He stares at me a moment, deathly still. A long pause. "I told you he's gone."

"I know."

"He's fucking gone, Clara."

"*I know.*" I scream it at him, as if to block out the sight of the man with his broken knees. It doesn't work. I don't think I'll ever be able to forget. It's tainted me, *touched* me. This place.

Gio's eyes seem to glow from inside, a dark vehemence I've never seen from him. Something cruel and determined. "I don't think you do know. Come inside, Clara."

My throat clenches tight. "No," I choke out. "I'll go back to my room."

He shakes his head, taking me by the arm. His grip isn't bruising anymore, but neither is it gentle. I can't get away as he pulls me around through the door, into the glare of the room.

Two guards are standing on either side of the door, making sure the man on the floor can't leave. Not that he can, with his knees shot to hell. I have no idea what they think about me being there, but they don't meet my gaze. I recognize one of them—a decent man, at least I'd thought so.

The man on the floor babbles when he sees me, pleas for mercy in a mixture of Italian and English. I clasp my hands to my stomach, afraid I'm going to wretch on the floor. I saw him through the window, but what I hadn't known about was the smell. The tang of metal saturates the air. *God.*

"Let me go," I whisper. Maybe it's cowardly not to want to watch a man die, but I'm not sure I'll survive. Especially if Giovanni is the one pulling the trigger. "Let him go too," I beg softly. "Just stop this."

"There's only one way to stop this, Clara."

"Giovanni, please."

His eyes have that flat, dead look again. "He's already dying. He's almost dead."

"Oh God. I'm going to be sick."

Giovanni looks at me, a brutal challenge in his eyes. Then he holds out the gun.

I stare at it, disbelieving. "No. I can't. I could never."

"You'd be taking mercy on him. He's in pain."

"You're a monster," I breathe. For doing this to him, for doing it to me. I don't care what excuse he has. I don't even care if the man really did come for me. This is wrong. It has to be wrong, because I don't know how to reconcile this—and I'm terrified that this place has changed me too.

That I'm a monster, too.

He presses the gun into my hand, almost tender, sympathy a hard light in his eyes. "Do it, bella. Put him out of his misery."

The man collapses into a moaning heap, perhaps finally understanding that he's fucked no matter what choice I make. The sounds coming from him aren't even human really. Pure animal instinct.

There's no help for him.

I point the gun at his head. It would be a mercy; I know that. He's going to die fast or die slow. That's the choice you face when you are born into the life. I should pull the trigger.

My hands shake so hard I can see the gun moving. There's no way I'll hit anything.

Reaching deep inside myself, I find some untapped strength. With a fresh surge of rebellion I swing the gun to point at Giovanni. My hands still shake, tears blurring my vision.

"That's right," he says, his voice rich with approval. "Pull the trigger. Stop me, bella."

I have this sick feeling that he actually wants me to, that some part of him loves me enough to want himself stopped—while the other part is evil enough to keep going. "I'll do it," I warn. "I'll kill every one of you."

"You might be able to do it," he says, musing and casual. "Take the west gate. There are keys in Alfredo's pocket. Head to Tanglewood and don't look back."

He really does want me to, I realize numbly. But I can't. I'm more terrified of being a monster than I am of dying. Let him hurt me. Let him kill me. My hands fall to my side.

With a low murmur in Italian, he comes to me.

His hands are gentle as he takes the gun. With his other hand, he draws me close to him. I bury my face in his rumpled tux, hurting enough to take comfort wherever I can find it. And God, his broad chest, his warmth, the spice of him piercing the blood in the air—it does comfort me. He holds me tight, as if he can ward away any demons, even himself.

I feel the slight sway of his body as his hand rises. Then the crack of a gunshot.

The moaning stops.

I press my face deeper into him. I don't want to look. Can't.

He was the one to show mercy after all.

CHAPTER EIGHTEEN

I WAKE AS if from a nightmare, my blood still racing from the fear, dark images flashing through my mind. Except it isn't a dream. The blood and grass staining my gold glitter dress prove that. That had really happened last night. And this morning…

This morning I'll get married.

Glitter rainbow stickers frame my face in the vanity mirror. It feels like a lifetime ago that I decorated everything with color and flash, childlike enthusiasm laced with a burgeoning femininity. A lifetime ago, but what's really changed? I'm back where I started, living the life I was born to.

Back then my only purpose was to marry a strong Italian man and make strong Italian babies. It was a fate I fought and escaped, only to end up right back here. I was never one to believe in destiny, but I can't deny its power as I contemplate the expanse of white fabric draped over the bed.

Two hours later, my makeup and hair are finished, my corset and stockings in place.

The only thing left is the dress.

The gown is couture, of course. Very expensive, with

a slender wrapped bodice and artful ruches in the wide skirt. There's something both architectural and delicate about the design, a contradiction that only enhances the allure.

It's a fairy-tale dress, but I know better than to believe in that.

There will be no white knight swooping in to save me today.

There's a small knock on the door. "Come in," I say absently, expecting Maria.

Instead Juliette wears a gorgeous silver sheathe and a hesitant smile. Romero stands at his usual post, holding the door open for her. He's been pretty pissy with me after last night, but now he's busy looking at Juliette with lust—and maybe a little bit of longing.

She pulls me into a hug. "Oh, Clara. You look beautiful. Radiant."

"Now I know you're lying," I say drily. "Considering I slept all of two hours last night."

Her expression is sympathetic. "Nervous?"

"Something like that." I decide to skip the retelling of last night. I'm not even sure I can get the words out. And if I start crying, I'll ruin the amazing eye makeup that Maria did. You can barely tell my eyes are puffy.

With a strange expression, Juliette holds out a small sky-blue compact. "For you." She glances behind her, but the door is firmly closed. We're the only ones here. "Giovanni asked me about something blue I was supposed to bring you?"

Shit. I take the compact and open it to reveal a small mirror. "Sorry about that. He heard the tail end of our conversation. I had to come up with something fast."

"Me too," she says, her cheeks pink. "I had to search my purse and act like I wasn't sweating it. It was either the mirror or my Adderall pills."

We share a look before breaking down into giggles. Lord knows I need a laugh after last night. It feels good to relax again, to have a friend. Maria, with her strange unexplained defensiveness of Giovanni, doesn't count. I miss Amy. I miss Honor. Both of them should be here for today, even if it is a fake marriage.

I get up from the vanity seat and move to the bed, using the square foot of space the dress isn't occupying. Juliette comes and sits next to me. This spot has the added advantage of being farther away from the door, so there's less chance of being overheard.

She speaks low, holding my hands in hers. "I called the number you gave me and spoke to a girl."

"Candy?"

"She didn't tell me her name. She was pretty hostile, actually."

"I'm sorry. She's really fierce about protecting her friends, and I've been missing for days now."

"I know. I told her what you said, that you were okay. That you were safe." Juliette makes a face. "She asked for proof of life."

"Oh my God. I do love that woman." I sigh, missing all of them at once. It hits me like a freight train. "Well, she'll tell my sister, and at least they'll know I'm alive. And she'll know to be on her guard."

Juliette hesitates. "I told her my name."

"Oh, but why? You didn't have to do that." I know how much she's risking helping me.

"So that she could get in contact with me. I haven't heard anything yet."

I bite my lip. "I'm sure she'll contact you."

"What about the wedding?"

"What about it? I don't have a choice."

"I know, but it's so messed up that you have to go along with this. What if you said no? I mean, Giovanni would be mad, but it's not like he can make you marry him. Father Michaels wouldn't pronounce you husband and wife if you don't say 'I do.'"

Father Michaels is the priest who officiates most of the family's ceremonies. He has a larger church in Vegas proper, but for a private family affair like this one, he'll use the chapel that's on the property. He baptized me and gave me my first communion. I never had much love for the man or the hypocrisy of strict religious rules in a family of monsters, but he had to be past eighty-five.

Last night I held Giovanni's body while he shot a man in cold blood, felt the complete lack of reaction. He's capable of anything.

"No. I'm not going to risk anything happening at the wedding. If I was going to put up a fight, I'd do it here, in this room…" I look over at the dress. *Fairy tale.* "But I don't really see the point in that either. He'll get what he wants either way."

Her eyes are troubled. "I feel bad I can't do more."

"You've already done plenty." The phone call is a huge weight off my mind. I know that Kip will keep Honor safe once he understands the nature of the threat. Not some random psycho on campus but a targeted kidnapping connected to our past.

For that matter Honor has done plenty too. She protected me the best that she could, and in my own way, I protected her back. There were things she didn't need to know, things that would only have endangered her. Things my father did. And now this.

It seems that my father and Giovanni are alike after all.

✧ ✧ ✧

JULIETTE WALKS WITH me from the mansion, helping me keep the hem of the gorgeous dress off the dirt path. I'm not sure why it matters, but that's how the family operates—propriety first, consent second. The blue compact is tucked into my garter belt, snug and secure. I figure it counts for both borrowed and blue. The dress and everything else are new. I don't have anything exactly old, but three out of four isn't bad.

We're escorted by Romero, who spends most of the walk pretending not to look at Juliette. He waits outside as we go in.

I expected the crowd to be small. What I didn't expected was to see only three people in the chapel.

Giovanni stands halfway down the aisle, still and almost contemplative. Behind him I can see Father Michaels between the pews. Beside him stands a man I vaguely recognize as Lorenzo, Giovanni's cousin. I remember that they were close even though Lorenzo's parents weren't officially in the life.

Giovanni comes down the aisle to meet me. "You look beautiful," he says soberly.

I nod my thanks. "So do you."

His lips quirk. "I know this isn't what you dreamed of."

This isn't what any woman would dream of. No matter how beautiful the chapel or the dress or even the man himself, the wedding feels cold. "Is that your way of letting me off the hook?"

He shakes his head slowly. "I didn't dream of this at all, bella. It presumed too much, more than I deserved. But now that I have you, I can't let you go."

His words move me more than they should. In the clear light of day, in this dress, with this man in front of me, I want more than anything to forgive and forget. To give us a real marriage, no matter how it started. But I can still see the mottled flesh of that man's knees, still smell blood in the air. Even if I can somehow forget the kidnapping, I can't forget death. It hangs over the ceremony like a shroud, the worst possible omen to a lifetime together.

Giovanni reaches into his pocket and pulls something out. "I should have given you this earlier."

The small antique ring takes my breath away, the diamonds glittering, the setting both stately and demure. It's exactly the kind of ring I would have dreamed about.

"You picked this out?" I ask, my voice wavery.

"It was my mother's." He looks unspeakably earnest and young in that moment. "Something old. For good luck."

It feels like there's a massive weight on my chest. I can't draw in enough air to respond, but I wouldn't know what to say anyway. I love that he feels there's hope for us, even while I know there isn't. I love *him,* even knowing the monster he's become.

In the end I don't have to say anything. He takes my hand and we walk down the aisle together to where the others are waiting. Juliette looks nervous, but she tries to cover it up with a smile. Even Lorenzo seems concerned, looking me over as if checking for injuries.

Only the priest seems oblivious to the tension. With his thick glasses and squinted eyes, I'm not sure how well he can see us.

Giovanni holds my hand while Father Michaels speaks. Maybe he thinks I'll bolt if he doesn't hold me. But the way he brushes his thumb across my palm, back and forth, feels more reassuring than confining.

"Do you take this woman to be your lawfully wedded wife?"

Giovanni doesn't hesitate. "I do."

Father Michaels continues with his speech, about honoring and obeying, loving and cherishing. "Do you take this man to be your lawfully wedded husband?"

And the truth is, I do love Giovanni. I cherish him. That's not enough to make a marriage, not in this mansion, not in the life. What is honor when we're violent murderers? What is obedience when we're ruled by greed?

He squeezes my hand gently, his dark gaze unwavering.

"I do."

CHAPTER NINETEEN

A SENSE OF numbness buoys me through the ceremony and the small, tense wedding lunch. Giovanni excuses himself to handle some business, and I say my goodbyes to Juliette. That leaves me alone in my bedroom, awaiting my wedding night like some terrified virgin.

"What do you think?" I ask softly. "Should I forget what he did and try to move forward with him?"

Lupo doesn't move, just looks at me with those dark eyes. He was already sitting on the bed when I came in, having made himself comfortable. His tail is still tucked around his body, not wagging. He doesn't trust me completely, but sharing this comfortable prison has brought us closer together.

"Still mad at me for trying to leave? I don't blame you. But I would have come back for you, I swear."

He rests his head on his paws.

I sigh and turn back to my drawing pad, where I'm shading his fur. There's a lot of it, which makes it a fun and challenging exercise. Something that should take my mind off tonight but doesn't.

"I'm giving up on men," I say, putting down my

pencil. "It's dogs only for me. I'll put a sculpture of you in the conservatory. What do you think?"

He growls low in his throat.

"Or maybe not."

Then I realize someone's coming to the door. Lupo growls and slinks off the bed to hide underneath.

The lock turns, and Maria walks in carrying a large white box with silver wrapping paper hanging off. She looks apologetic as she holds it out. "A wedding present from Juliette. Romero had to open it first."

To check for weapons. So much for forgetting the past. I'm still living in it.

I take the box and push aside the wrapping paper. Sapphire satin cups nestle against thin tissue paper. Delicate cream lace lines the bottom and the straps. Oh God. She got me lingerie. For my wedding night.

A blush heats my cheeks. Romero and Maria saw this. "So I don't even get privacy now?"

Humiliation burns, mixed with anger that I'm trapped here, that I gave up my one chance to escape for a man who died anyway. A man who was probably here to hurt me. Everything is twisted and upside down.

"I'm sorry," she murmurs.

"Don't pretend like you care about any of this. You're helping him keep me here."

"He won't hurt you."

The frustration inside me hardens, sharpens. "That wouldn't make it okay even if it were true. And it's not. Tonight he's going to *consummate* this marriage, whether

I want to or not."

Worry passes over her expression. "He…he wouldn't."

I laugh, rough and cold. "Then you're even more naive than I am."

That may not be who Giovanni was before. I know it wasn't as well as anyone. But I saw what he was capable of last night. This place has changed him. I think it changed me too.

Running my hands over the satin, some of my anger dissipates, leaving only sadness. "What do you think this is for, Maria? A romantic evening between lovers?"

Even though my voice is softer, she flinches.

I lift the lace strap with my forefinger. It's kind of a sweet present from Juliette, even if it is unexpected. As I pull the bra from the box, a slip of blue paper flutters to the bottom. A message. My gaze flies to Maria, but she's crouched by the bed making soft noises for the dog. She didn't see it.

With a casual movement, I drop the bra back into the box and shove it onto the bed. "Can you at least leave while I change? Or do you need to watch me do that too?"

I feel a little bad that she looks guilty, even though she *is* helping to keep me captive. Mostly I just need her gone so I can read what's on that paper. It might be something completely innocent like a note of best wishes. Or even laundry care instructions for all I know.

"I have to take Lupo," Maria says, not meeting my

eyes.

So we can have privacy? I hold back a shiver. Partly I'm defiant about what's going to happen, but mostly I'm scared. "Better you than Romero. He's still pissed at me."

Her smile is small. "Mr. Costas gave him hell."

"I bet."

She sobers. "I wanted to tell you…what happened to me. But I've never told anyone else before."

I shift, uncomfortable with where this is going. I don't want to care about her. And I have a sinking feeling this has to do with Giovanni. Except she's looking too vulnerable, and I can't be mean to her right now. I nod my head toward the small table, at least getting her away from the lingerie box.

She sits down as if preparing for execution. Her eyes are trained on the empty table, her slender hands clasped together in front of her.

The seriousness of her pose settles any remaining temper I've been feeling. I reach across and place my hand on top of hers in comfort. "What is it?"

Her lips press together for a long moment. "When I was sixteen, I was sold to a man my family owed money to."

"Oh my God."

"It wasn't entirely a surprise. My sister had disappeared two years earlier. And I knew they were struggling. Their only hope was for my brother to go to school and support them when he got out."

"That's awful, Maria. I'm so sorry."

Her eyes glisten with tears. "You may be wondering why I'm helping Mr. Costas, considering what happened to me."

"I…" I blink rapidly, trying to reconcile this with her previous words. "I guess you might not have a choice."

She gives a small shake of her head. "Not exactly. I mean I don't have any control over what happens to you. But I could quit working here. He wouldn't stop me. In fact he offered to set me up with a house, a new life."

My stomach churns. That's the kind of offer men make to mistresses. "So you and he were…involved?"

Surprise passes over her face. "No. Oh no, definitely not. He saved me, Clara. He took me away from the brothels and gave me freedom. And he taught me to defend myself. I could have gone anywhere. Some women went back to their families, but I didn't want to. I didn't want to face the world alone either, so I stayed here."

Sympathy slices deep within me. "I'm glad he saved you," I whisper.

That's the Giovanni I loved before. Is it possible that some of him survived?

How can it exist alongside the monster from last night?

She hesitates. "That's why I didn't…why I don't think he'll hurt you. He killed all the men who held us, the ones who beat us and sold us out every night."

Maybe only a man with both the lover and monster

could have saved those women. It takes a kind of brutality to face violence. It takes a monster to take down a monster.

"I understand." And I do understand why she believes in him after all that. I can't fault her for that. But I also know that things are different with me. I'm the one he kidnapped. I'm the one he married.

And I'm the one who has to face him tonight, alone.

"I'll help you get Lupo," I tell her. It takes both of us to lure him from beneath the bed and onto a leash. Then she's gone, leaving me alone with the box—and the note.

I toss aside the tissue paper and the bra. The blue slip of paper falls to the bedspread.

> *H is coming for you. Meet her in the pool house Saturday night.*

Chapter Twenty

I DECIDE TO wear the blue satin and cream lace set. There's a bra and matching thong, along with cream-colored thigh-high stockings with little fleurs-de-lis stitched in. It's definitely the prettiest underwear I've ever worn. I want to pretend like there's some other reason I'm doing this, like I'm just trying to appease my kidnapper, or maybe make sure no one questions the gift. The truth is that I want to look beautiful on my wedding night, no matter that it's fake. I want to look sexy for Giovanni, no matter how dark he's turned.

Only when I'm fully showered and shaved and dressed do I realize there's no robe. I find an old tie-dye pink robe in the back of my closet but decide that ruins the effect. And I feel too vulnerable standing in the middle of the room in underwear.

I turn off the lights and slide under the covers.

Butterflies flutter in my stomach, but I've decided not to fight Giovanni. He proved in the conservatory that he can make this good for me—better than I thought possible. I know it's going to happen anyway. So I'll lie here and look pretty and let him have his way. If I'm lucky, I'll get an orgasm or two out of the night.

That will be the end, because he told me it would be my choice after the marriage is consummated.

It will be almost a full week until Honor comes and rescues me. It's Sunday now, which means I have six days to get through. I'm a little surprised she's set the timeline for so long, but I'm sure it takes considerable effort to plan an escape with this kind of security.

So I'll wait and endure.

This is the very reasonable, logical, almost safe plan that I come up with between the time Maria leaves and the seconds in the dark when I hear the lock turn. Except my heart is racing faster than a shooting star. My palms are sweaty, my skin tight and hot. I regret not having sex with Shane or any of the college boys who would have happily, drunkenly hooked up—so at least I would have done this before. Instead I'm having a silent mental breakdown in the dark.

The door swings open, the faint light from the hallway obscenely bright. Giovanni darkens to pure shadow, moving without sound, with all the grace and danger of a panther.

He doesn't approach the bed. Instead he finds the vanity with ease, flicking on the lamp with a small *click.* His tux has rumpled since the ceremony, the jacket missing, shirtsleeves rolled up. His eyes are hooded with some emotion that makes me shiver.

"Clara."

I sit up, holding the sheet to shield my breasts. "I'm ready," I lie with all the sincerity I can muster. It sounds pretty convincing if you ignore the tremor in my voice. "You can do what you need to do, and I won't fight you."

"I see."

"Right, so…you can turn off the light now."

He turns away, and I see the flash of a smile. He finds this amusing? That's horrifying on multiple levels. When he turns back, his expression is serious. "Let's go."

"Um, what?"

"I'm not taking you here. We'll go to my room."

"Oh." Crap. Why didn't I think of that? Maybe it is a little weird to have sex on my childhood bed, even if it is big enough. Then again, having sex in the master bedroom—the place where my father slept—is actually weirder. And oh God, what if he didn't change the furniture in there either? "I'm not exactly dressed."

There's a pause, and when he speaks, his voice has lowered. "You're naked?"

Almost. "Juliette got us a present."

"I heard about that. I didn't think you'd wear it."

"Well, like I said. I'm just being practical about the whole thing."

"Ah." Now he's definitely holding back a laugh. "Practical."

My cheeks heat. "I can't believe you're smiling right now."

His smile fades a little, leaving him looking thoughtful. "You do have a way of making me smile when I least expect it. But we're definitely leaving this room. No one's in the hallway. No one will see you."

He sent Romero away? That's some relief. "You'll see me."

"But you're being practical about that," he reminds me.

Damn him. Keeping my head held high, I push the sheets off and stand up beside the bed. His gaze drifts over my body, eyes molten, jaw tight. It's a struggle not to cover my breasts or put a hand between my legs. There's fabric covering me, but it's thin and designed to show more than it hides. A blush spreads from the center of my chest, pinkening the slopes of my breasts, spreading up my neck.

I take a deep breath and one step forward. Then another.

I refuse to be embarrassed by him, but the way he looks at me isn't embarrassing—he looks at me like I'm the most incredible thing he's ever seen, like he has to hold himself back from snatching it. He looks like a man at the edge of his control. "Lead the way," I whisper.

He stands as if turned to stone. It's in slow, almost painful degrees that he moves away. The hall is empty, and I look the opposite direction, toward the staircase.

Giovanni stops and regards me with an assured curiosity. I might try to run, but he'll catch me. Whatever I do next, I'll end up in his room and on his bed. The only thing I can do now is be...practical.

It's a relief to see that he's changed the bedroom completely. I didn't spend much time in here, but I had at least seen my father's severe black furniture with gold trim and glass surfaces. The room has been redone with thick cherrywood in a conservative style. Wood the color of cinnamon is topped by white sheets and a cerulean down comforter.

Against the side wall there's a table with two chairs—and it's set with platters. As I step closer, I see cheeses, olives, and herb-filled bread. On another tray there are chocolate-dipped strawberries and candied pecans artfully arranged. Candlelight licks the metal latticework on the small plates.

"I'm not hungry," I say.

"Maria told me you skipped dinner." I hear the note of disapproval in his voice. "And lunch."

Food didn't seem like something I could digest. It's like getting married has changed my DNA, turned me into some other creature. I still feel like that, but Giovanni stands behind a chair, waiting for me to sit. The alternative to this is sex, and even though I've decided to do it, I can't bring myself to hurry it along.

I sit, the wood cool against my butt. My almost naked butt.

Giovanni sits opposite me, looking completely unconcerned by the fact that he's dressed while I'm…not. Of course I did this to myself. I thought wearing the lingerie would smooth along the process. He does seem appreciative of the view, watching me with heavy-lidded gratification; we seem to be moving at a glacial pace.

"Champagne?" he asks.

"Please." Alcohol sounds amazing. In fact if there were women walking around with neon-green test-tube shots, I'd grab three.

He pours three fingers in a slender flute.

I swallow the entire amount before choking on the fiery bubbles. "Oops," I cough.

With a quirk of his lips, he refills my glass, then fills his. "Tell me about school."

I eye the flute of champagne like it's my enemy. I want the numbness that comes with being drunk, but I'm not sure I can survive another round. Especially on an empty stomach. So I grab an olive and nibble on the salty flesh. "I thought you'd have read everything about it, considering you were following me."

He doesn't look repentant. "I know your course load and your GPA. I want to know what you think about it. What you loved. What you hated. What you dreamed about."

Is this a seduction? I want to tell him it isn't necessary. I want to tell him that stealing my body doesn't give him the right to my soul. Instead I find myself telling him the truth. "I loved all of it. Sculpture and sketching, composition and even calligraphy. What I didn't love was the campus politics, trying to fit in when everyone has an agenda."

"There was one person you'd usually share studio time with."

After I finish off the olive, I realize I'm actually pretty hungry. I pick some of everything for my plate. The bread is warm and fragrant, the chocolate strawberries cold and hard. "Amy. I love her. She's a great artist, even if she sometimes doesn't think so. It's just that she has lots of interests. The art thing is more about messing with her parents."

"They don't approve."

"Nah, they wanted her to do engineering or be a doctor or something. And sometimes I think she would have enjoyed that. I'm not like that. Art is my passion. Anything else would be a struggle. It would feel like work, instead of…"

"Instead of?"

"Instead of being home," I say softly.

His expression darkens, and I know he thinks I'm missing Tanglewood. That's kind of how it sounded, but it isn't what I meant. I do miss my sister and my friends back there. But art is not something that belongs to a certain place. It's not a church. It's inside me. Whether I'm sketching on a drawing pad or planning a sculpture for the conservatory, I can do that here.

"What about you?" I ask, turning the tables. "What do you love about the life? What do you hate?"

His stare is brooding. Long fingers drum on the table gently. Then he takes a swig of champagne—without coughing, the show-off. "I hate everything about it. The violence, the money. The way it brings out the worst in people."

I swallow, hearing the sincerity of his words. "Then why do it?"

"I get to have you," he says, his voice rough.

"You could have already had me. If you had shown up at my door as yourself, the boy I loved, I would have been with you in a heartbeat. I'm not why you do this. I'm just the pawn you're using to help you do it."

I hadn't meant to lay it all out there, but now that the words are out, I don't regret them.

"You're right."

"Then why, Gio?"

"They have her. My mother."

Shock slides through my body. "What are you talking about? Who has her?"

He stands and holds out his hand. "I'll tell you what you want to know, but not like this. Not across a table."

Only because he offers me the truth do I take his hand. He leads me to the bed. His movements are cordial, almost stiff, until he sits down. Then he draws me onto his lap, crushing me with his strong hold. I can hardly breathe, but I don't fight him—and not because it's practical. Because I sense that he needs this, needs me, and I can't deny him.

"They took me because they thought I might have information about where you and Honor had gone."

I don't mean to flinch, but I do. "Gio—"

"No," he says roughly. "I don't blame you. That was how it started. And then, Javier Markam is a sadistic motherfucker. I knew he was going to kill me, but he wanted to drag it out."

I swallow hard because I'd felt firsthand the cruelty

of that man. He pinned me down at my sister's engagement party. Giovanni was the one to save me that night, in more ways than one.

"I was gone for long enough that everyone assumed I'd been killed. The family would have swept me under the rug, but my mother insisted that they have a proper funeral." He laughs, raw and humorless. "There's still a headstone for me in the cemetery."

"Oh, Gio."

"That's why you saw an obituary. No cause of death was listed because they hadn't found my body. They held me in the basement, doing things that were…let's just say I was looking forward to dying."

I wrap my arms around him, pressing my face into his neck. I don't know whether I'm offering comfort or receiving it, but his arms tighten around me.

"Then your father was killed. There was a power struggle, but in the interim, your father's consigliere had control of the mansion. He found me in the basement. I was so weak at that point I think he expected me to die. Maybe putting a bullet in me would have been the greater mercy, but he brought me upstairs, tossed me in a bedroom, and waited to see what would happen."

"You didn't die," I whisper.

I feel him shake his head. "I didn't die, and what's more, I had heard Markam on a hundred different phone calls over those few months. He didn't guard what he was saying around me because he assumed it wouldn't matter. I sold the information to the family in exchange for reinstatement."

I pull back, not understanding. "But I thought Markam worked with the family. That's why they let him use the basement."

Giovanni nods. "They had a partnership, but the family never trusted Markam completely. And he never trusted them back. There were secrets on both sides."

"Because what matters most is blood," I say, my stomach clenching with the familiar refrain.

"That's right. The family in New York stepped in when everything went to hell. Officially Bartolo Vicente became the head of the Vegas operation, but Romero ran operations."

"And you?"

"I was the punk kid with leftover bruises and too much information to kill. I also had a pretty big chip on my shoulder after coming out of the basement. Bartolo took a liking to me, let me sit in on some big meetings. Between my information on Markam and the meetings with Bartolo, it got to where I knew more than Romero."

Now I understand why Romero's an enemy.

"When Bartolo got killed during negotiations with the Albanians, the *Rudaj,* I was the only one who knew the intricacies at play. They let me stand in temporarily."

"And how do I figure in?"

"You're going to make this permanent. With my status and your family tree, they won't dare throw me out of the mansion. As long as I'm here, I'm in the best position to find my mother."

"Who took her?" I remember the cruelty. "Markam."

"He didn't die with your father, but he was very pissed when I sold his secrets. He retaliated by taking my mother. And he's got a large network of places to hide women against their will."

My breath catches. "That's why you're taking down the brothels."

"They're disgusting. A stain on the family. I would always have taken them down if I had the chance, but doing it so quickly has raised some eyebrows. And I've already been through the ones owned by the Vegas operation. I need to expand outside my territory. That's why I need to solidify my position quickly. That's why I need you."

Chapter Twenty-One

WE STAY LIKE that for a long time, me sitting in his lap, my arms wrapped around his neck. I don't want to let go of this Giovanni who abhors violence but protects his family at any cost—the Giovanni I once loved. Through the thin fabric of his shirt I feel the crisscross of his scars. I can't help but stroke him in part sympathy, part wonder, reading the raised skin like braille.

There's a kind of intimacy in telling the truth, a seduction with every layer and lie fallen away. It leaves me aware of his body in a deeper way, the warmth of his skin at his neck, the hard muscles of his shoulders. It also leaves me aware of the hard ridge beneath my hips.

My heartbeat seems to thrum through every part of my body, through my fingertips and between my thighs. Meanwhile my body stills, even the natural motion of breathing held in restraint.

"I won't hurt you," he murmurs against the wild jumble of my hair.

"You might." I'm not only thinking about his body, the hard planes of him, the size with which he presses against the soft flesh of my ass. I'm thinking about the wedding vows he made to me. I'm thinking about what will happen when my purpose here is over.

"There are things I want to do to you, bella. Things I dreamed about when you were too young for anything at all. And then you hide under the blankets, and I realize you're still too young."

I pull back then and meet his dark chocolate eyes. "I'm a grown woman."

His gaze wanders over my bare shoulders, my breasts clad in satin. The place between my legs cupped with a strap of lace. "Your body, yes." He brushes a thumb over my temple, smoothing my hair. "Not up here. You hold yourself like you're bracing to be hit. I know your father was a cold son of a bitch, but I didn't think he—"

"I don't want to talk about my father." He's the last thing I want to talk about while Giovanni is holding me this way. The air is too inviting after his earlier confessions, teasing out my truths. When I was younger, I kept those secrets to protect the people I loved. Now I keep them to protect myself.

But I don't need protection from sex. And I don't really want it. I held myself back from closeness with Shane, with other boys, saving myself for a man who didn't exist. Now he's here, in my arms.

"Show me," I whisper. "Show me what you dreamed of doing."

He holds me, silent and still. I can only wait for his decision, body strumming with a lifetime of desire.

When he shifts my feet to the floor, my heart plummets. He's rejecting me.

Except he keeps me in the V of his legs, standing before him, held captive by a single hand linked to me. His eyes are trained to mine while his other hand works the notch of his belt. My eyes widen because I'm about to see his naked body for the first time.

Except he doesn't undress. Instead he turns me gently to face the wall, catching both my wrists behind me. Supple leather wraps around my wrists and cinches tight enough to hold me.

"Gio?"

"Bella," he says, a wealth of meaning encapsulated in a single word. The love he once felt for me, the conflicted desire he feels now. The torture did change him, harden him, but I'm beginning to fall for the man he is now.

He gives a little tug on the leather at my wrists as if to see if it will hold. My body turns toward him, and he holds me there, sideways. I realize in those silent, breathless moments that there is no position more on display than that of my side, where I can't look at him, where I can't look away. My only purpose is an object for him to appraise, with his gaze and the featherlight brush of his fingers. He touches places that suddenly feel sexual—the tender skin behind my arm, the faint hollow beneath my breasts, the tops of my thighs.

His voice is uneven. "All these years I've thought about how you would look all grown up. But I couldn't have…there's no way I could have imagined this."

My throat constricts. I want so badly to believe him, but there's a voice in my head I've never been able to forget. *You look nothing like your sister. Your breasts are huge, like balloons. You look older. Maybe my whore of a wife lied about your age too.*

The only reason he wants me now is for my family tree, and even that is suspect. Maybe there is some fondness in him from how he loved me before, as children. I can't believe that he really wants this body. Shane and his friends wanted it, but they were horny college boys. They wanted anyone. For all that he doesn't want this role, Giovanni wears the mantle of powerful capo even better than my father. He must have been with a hundred different women, sophisticated and beautiful.

"I'm not… I can't…" I swallow hard. "I know I'm not as pretty as other women. You don't have to lie to me."

He turns me to face him, searching my face with a mixture of shock and fury. "Men have died for calling me a liar, bella."

I raise my chin, knowing that in this, at least, I am safe. "I don't need a fake seduction."

"Fake," he says softly. "Lies. You don't believe that I want you. Even though my body proves it."

He means his erection, but I know how easy those are to be found. I felt them on my father, who had no right feeling that way about me. I press my lips together, forcing the truth back.

Giovanni moves from the bed, and I flinch. He lowers to his knees in front of me, holding my hips in both hands. Even with my hands tied behind me, I feel like a goddess standing in front of him. The way he looks at me, I feel worshipped.

"I have dreamed about you every night," he says, his voice hoarse. "Now that you're here, it almost hurts to look at you. You're so bright and beautiful and good."

My breasts rise and fall between us. "You mean it," I say, with some wonder.

"I would have gone to my grave never knowing a woman if I hadn't taken you."

I blink slowly, the words percolating through my brain like a hot summer rain in parched earth. "What do you mean?"

"I mean that you're everything, the end and the beginning. I've never touched another woman, never wanted to. It was always going to be you or nothing at all."

It feels impossible. "You've never had sex?"

His thumbs brush gently at my hips, slipping beneath the lace. "You don't have to worry that I'll hurt you. I'll be so careful with you. I'll learn your body until you come apart."

I already know he'll make me feel good. "Then that night? In the conservatory?"

He moves his hands to frame the triangle between my legs. "You taste so good, bella. One night and I'm already addicted. I want to feel your sex tremble against my tongue. I want to lick you until you scream my name."

A shiver runs through my body, quivering at my core. "God, please."

That was his first time tasting a woman, and he tore down all my defenses, ripped them apart and put me back together again. What would he do with practice? I won't survive it.

He kisses my mound over the small scrap of lace, then opens his mouth and bites gently against my skin. I shiver, unable to push him away, unable to pull him close. He nibbles his way down to my clit, teasing me through the fabric—which suddenly feels as sharp as a briar patch. My gasp sounds loud in the secret of the room, my breathing giving away more than words.

I wait impatiently for him to pull down my panties, but he doesn't. Instead he moves up my stomach, sucking pale skin, leaving red marks with the shadow of his jaw. He stands and pulls me flush against him, supporting my back with his arm, bending me so that he can nip at the exposed flesh of my breasts.

"Beautiful," he groans, tracing the lacy curve with two fingers.

With the severe facets of his face, the tone almost like gratitude, I can't deny the truth of it. And there's something sweetly vulnerable about being almost naked, with my hands at my back, while he is fully clothed. He could do anything like this—hurt me, take me. Instead he touches me as if that is the end goal, as if he cannot get enough.

My hips rock against him in silent plea.

I expect him to smile, maybe tease me about my impatience. It's what he would have done years ago, I think. But when he looks up at me, there isn't a hint of mirth in his expression. Only stark need, and I realize how much control it's taking for him to hold himself back.

"It's okay," I murmur. "You can do it."

Then he does smile, though it's strained. "Always rushing me. First in your room and now here. You aren't in control here, bella."

The sigh that escapes me is both resignation and relief.

He cups the back of my head, and I let myself fall into his embrace. His lips meet mine in a slow, inexorable claiming, every light touch of his tongue infused with possession, every subtle scrape of his teeth marking me as his. I'm not allowed to control this, can't fight it any longer.

I let myself sink into the space he made and find it to be shaped like me. Only enough space to feel, to breathe, to moan as his hand slides between my legs. Maddeningly, he remains over the lace, using it to gently abrade the sensitive skin, dragging it over my damp flesh like a sandpaper tongue.

"Please," I whimper. "Undress me."

"I could have looked at you like this all night," he says, one finger trailing over the curve of my butt. "I can't deny you, though. Not when you're so wet for me."

He hooks two fingers into my panties and tugs them

down around my thighs. They're actually more restrictive this way, biting into my skin when I try to spread my legs. I can't help it when he pushes two fingers around my clit on either side. I fight the bonds at my wrists, at my legs. Even the bra feels like bonds, restraining me.

Giovanni gently pinches my clit between his fingers, and I squirm, still supported by the iron band of his arm from behind. He dips his head to nip at my collarbone. I gasp, moving against him in a rhythm I know his body understands. He's hard and burning hot even through the fabric of his slacks. I press my tummy against him, wishing I could feel him somewhere else.

"Christ," he mutters, hands tightening.

It's a delicious squeeze, and I shudder in his arms. "I'm ready. I'm ready."

He shakes his head slowly, and I could cry. *You aren't in control here, bella.* And I feel out of control, my body burning hot and moving against him on its own, my mind a haze of kisses and warmth. I've never felt a man inside me before, but there's a new emptiness, my inner muscles clenching around nothing.

"I plan to use you all night, understand? I'm going to touch you everywhere, taste you everywhere." He pulls something from his pocket, small and black. I flinch when a silver blade flips open.

He places the pocketknife beneath the lacy bra strap, dull metal against my skin. A quick slice and the cup leans away from my breast. He cuts away the other side and the material drifts to the floor.

I flush as he draws a fingertip over the slope of my breast. He catches a nipple between his forefinger and thumb, pinching softly. He saw me the other night in the conservatory, but it was dark there. While not completely bright, there's enough light from the lamp by the table that he can see me clearly. His touch is achingly thorough, circling the full weight of my breasts, teasing my nipples to hard peaks.

He explores my shoulders and back and stomach with the same intensity, as if mapping my body's terrain. When I shiver, he stops and teases out another reaction—and I realize he *is* mapping me. He finds the places that make me sigh and shiver, that draw a whimper from me, that drag a groan from my throat.

He turns me away from him, and I feel a large palm caress down my back. He strokes my butt softly, finding every inch of the plush curves. Then his finger presses between to the tight knot of skin.

I yelp, pulling my hips away to escape.

"Shhh," he says. "Not tonight."

Even the suggestion leaves me shaken. I'm not as scared of him touching me there as I am of facing away from him. Then he does something even scarier. His hands are gentle as he bends me over the bed. He runs light touches down the side of my body and cups my butt.

He's not hurting you. I can't help the way I freeze up or the slight moan of despair that escapes me.

He stops moving behind me, and I feel his concern in the silence that follows.

"Clara?" he asks, his tone careful. "I'm not going to make you do this. I won't touch you back here."

His words are gentle. I know he's not making me do anything right now, but panic claws at my throat. It's too alike, being in this house, being bent over. I fight the bonds at my wrists as hard as I can, struggling to get free. There are horrible gasping sounds coming from somewhere, and I realize it's me.

Spots dance in front of my eyes. I can't move, can't breathe.

I find myself in Giovanni's arms, right-side up. It takes me a moment to realize that it's only his hands holding me now, that he's keeping my arms down but only so I don't flail. When I quiet, he releases me, using his hand to soothe me, cradle me, love me.

"I've got you," he murmurs against my temple. Some of the words he says in Italian, others I understand. "You're okay. You're with me, and I'm not going to hurt you. I'm not going to let anyone hurt you."

My breathing evens out in slow, painful degrees. I clutch at the fabric of his shirt, not caring that I'm naked, not caring that he's my enemy. Right now he's the only solid thing in a world made of waves and blistering sun. He's my anchor.

My voice is shaky when I manage, "I'm sorry."

"No, bella. Don't be. It's my fault. I went too fast. I wasn't careful with you."

I don't want to explain that it wasn't his fault, because then I'd have to explain whose fault it is. He sounds so genuinely regretful that it's hard not to spill the truth. "Can we pretend like that didn't happen?"

His laugh is rusty. "I'm not sure I can forget that. Not ever."

This is exactly why I didn't want him to know. He would look at me differently. And I'm afraid that if someone else knew, I would look at myself differently too. "Please."

He pauses, contemplative. His surface is calm, but I can sense something hot roiling within him. "Clara, I have to ask you. The way you reacted just now. It makes me wonder… Has anyone ever hurt you?"

A ripple of fear runs through me. No no no.

"I've never… I'm a virgin, if that's what you mean." At least that much is true. He seems like he's going to push the matter, so I reach up and press my lips against his. "Gio. I want to be with you."

Part of me knows I'm falling into my old habits, pleasing someone out of fear. It's not the same as it was with my father, but in some ways it is. He trained me to be the perfect Italian wife, and I've learned my lessons well.

Giovanni shifts, and I think he's going to kiss me. Or maybe bear me down onto the bed, take what we both want him to. Instead he sets me gently on the cool sheets. Then he reaches down for the blanket, tucking it around me.

I shove away the butter soft cotton. “Wait. No.”

He’s already walking away from me, showing his broad shoulders and trim waist. God, he must have put on fifty pounds of pure muscle since I saw him last. He’s different in so many ways, vital ways. I can’t love him as the boy he was before. I can only love the man he is now.

He flips off the lamp, casting the room in pale shadows. “It’s late,” he says gently, heading for the door. “You need to rest.”

And I know suddenly that I can’t let him walk away. Can’t stand to lose him.

Not Giovanni, the boy who grinned with abandon. He’s already lost. Now there’s only a man of intensity and passion, of determination and fierce loyalty. My husband.

“Gio.”

He pauses at the door without turning to face me. “Sleep.”

I cross the room and circle him, taking in the dark gleam of his eyes and the bronze skin revealed by his shirt. Moving a finger down his chest, I revel in the raised muscles that slow my path. When my finger touches the empty belt loop, he grasps my elbow in a taut grip.

“Clara. You don’t have to do anything.”

I keep my eyes on him as I fumble with the button. He makes a low sound as my fingers brush hardness underneath. The placket strains against his erection. With careful deliberation, I slide down the zipper and push the soft cotton briefs down. He makes quick work of his shirt, unbuttoning it and shrugging it to the floor.

We're both naked now, both clasped in moonlight. Both of us vulnerable.

Standing in front of him, I run a finger through the coarse patch of hair beneath his flat belly. Then I touch something achingly hot and smooth. He shudders but makes no move to stop me. His shaft pulses with life, as strong as a heartbeat. I trail my finger down the length and around his girth.

Then I touch my fingertip to the cool damp on the tip.

He sucks in a breath. "God, bella."

I fall to my knees, knowing another way I might please him.

He catches me with a hoarse sound and returns me to standing. "If you kiss me there, I won't be able to hold back, and I want to be inside you when I come."

A flush subsumes my cheeks, as hot as the hard flesh of his erection. "Oh."

With a knowing look, he takes my hand. When he lays me down on the cool sheets, I stretch out. His body reaches over me, large and dark and powerful. He plants soft kisses on my eyelids, my nose, my chin. Wordlessly I spread my legs for him.

He notches himself against my sex, heat against heat, wet against wet. I hover on the precipice of something both carnal and divine, knowing that the next few moments will change me forever.

His hands are gentle as they gather mine above my head, my wrists held loosely in the cage of his fingers. "Is this okay?" he asks softly.

I know he's thinking about earlier, wondering if it was the restraint that upset me. But that was something else. The feel of being spread open to him, unable to stop the press of him, the push, excites me. My hips roll against him, more proof that I want this. "Gio, please. I need more."

He enters me in slow inches, a stretch I feel deep inside. I gasp as he reaches farther, and he pauses. His head lowers to kiss my chest, my breasts. He sucks my nipple until a sharp pleasure-pain lashes my core, and I relax enough to let him in.

It feels like he's impossibly deep. "How much more?" I ask, trembling.

He slides his free hand down my stomach to the slippery skin. Gently he teases my clit until I sigh in pleasure. It still feels full, but if he keeps touching me like that…

"About halfway," he says, his voice like falling rocks.

Oh God. I hadn't seen before how his muscles ripple, hadn't seen how hard he's working to hold himself back. He wants to thrust all the way in, I can tell, but that would rip me apart. Halfway? How is that possible? A laugh of incredulity and wonder rends the air.

Then he laughs too, soft and bemused. "Your body, Clara. It haunts me."

"Turnabout is fair play," I say, voice tight. My whole

body feels tight, stretched to the limit. I'm not sure I can fit any more of him in. His hips are narrower than his shoulders, but even so my hips have to open wide to accommodate him. My arms are above my head. And inside, I'm incredibly full.

His fingers work at my clit in lazy circles. He swoops down to kiss my lips, his tongue matching the rhythm of his hand, the short pulses of his erection. The orgasm comes upon me like tendrils of ivy on ancient stone, slow and inexorable, taking over until I'm caught in its grip. Tremors shake me from the inside out, grasping at him, pulling him deeper.

He groans softly. "I'm not sure I'll survive you, bella."

"Let go," I whisper, but I'm the one who has to let go. To relax into his hold, conform around his body. It feels a little like splitting apart, like breaking and being re-formed in some new way.

When he presses all the way inside, I feel the rough hair of him against me. I feel the choked gasp he makes, the shudder deep inside him. "I won't last," he gasps.

"Then don't."

His hand tightens on mine, keeping my arms up. His other hand plants on my hip, holding me steady. Then he pulls back and surges into me, the fullness so intense I bite my lip. His thrusts grow faster, harder, the force of him shaking the bed. I rock with him because it's the only thing I can do, my body rising to meet him, reaching for his peak more than my own.

His body stiffens, and he grinds against me, pulsing deep inside. His expression is harsh, pain lining every feature. He clasps at me as he's falling, as if *I'm* falling and he'll never let me go.

When the clench releases him, he slides into me with languid strokes. His lips grow soft against mine, almost playful. His hips drop, changing the angle inside me. He finds some secret place that makes me push up on my toes.

I'm breathless. "Gio. Aren't you…"

"Finished? Christ, I'll never be done with you. I'm not sure I'll ever be able to leave your body."

I thought that men had an orgasm and were finished. That's what Amy told me, anyway. He still feels hard inside me, though less urgent. His hands release mine, and I hold on to his muscled shoulders.

He presses that spot, watching my face with dark cunning. My mouth opens on a silent cry. I don't know what's happening. This isn't like when he touched my clit, nothing like when I touched myself. It's a forced surrender, this orgasm, wrenched from my body like it belongs to him instead of me. Pleasure blankets me in muted waves, turning the whole world shades of purple and bronze, midnight eyes and hot skin in an endless expanse.

CHAPTER TWENTY-TWO

I WAKE UP with pale yellow across my pillow and something hard nudging my back. The memories come back to me in a rush, the dark shape of him moving over me, hours and hours, relentless, pleasure that morphed into pain and then back again. I moan, sore and aroused in a luscious cycle.

"You're awake," he murmurs.

He thrusts inside me, his way smoothed by a full night of his spend. My breath catches at the fiery ache of salt on abraded skin. Then he finds the spot that makes me moan, and my body rocks into him.

"I'm surprised you waited," I manage to say in a sleepy drawl.

"I said I wouldn't take you again. After the marriage was consummated."

A lazy smile touches my lips. "And the middle of the night?"

He pauses, his fingers tightening on my hips. "I don't want to hurt you."

I take the measure of my body, the whisker burn between my thighs, the tender flesh of my breasts. The bruises that circle my hips. He's awakened something inside me, something firmly woman, something powerful. "What if I want you to?" I ask, rolling my hips.

At that he pulls out and lays me flat on the bed. Pushing one leg aside, he thrusts into me. His eyes fall shut as if in intense relief. "I want you to like it."

"Then find that place inside me again."

His lips curve in a brutal smile, one of both surrender and domination. He pulls out of me and works his way down, over aching muscles and reddened flesh. Two fingers explore the inner wall of my body until I gasp. With a wicked glint in his eye, he bends his head and kisses my clit. His fingers and his mouth work in tandem, bringing me to the brink again and again until I'm wrung out, collapsed on the bed, unable to move a muscle as he slides inside and thrusts hard.

The sun has boiled into peak afternoon by the time he withdraws from the bed. His expression is regretful as he heads for the shower. "I have some work that can't be postponed."

I sit up and pull the sheet to cover me, a little cold without his body. "To call New York?"

He pauses. "Yes."

Of course he'll want to let them know that the marriage is complete. That it was consummated. The family values marriage and blood ties. Now he has both. He'll be able to continue the search for his mother, which is important. So why do I feel suddenly hollow?

I wish he didn't look so strong, so virile. Shouldn't nakedness be a position of weakness? He looks like a warrior, as if he could take on an army without a single piece of armor.

"You can sleep here," he says, gesturing to the bed. The room. *His room.*

I shouldn't ask questions I don't want to know the answer to. "Will the door be locked?"

He hesitates only a moment. "Romero will escort you anywhere you want to go."

✧ ✧ ✧

WE FALL INTO a pattern of sex and absence. He spends most of the night inside me, moving, thrusting, pulsing in the clasp of my body. In the daytime he's mostly gone, either working in the office or visiting one of the businesses.

I feel changed in some elemental way. Maybe because I'm married. Or maybe because I've fallen in love. Either way, dread creeps through me every hour I spend alone.

My sister is coming for me on Saturday. Romero still shadows my every movement, more vigilant now after my first escape attempt. And I think he's mapping the tunnels of the house. I'll have to think of a new method to get away from him on Saturday.

No matter how Giovanni has changed me, no matter how much I love him, I'll meet my sister in that pool house. Because of all people, I know that love doesn't conquer everything. Living as a prisoner in the house of my nightmares isn't a foundation for a marriage.

All I have to do is wait until Saturday night.

In the meantime, I need a new way to escape from Romero.

But Giovanni fights against my plan without even knowing it.

On Tuesday he takes me to one of the sitting rooms in the guest wing. The dusty furniture has been cleared out, the floor replaced with hardwood, heavy draperies torn from the windows and replaced with breezy white linens.

On one side of the room, large blocks of stone of various sizes and colors catch the light. I recognize soapstone and granite, and a particularly large prism of red alabaster that takes my breath away.

"I didn't know what kind of stone you prefer," Giovanni says, sounding hesitant. "If you like any of them, I can get more."

Distantly I see an antique wooden hutch with gleaming tools arranged inside. My eyes are all for the stones. Most of them come only to my ankles, a few to my knees. They're small pieces, but even a cursory inspection tells me they're rare—and this variety could never be local.

Granite and sandstone are plentiful at a quarry about an hour south of here. I went there before on a rare outing with Honor. But all of these types and colors and striations couldn't be found in one place. Even the selection at my art school isn't this wide.

It would take me years to sculpt all these pieces, and I can't wait to start.

I turn to face him, heart beating wildly. "Gio, these are amazing. Where did you get them?"

One large shoulder lifts, dismissing the effort. "Here and there."

Circling the red alabaster piece, I see the remnants of a sticker. *El Amarna*, it says. Customs. There's no way he sourced this stone and had it flown in since I've been in this house. "You ordered this before I got here," I say, running my finger along a jagged edge, deep red striated with black.

His cheeks darken faintly. "I started collecting them when you entered art school."

ON WEDNESDAY WE take his Shelby convertible to the Rock Canyon National Park, Lupo in the backseat beside a wicker basket. A thirteen-mile scenic drive with the top down puts a thousand knots in my long hair and a goofy smile on my face. Giovanni doesn't quite smile—I'm not sure he's capable of regular emotions like happiness anymore. But he does seem far more relaxed than he does at the mansion.

We take an easy hike route and avoid a large rainwater pond. I give him a questioning look.

"I don't like the sound of water," he answers.

When our legs are tired we find a plateau overlooking the valley and eat chicken-salad sandwiches while a gray northern harrier glides high above us. Lupo chases a chorus frog into the brush and comes back with nettles in his fur. These are the moments I would have dreamed of when I imagined the old Gio and myself together.

It's almost, *almost* enough to make me stay.

Except that we have to go back to the mansion, to the life. To everything I despise.

He gets a phone call on the way back. I only hear his half of the conversation. "Hello? Tell him no, absolutely not. He knows what the alternative is. I wouldn't hurt a fucking fly. If he wants to commit suicide, that's his business."

EVERY NIGHT HE teases and tortures me with an ever-increasing erotic skill set. And I surrender with abandon, forgetting what he does during the day, ignoring the violence, pretending not to know who used to sleep in this room. It bothers me, though, especially in the clear light of day. I try to spend most of the time Giovanni is away from me in the studio, sculpting or sketching.

On Thursday brown paper bags stuffed with acrylic paints and high quality brushes appear in Giovanni's bedroom. I unpack the colors with glee, running my fingers over the cream hog bristles.

"I love them. But why did you put them here?" I would have thought he'd put them in the studio.

"There's more in that room, and an easel set up by the window. I thought you might want to paint the walls in this room." He pauses. "Only if you want to."

Tears prick behind my eyes, and I launch myself at

him, throwing my arms around his neck. He catches me with a soft exhalation of breath. His arms clasp me to him, squeezing tight enough to steal my air.

I could stay here, I think.

At least until Giovanni leaves and Romero appears to stand guard at my door. Then I remember I'm a prisoner. How can I be bribed so easily with rocks and paint? But then again, if I have everything I ever wanted, how can I leave?

I spend the rest of the day painting the plateau where we ate lunch yesterday, remembering how it felt to have the wind on my face and Giovanni at my side.

ON FRIDAY GIOVANNI appears at the bedside, freshly showered and wearing a sharp custom suit.

"I'm up," I say sleepily, eyes barely open.

Giovanni has gotten into the habit of walking me to the studio before he begins working for the day. I don't love getting up early, but I do love the ritual.

Gio gives me an almost tender look. "Sleep."

I also prefer to be escorted by Giovanni rather than a guard. It's a little dampening to the creative spirit to be reminded that I'm not free. Tomorrow is Saturday, and I still don't know how to break away from him.

Even if I decide to stay, I rationalize, I would go meet my sister. She'll worry about me if I'm not there. And it would only endanger whoever comes to get me, whether Kip or Blue or someone else from his security company, if they have to break into the mansion itself.

I scrub at my eyes. "No, Romero will be here soon for the morning walk."

Lupo snores softly at the foot of the bed, his small body curled into a nest. He doesn't appreciate early mornings any more than I do, but we have to operate around Romero's availability for walks.

A light *clink* sounds as Giovanni sets the blue leash on the nightstand.

Awareness comes to me suddenly. I sit up, using the sheet to cover my naked body. "What's this?"

A muscle works in his jaw. "For you. Romero can still walk the dog if you prefer, but you can too."

My eyes widen. "Without a guard?"

"When you're outside, you need an escort. It's a security issue. Even with the fences and the patrols, I can't be certain you'll be safe." He pauses. "In the house, though, you can go as you please."

My heart stops beating for a full minute. This is it. He trusts me. He really trusts me, and I'm planning to betray him. I close my eyes. I can't think about it like that. I only want to see my sister, make sure she's safe and show her I'm safe too.

"Thank you," I whisper.

But he's already turned away, heading for the door.

Chapter Twenty-Three

I'M ANXIOUS AND restless throughout Friday night. Nightmares wake me up twice, once with a nameless, faceless person pinning me to the wall. The second one holds me in a cage, laughing demonically as I pull at the spindle bars.

A drowsy Giovanni wakes me up with soothing noises. "You're dreaming, bella."

My breathing comes in harsh pants. "Oh God."

"Shhh." He runs his large hand through my hair, brushing the strands between his forefinger and thumb. He cradles my head and runs kisses over my forehead, light and caressing, until I drift slowly back to sleep. I don't remember any nightmares after that, only vivid flashes of color and emotion that leave me unsettled come morning.

I wake up alone in bed with Lupo anxious to go out. It's almost noon and I'm still groggy from being up so much during the night. Showering quickly, I take Lupo out to the rose gardens just outside the west exit. A guard nods at me from beside the door, familiar with my new routine.

When I reach the studio with Lupo by my side,

Romero is waiting for me.

"Put the dog inside," he says, brusque and cold. "And come with me."

A shiver runs over my skin. This is how my father would summon me, one of his men plucking me from whatever I was doing with no preamble, harsh expressions and impersonal commands. "Sure. Okay."

There's a dog bed and bowl of water set up in the studio so that Lupo can sit with me while I work. I lead him inside and shut the door on his worried eyes.

"The office," Romero says.

My heart hitches. This is exactly like before. And then I'd get to the office and the door would close…but no. This is different. Giovanni is different. A little voice inside my head asks, *Is he really that different from your father?* He's been gentle enough with me, rough only in the ways I like best, but he's still a ruthless criminal. He has to be.

Dread grows with every step across the house until we reach the center.

I knock on the office door, my stomach in knots. *He doesn't know how this is affecting you. He has no way of knowing.* And I have to keep it that way, which means slowing my breathing back to normal.

"Come in."

Pushing inside, I'm dismayed to find him behind the desk. Anyone would feel like a naughty child at this point, being called in for some misdeed. After the number of times it happened to me, after the way it happened, my throat squeezes so tight I can barely force out a sound.

My hands clench and unclench behind my back. "You wanted to talk to me."

His gaze roams my body, impersonal and calculating. I know he takes in my too-fast breathing, the sheen of panic heating my face. Whereas last night he'd been full of calming softness, today he looks hard.

He tosses something on the shiny desk surface. "I found this."

It takes me a second to recall the folded blue slip of paper, the note from Honor. I shoved it between the pages of my sketch notebook, uncertain whether I'd need to keep it or not.

"You looked through my things," I say, halting.

He laughs, humorless. "Yes, that's me. The big bad wolf you need to get away from."

I swallow hard. "She was just trying to help."

"What I want to know is how she got this note to you?"

I remain stubbornly silent—but shit. Shit. He'll eventually track down who did this, and Juliette will be in trouble. Would he hurt her? I want to believe he wouldn't hurt a woman. Isn't that what Maria assured me?

I wouldn't hurt a fucking fly. If he wants to commit suicide, that's his business.

No, he's a dangerous man. I can't underestimate him. I just don't know how I'm going to protect Juliette.

"For that matter," he continues, voice flat, "how did she find out where you were? Have you been in contact other than this?"

Despite the butterflies in my stomach, I force myself to approach him, to circle the desk so I can appeal to the man I love—the one who held me during my nightmares last night. Not the one who makes homicidal threats over business negotiations.

"Please, Gio. Let me call her so she knows I'm safe. I'll tell her not to come."

A cold glint enters his eyes. "You don't want me to greet her in the pool house?"

My heart drops. "No. *Please.* She just wants to make sure I'm okay. I'll stay with you. I was already going to tell her I wanted to stay here."

Disbelief and fury war on his face. "How fucking stupid do you think I am?"

"I'm telling the truth!"

"Then tell the truth about where you got this note."

My lips press together.

"That's what I thought. Keeping secrets but I'm supposed to trust you."

"I'm not keeping secrets. I only want to keep my sister safe." Along with Juliette, for helping me. "I really was going to stay with you, I swear it. I'm being honest with you."

"Honest?" he asks softly. "While you're so busy being honest, why don't you tell me why you freaked out when I had you on your stomach?"

My stomach turns over. Flashes of memory assault me—the plush carpet underneath me, the faint smell of cigars and ink. All that's missing is hot breath and groping hands. It's too similar, too much. I stumble backward, almost falling against the shelves.

Giovanni reaches up to steady me, but it feels like an attack.

His touch burns me, and I twist away, knocking over a small side table. "No!"

"Tell me," he says, eyes dark and determined. "Someone hurt you, bella, and I'm not going to rest until you tell me who."

Tears stream down my face, blurring my vision. I trip over the edge of the rug, skidding on the hardwood floors. Pain shoots up my knees at the harsh impact burn. "You're hurting me."

Giovanni lifts me as if I weigh nothing, turning me in the air until we're back at the desk. We're on the other side, now facing the stained glass mirror at the back, but it's still too close. He turns me onto my stomach, facedown, palms pushing at the smooth surface. I'm gasping for breath, begging and pleading and threatening. The wood grain with the knot that looks like a scary face, the one shaped like an acorn. My memories slide down to a dark place. *No.*

He bends over me from behind, his breath warm against my cheek. "Who are you thinking about?"

"You, you," I cry out, ragged and breathless. "Let me go."

His hold on me is merciless. I can't lever away, can't move a single muscle. "Who hurt you? Was it someone at the university? That fucker I punched in the alley?"

"No no no." The words are small, almost a breath.

He presses his body against mine, erection hard and hot and familiar. "The one who married your sister? Someone touched you, bella. Tell me and I'll let you go. Who was it?"

"My father," I scream with a hard sob against the cool, unfeeling wood. How many times was I bent over this desk? How many times did I press my lips together not to make a sound?

Cold air washes over my back, and I realize I'm free. Giovanni stands a few feet away from me, looking shell-shocked. "Your father?"

I stand and wrap my hands around my stomach, shaking. "I never wanted you to know."

"I don't understand. I thought for sure it was someone after you left here. He was hurting you?"

"Just stop," I say, my voice dull.

He takes a step closer, his hand reaching out, and I flinch away.

He freezes. "Why didn't you tell me?"

"I couldn't, okay? I couldn't tell you or anyone. He told me he'd have anyone killed if I told them."

"Honor?" he asks between clenched teeth.

"I don't think he hurt her. Only me because I wasn't his real daughter. He told me I couldn't tell her or I'd be sent away. And I didn't want to leave her, even if that meant putting up with him."

"He…" A hard swallow. "He raped you."

"No," I say bitterly. "I was telling the truth when I said I was a virgin. He liked to call me into his office because I'd done something wrong. Maybe I had been sketching instead of doing my history homework. So he'd tell me to bend over the desk for punishment."

Giovanni's hands are clenched into fists, his large body trembling with rage. "Why?"

I know what he's asking. Not why did it happen, but why didn't I tell him. "What would you have done, Gio? If I told you my father would spank me without my panties on, that he would feel me up while he did it?"

"I would have killed him," he says, his voice rough with venom.

"I know," I say, suddenly weary. "I know you would have. I didn't doubt that. That's why I could never tell you. You would have killed him, but he had an entire army at his disposal. You would have been killed first—or if not first, definitely after."

"Who the fuck cares?" he asks roughly. "I was nobody. I was *nothing.* It didn't matter what happened to me. You should have told me so I could protect you."

"And what about me protecting you? I loved you, Gio, with everything I had. That was how I protected you and Honor. Both of you would have fought for me and suffered the consequences. So I didn't tell."

Giovanni runs a hand over his face, looking more troubled than I've ever seen, more *real* than he's been since I returned to the mansion. He stares at the stained glass, unseeing. "So all those nights when you came to meet me, he had put his hands on you. He had terrorized you, and I did nothing."

I take a step toward him, place a hand on his arm. "This is what I didn't want. This guilt."

"Guilt?" he says harshly. "I swore I'd protect you."

"It wasn't your fault, just like it wasn't mine."

He pulls away from me. "I wish I could kill him again. That fucker. I wish I could take him downstairs."

The basement, he means. I shiver. "It's over now. Done."

His expression clouds, and he looks at me like I'm a stranger. "Done," he repeats hollowly.

"I'm over it," I say gently, but we both know that's a lie. My freak-out in the bedroom proved that, and the knocked-over side table between us confirms it. "We don't have to talk about it again."

His eyes meet mine, and I see a grief so profound I can't breathe. "When they held me in that basement, I was glad. It meant you were free. Every second I spent down there meant they hadn't found you yet. So no one could put their hands on you if you didn't want them to."

Tears trace a hot path down my cheeks. "I'm so sorry, Gio."

"And it was for nothing."

"No. It was *everything.* You did save me. And Honor too. I love you for that, Gio. I love you for everything." I reach for him, but he pulls away with a slashing motion.

"You loved that boy. He's gone now."

Cautiously I reach for him again. I place a hand on his muscled arm, feeling the tension running through him. He doesn't move away, but he doesn't embrace me either. "I know you're different," I tell him. "I love who you are now too."

We remain that way for a long moment, as if in a black hole, floating without gravity, anchored only by the touch of my hand to him. I can feel his breath, his anguish. His remorse.

His eyes are soulless, empty. "Romero will take you back to the studio."

My hand falls away. "What do you mean, he'll take me back? I know the way."

"He'll escort you. You aren't going to be at that pool house tonight. You aren't going anywhere without a guard."

CHAPTER TWENTY-FOUR

I ONLY RETURN to the studio long enough to pick up Lupo, who whines in a high pitch and licks my hand.

"Take me to my old room," I tell Romero, who looks uncertain but ultimately lets me go.

For the next hour I curl up in the old bed with flowered sheets and stare out the window. Gio looked so cold when he sent me away. And all the trust he had built in me is gone. I can't live this way. Even if he gives my freedom back, I'll always know he can take it away again.

The only way to get out is to see my sister, except I have no way out. Romero is standing guard outside the door. The window is secure. Will Giovanni hurt her when he meets her in the pool house? He might not hurt her, but he would definitely consider the men with her fair game. Soldiers, like him.

At dinnertime Maria enters the room bearing a tray. "Come and eat," she says.

"I'm not hungry," I mumble, pressing my face into the pillow.

I hear the door close and figure she's left the tray on the table. But I hear her making soft kissing noises to Lupo. When I peek behind me, he's sniffing close to a piece of meat she's holding out. He takes it and backs away, chewing and eyeing the plate for another piece.

At least someone learned to trust during my time here.

She approaches the bed and straightens a pillow. I don't care what she has to say. Giovanni is so great, he would never hurt me. I know now that it's partially true. He doesn't try to hurt me, not with his hands. He hurts me anyway, by treating me like a captive. By keeping me from my sister. By forcing me to face truths I prefer to leave buried.

"Clara," she whispers.

It's strange that she's whispering. Strange enough that I turn in bed to face her.

Her expression is worried as she looks me over. "Are you okay?"

I frown, a little confused. "What?"

Her brows draw together. "I went into the office to tell Mr. Costas something. I saw what he was doing to you. Romero made me leave, but…"

And she thought he was hurting me, raping me. Bent over the desk. I can imagine how it looked. He wasn't raping me, but he was violating a boundary I had fortified for so long. I'm not sure if she would help me if she knew he was demanding secrets instead of sex. So I don't tell her.

"Will you help me leave now?"

She glances toward the door. "Yes. What I was going to tell Mr. Costas… I was contacted this morning by someone whose name is Honor. She says she's your sister, and she offered me money to help her get you out."

My mouth opens. Closes. Why would Honor offer a ransom when she's planning on extracting me? Maybe it's a distraction. Still, something doesn't feel right about the timing.

"I wouldn't have done it," Maria says sadly. "Wouldn't have betrayed Mr. Costas for anything. But I can't leave you here after what I saw. I'm sorry I didn't believe you before."

I feel bad that she believes the worst of Giovanni. He's not a saint by any means, but he hasn't done what she's thinking. Still, I need to get out of here. Giovanni clearly will never treat me as an equal. And my sister might be in trouble if he meets her in the pool house.

That's a big *if,* because now I'm doubting whether that plan ever existed. Why would Juliette lie?

But if Juliette did lie, then something even more sinister is going on. She had Candy's phone number. It wasn't a direct link to Honor, but she could have used it to find her. Honor could be at some other meeting spot right now, expecting to find me but trapped instead.

Why would she want me to come to the pool house? Maybe that was just a feint, so I wouldn't be alarmed that my sister didn't contact me. She could have assumed I'd never get free of Romero anyway, so it wouldn't matter.

Then again, she might have hoped I would go to the

pool house. What would have been waiting for me there? Who would have been waiting?

A short knock comes at the door.

It opens to reveal Romero and, standing behind him, Juliette.

My heart races. "Romero," I say, my voice even despite my jangling nerves, "please call Giovanni. Now."

He wouldn't love being ordered around by me, but he seems to recognize the note of urgency and danger. Swiftly he moves his hand to his pocket where I know he keeps his cell phone.

And behind him, Juliette pulls something out of her pocket.

"Romero!" I yell.

He turns around, his hand going to the sidearm under his jacket. "You," he breathes.

Juliette holds a gun steady, eyes glistening. "I'm sorry."

A shot echoes through the room, so loud my eardrums feel like they burst.

I watch as a dark stain forms on Romero's white dress shirt. He looks down in shock before his large body slumps to the ground. A low, mournful whine comes from beneath the bed.

"Oh God," Juliette says. "Oh God. Oh God."

Maria and I are frozen by the bed.

She looks at us, her eyes both shocked and remorseful. "Both of you. Let's go."

CHAPTER TWENTY-FIVE

JULIETTE DIRECTS US to the west exit where there's no guard by the door. There are other men to meet us, some of whom I recognize from the old days. Men in suits, with those same soulless eyes. A white van idles near the supplies entrance, its back doors open. A dark-tinted limo is in front of it, engine purring softly.

"Get in," one of the men says, gesturing to the van.

When neither Maria nor I move quickly enough, he shoves the butt of a gun into my back. Pain shoots through my spine, and my knees threaten to buckle. I force my lips together, determined not to make a sound. I accused Giovanni of being like my father, but he wasn't. He'd never hurt me.

These men are like my father—ruthless and cruel.

I climb into the van and help Maria, who looks like she might be going into shock. Her face is extremely pale, her eyes not focusing on anything. I squeeze her cold hands in mine and whisper, "It will be okay."

Juliette steps into the back of the van with us, still holding the gun she used in the house.

No silencer. So why didn't Giovanni come running? Clearly this is a well-executed takeover. I just hope Gio got distracted—and that he isn't hurt. My mind flashes to Romero's bleeding body. *God.*

The van rumbles as it turns on, but we idle there.

"Why?" I whisper to Juliette.

She looks despairing, helpless. "It was supposed to be Romero. He would be the head of the family, and he would marry me. My family would get the status we deserve."

I stare at her, shocked. He would have been her husband. "You *shot* him."

"I didn't want to do that," she says, hands trembling. "I didn't have a choice."

Fairy tales were for girls who didn't have a choice, ones bent over desks and locked in rooms. Stories we could believe in, when real life let us down. We didn't have a choice, but Juliette did. And I had seen the way he looked at her. She had written her own tragedy.

"Did you ever call Candy?"

Her eyes fill with tears. "Yes. And they were taping it the whole time."

I don't understand why she would betray both Giovanni and Romero. They were the two possible leaders of the Vegas operation. The New York family would back one of them or the other. "Who's behind this?"

Juliette's pretty eyes flicker toward the limo in front of us. "Javier Markam is going to bring the family into the twenty-first century."

So that's who is behind this. She's on crack if she thought the family would accept an outsider. "And he's going to repay you for your loyalty."

Fury flashes in her eyes. "Go ahead and judge me. You got to grow up the daughter of a capo, the biggest house, the best cars, the clothes. You have no idea what it's like to be me."

I never had flashy clothes or cars before Giovanni. And a big house feels very small when your door is locked. My birthright has always been more of a curse than a blessing, but I don't bother to explain that to her.

"The family will never accept Markam," I say instead. "Especially once they learn he planned an attack on the mansion."

"They won't ever know," she says fiercely. "You and Giovanni will run away together while stealing the family's money. You'll never be found, but Markam will step in to save the operation."

"And Romero?"

Her lower lip trembles. "Oh God."

The gun she's holding shakes so badly. She's going to drop it. It could hit the metal floor and go off, shooting any one of us.

One of the suits steps into the back with us and shuts the door. He mostly ignores us. As the van pulls away, he focuses on the mansion through the high tinted windows.

"I won't go back," Maria whispers, holding my hands so tightly they ache.

She must be remembering her time in that horrible brothel. I actually suspect there's a worse fate planned for us, to make sure we're truly never found. But I doubt that would be reassuring.

I squeeze back. "We need to get out of this van before it goes too far. On my mark?"

She stares at me blankly.

Shit. I know it's asking a lot of her, considering she seems close to a breakdown, but I need all the help I can get. I don't have any special skill with fighting or a gun, and we're working against trained killers here. Part of me wonders whether we should wait and see if Giovanni can find us, my fairy-tale white knight. Except I can't be sure that he's still conscious at the moment or even alive. The farther away from the mansion we get, the worse our chances.

Fairy tales are the stories we tell ourselves when we need them. They serve their purpose. Hope. And I need all the hope I can get right now. I was raised a mafia princess, bred to marry a king. That makes me the queen, and I'll be damned if I let Juliette ruin my ending.

"Now," I whisper.

I go for Juliette's hair, yanking hard. She screams, the gun clattering to the floor and sliding. I dive for the gun and grasp it, but she's already on my back, clawing me. I get in a hard elbow to her stomach, and she falls back with a *thunk* on the metal bench. In the space that follows, I grasp the gun—ready to shoot the man at the back door.

Except he's already on the floor out cold. Maria

stands over him, hyperventilating.

"Wow," I say, impressed. "You can fight."

"Learned," she says, panting. "Can't breathe."

"Okay, okay," I try to soothe her. "Nice and slow. Focus on me. We're going to get through this."

The brakes slam on the van, and we all slam into the divider. So much for nice and slow.

We can hear the front doors open and shut, footsteps around the side. They're coming for us. "Lock the doors," I tell Maria.

She locks them just as the handle creaks. Someone bangs hard on the outside. "Open the fuck up!"

"They'll get the key," I mutter.

This is a problem. I have a gun now, but so do they. I doubt Juliette or this unconscious guy would make a valuable hostage to them. Our best bet is staying out of their hands.

A whistling sound fills the air while Maria pulls the belt from the guy's slacks. She wraps it around the double handles with cold efficiency and pulls tight. More banging from the outside, but the makeshift lock seems to hold.

"Remind me never to get on your bad side," I tell her.

"They'll get in eventually." She looks deathly pale now, leaning against the wall of the truck.

I dig in Juliette's designer clutch and pull out a cell phone. What would be really handy right now is Giovanni's cell phone number, but I don't see it listed in her contacts. I do see Romero. My heart squeezes, remembering him lying on the floor. Maybe someone in the mansion has found him? They might be able to patch me through to Gio. But we only have minutes, seconds. *Think, think.*

I dial a cell number I've called multiple times a week.

My sister's voice feels like a cool mist on a scorching hot day. "Hello?"

"Honor?"

"Oh my God, Clara! Is that you? Are you all right? Where are you?"

I laugh, a little watery, at the rapid-fire questions. "Kind of in a tight spot, actually. Don't suppose you're anywhere near the mansion?"

"No," she says. "Oh no. Juliette said you were in New York. That the family had you for ransom."

A very terrifying burning smell seeps in through the cracks around the door. More banging on the metal. "Better come out," a voice says.

"Don't believe anything she told you," I say.

"She said Giovanni is alive, that he kidnapped you."

"Okay, that part is true. But he's also the only one who can help me right now. I need you to get ahold of him and tell him to look for a white van that left through the supplies entrance. Preferably as fast as possible."

She speaks rapidly to someone else.

Maria huddles on the hard bench, having gone from pale to faintly green. "They're burning the truck," she says. "They're burning us. Alive."

I have to admit, it looks bad. Little tendrils of black smoke sneak in through the bottom of the doors. "All we have to do is hold out until Giovanni comes. Which will be soon."

Her eyes are wide like saucers. "How do you know?"

"You were the one who said he wouldn't hurt us. That goes for letting us get hurt too."

"That was before I saw him holding you down over a desk!"

"There's a story behind that," I say, gesturing to the man on the floor. "Check him for other weapons? We might need a backup plan."

"Okay," my sister says, breathless. "They contacted him. He's on his way."

"Great. Listen, Honor. I love you. You're the best big sister a girl could have."

Her voice is trembling. "Clara, what's happening there?"

The details would only freak her out worse than the vague things she can guess now. "We'll hug later, I promise. But just in case I'm wrong, name the baby after me. Even if it's a boy."

I hang up, knowing she'll kick my ass for that later. I'm just praying that she actually gets to.

Maria comes up with a knife from the man's boot and pepper spray from Juliette's clutch. Not exactly an arsenal, but it will have to do. At least there are only two of them. And we have the element of surprise.

"Between the two of us, you're the one who can

fight, so you're the one who needs to play dead." I detail a short and sweet plan to Maria, who nods but doesn't say much.

Should I use pepper spray on my eyes? That's probably overkill. Instead I slam the soft flesh of my arm into the corner of the bench, making tears spring to my eyes.

Then I open the door.

There are immediately two very large guns pointed at me by two very angry men. "I'm sorry," I say, crying. "Please don't hurt me."

One of them leers at me. "You'll be wishing you hadn't done this in about an hour."

I back up, almost tripping on Juliette's body. "Giovanni Costas kidnapped me. I just want to go home."

One of the men follows me into the truck, reaching for me.

That's when Maria strikes, hitting him on the side of his knee in a way that sends him sprawling to the floor. I follow up with the pepper spray, making him howl and flail. I jump onto the bench to avoid being snatched by him and hop out of the van.

The last man has his gun trained on Maria. I aim for him, but we're at a stalemate.

"Drop it," he warns. "We don't need this bitch. Just you."

Shit. I know I don't have a choice. I've seen those eyes before. He won't hesitate to shoot her. I couldn't have stood by and let her get hurt even before she was going to help me escape.

Reaching down, I slowly lower the gun to the floor.

"No," Maria says, snapping out of her trance. "It's not worth it. Shoot him."

I set the gun on the ground and nudge it away with my foot. "And let you get hurt? I don't think so."

The man gives a cruel smile. "Javier only needs you, sweetheart. I was going to have some fun with this one. But now I think the two of you are too much trouble."

My mind barely interprets his meaning before I see his finger twitch. Then I'm throwing myself onto Maria. A loud *bang* blasts through the air; pain blooms like crimson flowers as I land on the hard-packed dirt.

Tires squeal, and I wonder if the van is leaving. From the corner of my eye I see the black limo speed away, filling the air with dust. It floats across my vision like glitter.

More shots ring out.

I stare at the blue, blue sky above us and wonder if it's always been that wide. Where is the sun? It seems bright out, but it feels incredibly cold. I'm shivering.

"Clara. Clara!" Giovanni's face appears above mine.

His hands are all over me. Doesn't he know I'm not in the mood? Men. Then something sharp pierces the cloud I'm floating on. *Ouch.* Don't like that.

"Stay with me." He sounds frantic. Panicked, really. It's strange coming from him. He's always so confident and composed. "Can you hear me?"

"Nice and easy." It seems like the thing to say.

"Christ. She's losing too much blood. Stay with me!"

Is he still talking to me? It's not clear. Everything is pretty fuzzy, like I'm looking through a stained glass window. I hope my sister doesn't take me seriously about naming her baby boy Clara. "I love you, by the way."

Then I close my eyes and rest.

CHAPTER TWENTY-SIX

"KIP LIKES THE name Alfred. It was his grandfather's name. I think it kind of sounds like a grandfather's name, don't you? I can't imagine a baby face named Alfred. Like he'd need a tiny butler suit."

My sister's voice drifts over me, comforting as the artificial haze of whatever medication wears off. There's a sharp pain in my shoulder that I don't really want to think about right now, so instead I focus on what she's saying.

"I'm thinking of Alessandro. What do you think? It's pretty, right?"

Another thoughtful pause.

"Not as pretty as Clara, mind you. But I hope you weren't serious about that, if it's a boy. I suppose we could have gone with Claro, but that's worse than Alfred." Her words grow thick. "If it's a girl we are definitely going to name her Clara. If she gets even half your strength, we'll be glad."

"Strength," I manage to say, my voice rusty. "I remember you calling it stubbornness."

She appears above me, her eyes shining with tears. "You're awake."

"Especially when I wanted to move out."

"The world is a very scary place."

"I'm not going to argue with you just now."

She bites her lip, worry infusing her brown eyes. "How do you feel?"

"My shoulder hurts. Tell me I just landed on it wrong."

"You probably did," she says. "After you got shot."

I groan. "I'm going to need harder drugs."

I'm back in the bedroom—Giovanni's bedroom, with the expansive vista of the Red Rock Canyon painted on one wall. My limbs are heavy, my eyelids somehow sore. Honor has pulled up one of the wooden chairs from the table to my bedside, a small basket bursting with pink and blue and pastel green yarn bundles at her feet.

"I'll get the doctor. And I'll tell Giovanni you're awake."

"Wait." I grasp her arm with my good hand, the one that doesn't feel like it's weighted down by two tons of cement. "You're okay with him?"

Her eyes flash. "I'm furious with him. But he did save your life. You know…after drugging you, kidnapping you, and forcing you to marry him."

"Oh. You heard about that." I'm picturing an explosion when someone told her. Followed by a nuclear winter. It might have been good to be unconscious for that.

"I had some things to say to Gio about that, I can promise you. And that sham ceremony is absolutely not a real marriage. But I've watched the way he's been these past two days."

I'm a little afraid to ask. "How has he been?"

"He's been outside the room nonstop since you've been in here. He won't even leave to eat or shower. He's a mess. But he won't come inside the room either."

As much as I love my sister, I'm honestly a little disappointed not to find him here. "Why not?"

"I think…he thinks he's responsible for what happened to you." A delicate flush paints Honor's cheeks. "I might have said that to him, actually. Repeatedly."

I can imagine. "I want to see him."

Honor studies me. "Are you sure? Because if you're afraid of him, or if you just don't want to see him for any reason, you don't have to. You don't owe him anything."

She's such a fierce protector. I reach for her hand and squeeze it. "Thank you for that. But please. I want to see my husband."

✧ ✧ ✧

I FIRST MET Giovanni as an eighteen-year-old boy, with lean muscles and beautiful eyes.

Then I saw him again as a grown man. His chest and shoulders had filled out with muscle. He seemed taller even though that shouldn't have been possible. The biggest changes were the hard angles of his face—and the harsh scars on his back.

When Giovanni walks into the bedroom, he's aged ten years.

There's a beard growing on his face, in only two days' time. His eyes are bloodshot, rimmed with red. His clothes hang rumpled on his large frame.

He approaches the bed the way a man faces his execution. "Clara."

I reach for his hand. After staring at it for a beat, he takes it. His hand is cool and dry, loosely framed around mine. "Are you okay?" I ask, hesitant.

His lip quirks in that familiar way. "I think that's my line."

Some relief fills me to hear him sound normal. "I'm okay. Or I will be, once I have a test-tube shot."

"A what?"

"Green. Lime green. Never mind."

He looks away, his jaw clenched. "Clara. I want you to know, I won't hold you to the vows. Obviously they weren't real."

My heart clenches, and I don't think it's only the throbbing in my shoulder. I try for levity. "Is this because my sister's scary?"

He gives a short laugh. "She is. But I decided you had to go before you were taken."

A dark shadow settles over me. "Because of what I told you."

"Yes."

"I didn't want you to look at me differently."

He runs a finger across my cheek. "I look at you like you're the strongest woman I've ever met. It's an honor knowing you."

"That sounds like a goodbye."

"As soon as you're healthy enough to travel, you can go back home."

"But your mother…"

"I'll keep looking for her one way or another." His smile is sad. "Having you would solidify my standing with the family…but the truth is I took you for myself. Because I wanted you. I wanted you the entire time, and in a moment of weakness, I let myself have you."

My eyes prick with tears. "Gio."

"I know I should apologize for that, but I'm not sorry for that. I'm only sorry I have to let you go." He pulls his hand away, leaving me bereft.

He turns away, showing me his broad shoulders. Both my sister and Gio called me strong today, but I don't feel strong. All my life I've used my art to express my hopes, my dreams. And now I'm watching my greatest hope walk away from me.

"Wait," I whisper.

He stops at the door without turning.

He's only a few feet away, but it may as well be miles. I'm locked in a castle, and he's on the outside. Except that was the past. He says the boy he was is dead, but I think that princess is gone too. I'm someone else now. Someone who can fight for what she wants, for *who* she wants.

"I want to stay."

There's a pained pause. He turns to face me, his expression unforgiving. "You don't know what you're saying. I drugged you, Clara. I held you captive. I know you may have softened toward me at the end—"

"Fell in love with you," I say softly.

He flinches. "That's not possible."

"I think there could be a million different incarnations of you, and I'd fall in love with every single one."

He's almost vibrating with tension, a man at the end of his rope. "God, Clara."

"So I want to stay with you." Some of my confidence falters. He's not the only one who changed. I'm not the girl he knew before. "Unless you didn't fall in love with me."

His expression is stark with need as he nears the bedside. "Fall in love with you? How could I fall in love with you when I loved you with every breath, every heartbeat, every lash of the fucking whip? When you invaded my dreams, my hallucinations. I can't stop loving you, bella. I've tried. God help me, I've tried."

Tears blur the vision in front of me, the haggard man, the fallen knight. "Gio."

He clasps my hand between his and rests his forehead on my unharmed shoulder. "I didn't know how to have you. I didn't believe I deserved you. So I took you, and you…God, you were shot. Because of me."

"No one said marriage was easy."

His laugh is unsteady. "I know I don't deserve you, but I'll keep you. If you want to stay, I won't be able to let you go."

I close my eyes, knowing that my demons have

fought alongside his. We have our own battles, the both of us, but we can fight them together. "The mansion had so many memories. So many monsters. But you vanquished them, one by one. Only you could have turned this place into a home, Giovanni."

"We can leave here. We can run away together, you and me."

That was what I'd always wanted. Running away together. It sounds romantic, but the truth is, it's really just running away. "We'll stay here," I say softly. "So you can look for your mother."

It wouldn't be easy, dealing with the violence of the life.

Another battle we would fight together.

He kneels beside the bed. "*Ti amo, bella. Mi vuoi sposare?*"

Tears stream down my face. I don't know Italian like he did, but I know enough. "We're already married."

"Di nuovo," he says. "Again. For real this time."

I run my fingers through his hair, a wild mane now. "It was always real."

He bows his head over my hand, his voice low and fervent. "I know, bella. Always."

Epilogue

The mirror has blackened at the edges, turned misty in the center. How many brides have looked at themselves in this pane of glass? How many of them lived happily ever after?

My sister sniffles from behind me, her brown eyes glossy with tears. "You're so beautiful."

This ceremony is more for her than for me. For all of our family and friends who didn't get to attend the first one. I don't have any of the fear, the nerves that I had before.

I give her a soft smile. "If I am, it's because of you."

She applied my makeup, somehow making it both subtle and glittering. I don't know how she does it, but I'm grateful to have her. Now she's forming a wide braid with loose curls, twining strands of pearls and crystals that remind me of water droplets. Combined with the full skirt of my dress and the antique engagement ring on my finger, I feel more like a princess than ever.

Flowers spill over every pew and surface in the chapel—and also the small dressing room.

A knock on the vestibule door. Maria peeks inside. "Are you ready?"

"Almost," I tell her, picking up the sweeping bouquet of calla lilies.

"You'd better hurry," she says, her voice dry. "I think the groom is going to pass out soon."

That makes me laugh. "Cold feet? We're already married."

The past few months have brought us closer than I could have imagined. My recovery at the mansion, the birth of my nephew, Alessandro. We spend every day together, talking and laughing and dreaming. And every night, he explores new ways to make me shiver and moan.

Before I wanted to sculpt the counterpoint to the angel at the Grand, but only now I realize that isn't the archangel. It's a phoenix, rising from the ashes. The perfect use for the red alabaster stone.

Maria shakes her head, expression rueful. "I think he's worried you'll get cold feet."

I stare after her as the old wooden door shuts. "Silly man."

"Smart man," Honor says. "He knows what you're worth."

A small, plaintive cry comes from the corner. "Shhh," she soothes Alessandro, picking him up from the carrier. "Are you hungry, little one?"

He grasps at the silvery material of her dress, impatient.

"Oh, but they're ready for you," she says, biting her lip. "I think he could wait until after."

"Don't be silly. No nephew of mine is going hungry." I fight a smile and lose. "Besides, maybe five minutes will give Giovanni a little scare. It's nothing he doesn't deserve."

Honor laughs. "You really are his perfect match."

It turns out to be fifteen minutes instead, but I'm not worried. The afternoon is cool, the wind light enough to leave the chapel doors open. Only people who love us are in attendance—Candy and Hannah from the Grand, Amy from school. Giovanni's cousin Lorenzo returned as well, looking very relieved to have my consent this time. He also couldn't stop looking at Amy throughout last night's dinner.

Even Romero attended, having been given the green light to resume normal activity last week. His health has returned to normal, but his spirits remain subdued after Juliette's arrest. She took the fall for everything, with Javier Markam missing. But we knew the truth about what happened, and Giovanni was looking for him.

Men in suits and sunglasses are tucked into every corner. Security is high, but we're in the mafia. Security will always be high.

Maria waits at the foot of the aisle with Lupo, who looks disgruntled at the flowers she's looped around his collar. I laugh softly and give him a soft pat as I pass him.

The small chapel hums with conversation. Giovanni stands in front of the room, anxious energy vibrating around him. Maria wasn't exaggerating. He looks ready to tear into somebody.

He grows still, and I know he's spotted me. The entire crowd quiets.

Giovanni has a natural command of the room. The son of a foot soldier, he was never expected to lead. But he assumes his position with a grace and control that are enviable—and an innate respect for humanity that my father never had. He still hasn't found his mother, but I know he'll never stop searching, never stop until she's found or, at the very least, laid to rest.

The touching refrain of the wedding march fills the air, and I walk down the aisle. Flower petals catch at my dress. Friends and family watch me, some stoic, some with tears in their eyes. Everyone here wishes the best for me, and it feels a little bit like floating.

Giovanni's jaw is clenched hard when I reach him. He takes my hand in a firm grip, and I feel the tremors run through him. He looks like a man pushed to the brink. You wouldn't know we just had wild marathon sex this morning, not four hours ago.

The priest welcomes everyone and begins the ceremony, his droning voice booming through the rafters.

"You came," Giovanni says low enough that only I can hear.

"Did you think I wouldn't?" I whisper.

There's a pause. "Thought you might pay me back."

I bite my lip, holding in a laugh. "I thought about it."

His hands tighten, almost reflexively, before loosening. "I would have found you."

Only he could make a threat sound romantic. "I came, didn't I? I decided you were worth marrying."

The corner of his lip quirks up in that reserved way I've come to love. "Thanks."

When I was younger, I longed for freedom as if it were a place. I longed for love as if it were a person. In the end I found both back where I started, with the man who loved me all along. "And plus…this baby will need her father."

His gaze snaps to mine. "What did you just say?"

"I mean, I don't know if it's a girl. It could be a boy." With the hand not holding my bouquet, I run a palm over my stomach. I haven't started to show, but I knew I was pregnant before I took the test. "I have this feeling, though."

Giovanni's hands shake in mine, and I grasp them firmly. He looks at me, his eyes dark and completely, utterly open. I can see deep into every dream, every hope he hardly dared. I can see the way it shatters him, having everything he ever wanted.

I walked into this church calm and confident. I comforted my sister and smiled at my friends. I could have withstood almost anything except the way this strong man's eyes glisten with tears.

"No, Gio," I whisper, my eyes pricked with heat. "Don't be sad."

He doesn't say the obvious answer: *I am happy.* When you've been through what he has, when you've experienced that kind of loss, everything is tinged with sadness.

"I can't…I can't lose you, bella." He's gone completely pale, eyes stark with pain.

He's faced torture and violence, but the thought of losing me is tearing him apart. And it's breaking my heart. "You won't lose me. Or this baby, Gio. We're here forever. For always."

The priest's booming voice cuts in on us. "Do you take this woman to be your lawfully wedded wife?"

I do. That's his line, but he's fighting something deep and dark right now. A lifetime of denial, of grief. That horrible pleasure of having something you know you can't live without.

There will be more violence in his future, more suffering, because that's the condition of being human. And of being the head of the Las Vegas mafia operation. But he'll face that with me by his side, every step of the way. Including here, now.

Without waiting for him to answer, I throw my arms around him. He catches me and holds me to him without hesitation, as if this is where I belong. His lips move over mine, hungry and hard.

"I do," he murmurs between scorching kisses, between nips and licks that make my knees weak.

The priest sputters beside us, having finally realized that we've derailed off course. I pull back long enough to tell him, "I do too."

Then Giovanni drags me back, one hand at my hip, the other cupping my face, this kiss full of possessive intensity too raw for a church. And definitely too sensual for an audience. I start to pull away, but he holds me closer while Lupo barks circles around us.

My lips curve into a smile beneath his. "We're making a scene."

"I'm not letting you go, bella."

"Not even to take the dress off me?"

He presses his forehead against mine. "The dress definitely stays on this time."

My laugh rings out when he sweeps me into his arms. He carries me over the lawn and across the threshold of a mansion made new with heart, with family. There are a hundred walls to paint, a thousand dark memories to wash away. And we'll face them together.

Thank You!

Thank you for reading Hold You Against Me…

I hope you loved Giovanni and Clara's story as much as I do!

If you're new to the Stripped series, find out what happens when Clara goes on the run and Honor meets a darkly mysterious man in Love the Way You Lie…

> *"I've always been a fan of Skye Warren ever since I read Wanderlust. Her writing is flawless and tales captivating. Love The Way You Lie is no exception. 5 Stars."*
>
> ~ Pepper Winters, New York Times bestselling author of Tears of Tess

I'll do anything to stay hidden, even if that means working at the scariest club in town. Then he shows up, mysterious and yet strangely familiar. And so damn sexy.

When he looks at me, I forget why I can't have him. He's beautiful and scarred. His body fits mine, filling the places where I'm hollow, rough where I am soft.

He's the only man who wants to help, but he has secrets of his own.

He has questions I can't answer.

I'm running from my past, but his might catch me first.

Read Love the Way You Lie today!

If you've already read Love the Way You Lie, you can continue the series with Blue and Lola's story in Better When It Hurts and Ivan and Candy in Pretty When You Cry.

And don't miss the gritty and suspenseful Chicago Underground series. USA Today bestselling author Cari Quinn calls it a "must read." Book one, Rough is free on all retailers!

Sign up for my newsletter so you can find out when I have new books!

You can also join my Facebook group, Skye Warren's Dark Room, to discuss Hold You Against Me, the Stripped series, and my other books.

I appreciate your help in spreading the word, including telling a friend. Reviews help readers find books! Please leave a review on your favorite book site.

Turn the page for an excerpt from Love the Way You Lie…

Excerpt from Love the Way You Lie

IN THE FIRST moments onstage, I'm always blinded.

The bright lights, the smoke. The wall of sound that feels almost tangible, as if it's trying to keep me out, push me back, protect me from what's going to happen next. I'm used to the dancing and the catcalls and the reaching, grabbing hands—as much as I can be. But I'm never quite used to this moment, being blinded, feeling small.

I reach for the pole and find it, swinging my body around so the gauzy scrap of fabric flies up, giving the men near the stage a view of my ass. I still can't quite make anything out. There are dark spots in my vision.

The smile's not even a lie, not really. It's a prop, like the four-inch heels and the wings that snap as I drop them to the stage.

Broken.

A few people clap from the back.

Now all that's left is the thin satin fabric. I grip the pole and head into my routine, wrapping around, sliding off, and starting all over again. I lose myself in the physicality of it, going into the zone as if I were running a marathon. This is the best part, reveling in the burn of my muscles, the slide of the metal pole against my skin and the cold, angry rhythm of the song. It's not like ballet, but it's still a routine. Something solid, when very few things in my life are solid.

I finish on the pole and begin to work the stage, moving around so I can collect tips. I can see again, just barely, making out shadowy silhouettes in the chairs.

Not many.

There's a regular on one side. I recognize him. Charlie. He tosses a five-dollar bill on the stage, and I bend down long and slow to pick it up. He gets a wink and a shimmy for his donation. As I'm straightening, I spot another man on the other side of the stage.

His posture is slouched, one leg kicked out, the other under his chair, but somehow I can tell he isn't really relaxed. There's tension in the long lines of his body. There's *power.*

And that makes me nervous.

I spin away and shake my shit for the opposite side of the room, even though there's barely anyone there. It's only a matter of time before I need to face him again. But I don't need to look at him. *They don't pay me to look them in the eye.*

Still I can't help but notice his leather boots and padded jacket. Did he ride a motorcycle? It seems like that kind of leather, the tough kind. Meant to withstand weather. Meant to protect the body from impact.

The song's coming to a close, my routine is coming

to an end and I'm glad about that. Something about this guy is throwing me off. Nothing noticeable. My feet and hands and knowing smile still land everywhere they need to. Muscle memory and all that. But I don't like the way he watches me.

There's patience in the way he watches me. And patience implies waiting.

It implies planning.

I reach back and unclasp my bra. I use one hand to cover my breasts while I toss the bra to the back of the stage. I pretend to be shy for a few seconds, and suddenly I feel shy too. Like I'm doing more than showing my breasts to strangers. I'm showing *him.* And as I stand there, hand cupping my breasts, breath coming fast, I feel his patience like a hot flame.

This time I do miss the beat. I let go on the next one, though, and my breasts are free, bared to the smoky air and the hungry eyes. There are a few whistles from around the room. Charlie holds up another five-dollar bill. I sway over to him and cock my hip, letting him shove the bill into my thong, feeling his hot, damp breath against my breast. He gets close but doesn't touch. That's Charlie. He tips and follows the rules, the best kind of customer.

I don't even glance at the other side of the room. If the new guy is holding up a tip, I don't even care. He doesn't seem like the kind of guy who follows rules. I don't know why I'm even thinking about him or letting him affect me. Maybe my run-in with Blue made me more skittish than I'd realized.

All I have left is my finale on the pole. I can get through this.

This part isn't as physically strenuous as before. Or as long. All I really need to do is grind up against the pole, front and back, emphasizing my newly naked breasts, pretending to fuck.

That's what I'm doing when I feel it. Feel *him.*

I'm a practical girl. I have to be. But there's a feeling I get, a prickle on the back of my neck, a churning in my gut, a warning bell in my head when I'm near one of *them.* Near a cop. My eyes scan the back of the room, but all I can see are shadows. Is there a cop waiting to bust someone? A raid about to go down?

My gaze lands on the guy near the stage. Him? He doesn't look like a cop. He doesn't *feel* like a cop. But I don't trust looks or feelings. All I can trust is the alarm blaring in my head: *get out, get out, get out.*

I can barely suck in enough air. There's only smoke and rising panic. Blood races through me, speeding up my movements. *A cop.* I feel it like some kind of sixth sense.

Maybe he feels my intuition about him, because he leans forward in his seat.

In one heart-stopping moment, my eyes meet his. I can see his face then, drawn from charcoal shadows.

Beautiful, his lips say. All I can hear is the song.

I'm not even on beat anymore, and it doesn't matter. It doesn't matter because there's a cop here and I have to get out. Even if my intuition is wrong, it's better to get out. Safer.

I'll never be safe.

The last note calls for a curtsy—a sexy, mocking movement I choreographed into my routine. Like the one I'd do at the end of a ballet recital but made vulgar. I barely manage it this time, a rough jerk of my head and shoulders. Then I'm gone, off the stage, running down the hallway. I'm supposed to work the floor next, see who wants a lap dance or another drink, but I can't do that. I head for the dressing room and throw on a T-shirt and sweatpants. I'll tell them I feel sick and have to leave early. They won't be happy and I'll probably have to pay for it with my tips, but they won't want me throwing up on the customers either.

I run for the door and almost slam into Blue.

He's standing in the hallway again. Not slouching this time. There's a new alertness to his stare. And something else—amusement.

"Going somewhere?" he asks.

"I have to… My stomach hurts. I feel sick." I step close, praying he'll move aside.

He reaches up to trace my cheek. "Aww, should I call the doctor?" His hand clamps down on my shoulder. "I wouldn't want anything bad to happen to you."

I grip my bag tight to my chest, trying to ignore the threat in his words. And the threat in his grip. I really *do* feel sick now, but throwing up on him is definitely not going to help the situation. "Please, I need to leave. It's serious. I'll make it up later."

He'll know what I'm saying. That I'll make it up to him personally. I'm just desperate enough to promise that. Desperate enough to promise him anything. And he's harassed me long enough that I know it's a decent prize. I'm sure he'll make it extra humiliating, but I'm desperate enough for that too.

"Please let me go." The words come out pained, my voice thin. It feels a little like my body is collapsing in on itself, steel beams bending together, something crushing me from the outside.

Regret flashes over his face, whether for refusing my offer or forcing me that low. But this time he doesn't let me go. "There's a customer asking for you. He wants a dance."

Want to read more? Love The Way You Lie is available now at Amazon.com, iBooks, BarnesAndNoble.com and other retailers.

Excerpt from Rough

There's a certain sultry walk a woman has when she's bare that can't be faked. No hose and no panties. The nakedness under my skirt was as much about keeping me aroused as it was about easy access.

I'd perfected the art of fuck-me clothes. A surprising number of men asked me out, even at a grungy club on a Saturday night. Cute little college girl, they thought, out for a good time. I saved us all time by dressing my part.

Tonight's ensemble consisted of a tight halter and short skirt with cheap, high-heeled sandals, bouncing hair, and bloodred toenails. The scornful looks of the other women didn't escape me, but I wasn't so different from them. I wanted to be desired, held, touched. The groping fingers might be a cheap imitation of intimacy, its patina cracked with rust and likely to turn my skin green, but they were all I deserved.

My gaze panned to the man at the bar, the one I'd been watching all night. He nursed a beer, his profile harsh against the fluid backdrop of writhing bodies. His gray T-shirt hung loose on his abs but snug around thick arms, covering part of his tattoo.

Dark eyes tracked me the way mine tracked him.

His expression was unreadable, but I knew what he wanted. What else was there?

He was hot in a scary way, and that was perfect. Not that I was discerning. I needed sex, not a life partner. There were plenty of men here, men whose blackened pasts matched my own, who'd give it to me hard.

A woman approached him. Something dark and decidedly feminine roiled up inside me.

She was gorgeous. If he wanted to score, he probably couldn't do better, even with me.

I tried not to stare. She walked away a minute later—rejected. I felt unaccountably smug. Which was stupid, since I didn't have him either. Maybe no one had a chance with this guy. I was pretty enough, in a girl-next-door kind of way. Common, though, underneath my slutty trappings—brown hair and brown eyes were standard issue around here.

"Hey, beautiful."

I glanced up to see a cute guy wearing a sharp dress shirt checking me out. Probably an investment banker or something upstanding like that. Grinning and hopeful. Had I ever been that young? No, I was probably younger. At nineteen I had seen it all. The world had already crumbled around me and been rebuilt, brick by brick.

"Sorry, man," I said. "Keep moving."

"Aww, not even one dance?"

His puppy-dog eyes cajoled a smile from me. How nice it might feel to be one of the girls with nothing to worry about except whether this guy would call tomorrow morning. But I was too broken for his easy smile. I'd only end up hurting him.

"I *am* sorry," I said, wistfulness seeping into my voice. "You'll thank me later."

Regret panged in my chest as the crowd sucked him back in, but I'd done the right thing. Even if he were only interested in a one-night hookup, my type of sex was too toxic for the likes of him.

I turned back to the guy at the bar. He caught my eye, looking—if possible—surlier. Cold and mean. Perfect. I wouldn't taint him, and he could give me what I craved. Since Tall, Dark, and Stoic hadn't deigned to make a move on me, I would do the pursuing. A surprising little twist for the night, but I could go with it.

I squeezed in beside him at the bar. Up close his size was impressive and a little intimidating, but that only strengthened my resolve. He could give me what I needed.

"Hey, tough guy," I shouted over the din.

He looked up at me from his beer. I faltered a bit at the total lack of emotion in his face and fought an automatic instinct to retreat. His eyes were a deep brown, almost pretty, but remote and flat. Dark hair was cut short, bristly. His nose was prominent and slightly crooked, like it had been broken. Maybe more than once.

He looked mean, which was a good thing, but I was used to a little more effort. Even assholes provided a fake smile or smarmy line for the sake of the pickup. There was a script to these things, but he wasn't playing his part.

My club persona and beer from earlier lent me confidence. Whatever was bothering him—a bad day at the construction site or maybe a fight with the old lady—I didn't care. He was here, so he needed this as much as I did.

I planted my elbow on the bar. "I saw you looking at me earlier."

He raised an eyebrow. I shrugged. He was making me work for it, but I found myself more amused than annoyed.

"Buy me a drink?" I asked.

He considered me, then nodded and signaled the bartender.

The beat of the club reverberated as I took a sip. "So do you talk?"

His lips twitched. "Yeah, I talk."

"Okay." I leaned in close to hear him better. "What do you talk about?"

He ignored my question—or maybe answered it—by asking, "What are you doing here?" Almost like he was asking something deeper, but that had to be the alcohol talking.

"I'm trying to get laid, that's what I'm doing here." I pulled off a breathy laugh I was pretty proud of.

He didn't react, didn't appear surprised or even interested, the bastard. He just looked at me. "Why?"

I decided on honesty. "Because I need it."

He seemed to weigh the truth of my words, then nodded toward the exit. "All right, let's go." He got up and threw some cash on the bar.

His easy acceptance caught me off guard, just for a moment. But it shouldn't have surprised me, because…well, because men always wanted sex. That's what I liked about them—they didn't even bother trying to hide it. It was worse when I hadn't seen it coming, when it had sneaked up on me—Now wasn't the time to think of that. It was never the right time to think of that.

He tucked his hand under my elbow, guiding me. He used his body to maneuver us through the crowd, almost as a shield. The whole thing was so gentlemanly, given what we were about to do, that I wondered if he'd heard me right. Maybe he'd want to get coffee or something, and wouldn't that be awkward all around?

But he was a man, and I was a woman wearing fuck-me clothes—this could only end one way.

When we exited the club, I couldn't help sucking in several deep breaths. Even the faint smell of street sewage was refreshing, washing the stench of smoke, alcohol, and countless perfumes from my lungs. I never liked the crowds. The press of bodies, the mingling smell of sweat, the small bumps from all around. Tiny violations that were somehow okay since everyone did it.

As my heart rate settled, he inspected me as if he could read me. He couldn't. "What's your name?" I asked to distract him.

"Colin. Yours?"

"Allie."

"Nice to meet you, Allie. Your place or mine?"

I was comfortable again. I knew this play: horny girl who can't wait to get naked.

"We don't need to go anywhere. Let's get started right here." I let a soft moan escape me and clasped myself to the brick wall named Colin. Never mind that I was dry as a bone. He wouldn't notice. They never did.

He raised his eyebrows. "In the parking lot?"

"Or in my car. Whatever. I just want you to do me."

"I'm not fucking you in a car. It's forty degrees out."

I was hardly in this for comfort. I'd done it in colder weather just this past winter. "I don't mind."

"Well, I do."

"Fine." I was willing to give him so much. Why couldn't he take it the way I wanted? "Then we can go to the motel over there. You're paying."

He didn't look happy. I wasn't either, but I couldn't budge on this. Going to an apartment might be the norm for hookups, but my hookups weren't normal.

Going to their houses where they might do God knows what was out of the question. And I wasn't about to bring one of these guys home.

"Not there," he said. "I'll pick the place."

✧ ✧ ✧

I FOLLOWED HIS truck in my car to a motel about ten minutes away. When I pulled in, he waved me to a parking spot next to his truck and went into the office.

The place wasn't fancy, but the manicured shrubbery and freshly painted building proclaimed this was an entirely different kind of establishment than the dump by the club. No renting rooms by the hour here.

The sign out front advertised $119.99 a night. A typical price for Chicago, but I sweated the cost. The extravagance of my six-dollar drink from earlier paled in comparison.

What if it was too much money? I might not be worth it.

I kept watch on the frosted office door like he might disappear. Eight minutes later, he came out. My stomach clenched. He flashed a key and nodded toward the back before getting into his truck. I followed him in my car and pulled up beside him again.

It was dark back here. Deserted. The only light came from flickering, yellow lamps dimmed by tiny hordes of bugs. Scattered buildings slumbered around us like a nest of dragons, their snore the low drone from the appliances. It wasn't exactly safe. Technically that was what I wanted, but the allure of danger only worked up to a point.

He didn't come to my car. Instead he opened the motel room door and waited.

I could drive away. He probably wouldn't even come after me. Even if he could, if I drove somewhere safe—assuming there was such a place—there'd be nothing he could do.

But his solemn patience gave me the courage to open

the car door and join him.

The stale air and harsh edge of cleaning supplies softened me. I'd ridden along with my dad in his 18-wheeler once. He usually slept in truck stops, but with me he'd gotten motel rooms. This was just an empty room, but it felt strange to use a place for casual sex that I associated with childhood memories.

Once inside the room, I set down my purse on the floral fabric chair.

Colin reached out and trailed his finger along my jaw. His eyes, almost black in the dark motel room, searched my own. I thought he was going to fuck me then, but he said, "I'm going to make coffee."

I blinked. Shit, coffee. "Okay."

He went to work at the coffeemaker. Unsure of what to do, I sat down in the chair, clutching my purse in my lap like I was waiting for a doctor's appointment instead of rough, dirty sex.

He poured a cup of coffee, adding the cream and sugar without comment, and handed it to me. I took a few sips. It soothed some of the skittishness I hadn't realized I had. He didn't take any for himself.

Enough of this.

I set down the cup on the cracked countertop and stood to kiss him. I started off light, teasing, hoping to inflame him. This was all calculated, a game of risk and power.

He kissed me back softly, gently, like he didn't know we'd started playing. He held his body still, but his mouth roamed over mine, skimming and tasting.

It wasn't a magical kiss. Angels didn't sing, and nothing caught fire. But he wasn't too rough or too wet or too anything, and for me it was perfection.

I rubbed against him, undulating to a rhythm born of practice. His hands came up, one to cup my face, the other around my body.

I sighed.

He walked me backward, and we made out against the round fake-wood table, his hands running over my sides, my back. Avoiding the good parts like we were two horny teenagers in our parents' basements, new to this. I shuddered at the thought. This was all wrong. His hands were too light. I was half under him already, my hips cradling his, so I surged up and nipped at his lip. Predictably his body jerked, and he thrust his hips down onto me.

Yes. That's what I need. I softened my body, surrendering to him.

"Bed," he murmured against my lips.

We stripped at the same time, both eager. I wanted to see his body, to witness what he offered me, but it was dark in the room. Then he kissed me back onto the bed, and there was no more time to wonder. The cheap bedspread was rough and cool against my skin. His hands stroked over my breasts and then played gently with my nipples.

My body responded, turning liquid, but something was wrong.

I'd had this problem before. Not everyone wanted to play rough, but I was surprised that I'd misread him. His muscles were hard, the pads of his fingers were calloused. I didn't know how he could touch me so softly. Everything about him screamed that he could hurt me, so why didn't he?

I wanted him to have his nasty way with me, but every sweet caress destroyed the illusion. My fantasy was to let him do whatever he wanted with me, but not this.

"Harder," I said. "I need it harder."

Instead his hands gentled. The one that had been holding my breast traced the curve around and under.

I groaned in frustration. "What's wrong?"

He reached down, still breathing heavily, and pressed a finger lightly to my cunt, then stroked upward through the moisture. I gasped, rocking my hips to follow his finger.

"You like this," he said.

Yes, I liked it. I was undeniably aroused but too aware. I needed the emptiness of being taken. "I like it better rough."

Colin frowned. My eyes widened at the ferocity of his expression.

In one smooth motion he flipped me onto my stomach. I lost my breath from the surprise and impact. His left hand slid under my body between my legs and cupped me. His right hand fisted in my hair, pulling my head back. His erection throbbed beside my ass in promise. I wanted to beg him to fuck me, but all I could do was gasp. He didn't need to be told, though, and ground against me, using my hair as a handle.

That small pain on my scalp was perfection, sharp and sweet. Numbness spread through me, as did relief.

The pain dimmed. My arousal did too, but that was okay. I was only vaguely aware of him continuing to work my body from behind.

I went somewhere else in my mind. I'd stay that way all night.

At least that's what usually happened. Not this time. Instead I felt light strokes on my hair, my arms, my back. His cock pulsed hot against my thigh, but he didn't try to put it inside me, not in any of the places it would almost fit. His hands on me didn't even feel sexual. He petted me, and I arched into his caress.

Other Books by Skye Warren

Standalone Dark Romance

Wanderlust

On the Way Home

His for Christmas

Hear Me

Take the Heat

Stripped series

Tough Love (free prequel)

Love the Way You Lie

Better When It Hurts

Even Better

Pretty When You Cry

Caught for Christmas

Chicago Underground series

Rough

Hard

Fierce

Wild

Dirty

Secret

Sweet

Deep

Criminals and Captives series

Prisoner

Dark Nights series

Keep Me Safe

Trust in Me

Don't Let Go

The Beauty series

Beauty Touched the Beast

Beneath the Beauty

Broken Beauty

Beauty Becomes You

The Beauty Series Compilation

Loving the Beauty: A Beauty Epilogue

About the Author

Skye Warren is the New York Times and USA Today Bestselling author of dark contemporary romance. Her books are raw, sexual and perversely romantic.

Sign up for Skye's newsletter:

www.skyewarren.com/newsletter

Like Skye Warren on Facebook:

facebook.com/skyewarren

Join Skye Warren's Dark Room reader group:

skyewarren.com/darkroom

Follow Skye Warren on Twitter:

twitter.com/skye_warren

Visit Skye's website for her current booklist:

www.skyewarren.com

Copyright

Print Edition

Cover design by Book Beautiful
Photograph by Allan Spiers
Cover model Alan Valdez
Formatting by BB eBooks

Made in the USA
Middletown, DE
18 June 2016